SOMNIUM

DEIRDRE SWINDEN

Let the world know:
#IGotMyCLPBook!

Crystal Lake Publishing
www.CrystalLakePub.com

WELCOME
TO ANOTHER

CRYSTAL LAKE PUBLISHING
CREATION

Join today at www.crystallakepub.com & www.patreon.com/CLP

Dreams can last from seconds (non-lethal) to as long as 20 minutes (highly lethal). Sleep Subjects should be guided toward the shortest resolution, and the dream state disrupted as quickly as possible. Should the dream state exceed these limits, Operators are instructed to remove MCLs prior to jump termination. Note: Forcible expulsion from the dream reality may cause irreversible damage to both MCL and Sleep Subject.

—Excerpt from the Mearan-Cadail Laoch (MCL)
Dream Jump Instruction Manual

Sometimes I wonder if she were to see me on the street, would she get the feeling she knew me? That maybe she had seen me in a dream? Would she be confused? Upset? Or would she watch me go by, wondering if I recognized her as well? Because I do. I am Mearan-Cadail Laoch. And my life is her worst nightmare.

—Excerpt from MCL Nathan Keller's Journal

Oh fuck, not again.

—Somnium Sleep Subject (SSS) 8924
upon entering the dream reality

PROLOGUE

RATS SWARMED THE tunnels of the ancient sewer system. The heady scent of fur-covered bodies forced its way into Jon Markway's nose. Shotgun blasts splattered smears of fur and blood on the narrow tunnel walls, and he put a hand to the folds of his companion's fleshy back.

"Move, goddammit."

Kevin Davis did just that, turning first left then right then left again, desperate to find a way out of the system. Close on his heels, Markway held the horde at bay, explosions echoing along the filthy walls. Skidding to a halt at a three-way junction, Kevin licked salt from parched lips.

"Which way, which way . . . "

Markway shoved him again. "Just fucking go."

To his left, a grate. A strand of grimy sunlight. Kevin curled his fingers around the bars and pushed with all the force of his substantial weight. Cursing at the well-secured iron, he turned back, the rush of feet coming ever closer.

They didn't have much time.

To the right, the last shell exploded. Rodents bounced like tennis balls, but the wave kept coming. Markway wrapped his hands around the hot metal and brandished it like a baseball bat, a questioning eyebrow to his companion.

"Dead end," Kevin said. "What do we do?"

"Wake the fuck up."

Startled, Kevin looked down and slowly curled his fingers inward to center his mind. Eyes shut, he pictured home. Pictured his bed. Pictured anything but the sewage tunnel where he didn't want to die.

It didn't work.

Instead he focused on a different tactic and reached into his pocket. Forcing his fingers through a thick, brown sludge, he withdrew a damp lighter and rolled the spark wheel, willing the flame to ignite with everything he had.

Once. Twice. Light sprang to life, sputtered and died.

"Dammit!"

Markway caught Kevin by the back of his shirt and drove him toward the final path as rat breath tickled his ankles. Another hallway, tighter than the last. Kevin's ample frame slid along muck-covered walls that stank of substances best not thought of. On the floor, a crumpled gas can. Kevin picked it up and shook it.

"Empty."

For the first time in his memory, Kevin caught a whiff of panic that didn't emanate from his sweat-drenched pits.

"I'll be goddamned." Markway shook the can for himself. Tossing it aside, he put his back to Kevin's. "Find us another way."

Feet moving once more, Kevin rounded the last bend. A door. There was nothing else to do. He plowed through. A closet, barely big enough to fit the two men, the angry horde subdued by the wooden barrier. It wouldn't hold. Claws scratched, teeth chewed, and the sheer weight of numbers would soon be enough to break through.

"Something's different," Kevin said as he caught his breath. "You feel it?"

Markway said nothing and searched the blank walls for a way out. Overhead, a vent grate offered opportunity. Tugging it open, he cursed again. "Filled. This junction is dead."

"Then so are we." Kevin sank to the floor, legs tented, hands dangling between his knees.

"Don't give up on me now, little man. Try again."

A trickle of foul liquid flowed over Kevin's shoulder. He shut his eyes and leaned his head against the dank stone. It wasn't the first time they'd been here, but more and more Kevin felt it might be the last. Slamming his head against the wall, he curled his hands into burly fists.

"I will not die covered in shit and piss."

The room shimmered, scorched by an unseen desert heat, and for a moment, Markway felt hope return.

It didn't last.

On the floor, Kevin slapped a hand against his own cheek again and again until Markway reached down to stop him. Resignation landed on Kevin like wet concrete. He thought of Markway. He thought of his mother. He thought of his lighter and rolled it again. A spark and nothing more. Slowly, he lowered his hands.

"I want you to go," he said.

Heavy boots stomped on tiny pink hands that reached with fierce hunger through the gap between wood and stone. Markway shook his head. "Not without you, little man."

Kevin faced him with calm resolve. "I don't want to play anymore. I'm done. The rules have changed. You feel it. I know you do. So go. Please. Just go."

"No can do. I will *not* leave you."

"We can't go anywhere else."

Unable to admit Kevin might be right, Markway squatted before his companion, clapped the boy's beefy neck and let his hands slide down to Kevin's. He took the lighter and turned it over, a soft flame springing to life as the door cracked down the middle. Markway set his back against it. "Always hated these fucking furballs. Much preferred the giant albino spiders. You remember those?"

Kevin couldn't help but grin. "Not sure I'll ever forget."

Withdrawing two cigarettes from his shirt pocket, Markway handed one to Kevin and sank down beside him. "Giant albino spiders. Now that was something to see." Smoke plumed from Markway's nose. "Didn't think this would be the way I went."

"Who would?"

Jon Markway struck the lighter once more, the flame bright in the gloom. "You give up too easy, little man. We're not done yet."

A spray of concrete dusted their shoulders and Markway looked up. White limbs extended like cranes over the empty space above their heads, eight black eyes dancing in the sputtering flame. Markway sent up a laugh as the door gave way and the lighter died.

"I'll be goddam . . ."

CHAPTER ONE

"I CAN'T BELIEVE you talked me into this."

Gillian Hardie looked up from her packing as Jenna Matthews kicked open the cabin door and threw her overnight bag on the couch.

"Talked you into what?" Gillian asked and tossed a pair of jeans into an open suitcase.

"They make movies about places like this, you know. And not one of them ends well for the big-chested blonde."

"Good thing you're not a real blonde." Gillian squeezed Jenna's hand. "Thanks for coming."

"I'll always come when you call, Gill. But please tell me you finished the bathroom?"

"See for yourself."

Crossing the spacious open floor of the one-room cabin, Jenna slid back a recently added barn door. She looked with pleasure on the renovations. "Son of a bitch! You actually did it. But I still think you could do with a few more walls. This place is . . . "

"If you call it a dump one more time, I'm never going to forgive you."

"Not my first thought." Jenna grinned. "But close."

Snickering, Gillian scratched a small black and white mutt behind the ears as he made himself comfortable on the bed. "It's only for a few days, and you know Jax will be better off here than in your apartment. He's got his toys, bed and a fenced yard. What more can a dog ask for?"

"A television? Wi-Fi?" Jenna collapsed onto the couch. "Anything more connected than the toaster? Hell, I'd settle for a transistor radio."

"It's the deep dark woods. The reception's shit."

"Leave it to you to want to live like a woman stuck in the 1800s."

"I have better dental coverage."

"But no cable."

"Keep it up and you'll have to rely on shadow puppets as your only means of entertainment."

Jenna propped her feet on an antique trunk that doubled as a coffee table. "How's my other mother?"

Paused in her packing, Gillian absently rubbed the worn surface of a green and black stone pendant. The ritual calmed her nerves as she prepared to venture into the world once again.

"Dad didn't say much. Just that I needed to get there."

The call had come two hours before. Her father's dire warning forcing Gillian to shove her fears aside, seeing her ailing mother far more important than any sleepless nights the journey might cause. *Hell*, Gillian thought as she resumed packing, *I might get a new book out of the trip.*

"She'll be all right," Jenna said.

"He wouldn't ask if it weren't serious."

"There's a name for it you know, fear of going out in public."

"I don't suffer from agoraphobia," Gillian muttered. "Technophobia, taphephobia and galeophobia, check, check and check. But I can go outside whenever I want. It's the wanting part that's not so easy."

"What the hell is galeophobia?"

"Fear of sharks."

"And that other one?"

"Being buried alive."

Jenna shuddered. "You're seriously fucked up, you know that?"

"Don't have to tell me twice. There's a reason I live in the deep, dark woods and it isn't to be the cliché writer."

"Oh, I know." Memories of the formative years of their friendship at Emory University were too distinct to forget. Jenna had been the one person Gillian could always rely on to sit up with her after one of her nightmares, the screams often waking more than her roommate. "You really think cutting out technology has helped?"

"I know it has," Gillian said. "So I'll stay secluded, thank you very much. You'll be okay?"

"Aren't I always?"

"I put fresh sheets on the bed."

Jenna got up to run her hand over the soft finish of an antique mahogany sleigh bed. Brightly colored sheets were a sharp contrast to the wooden frame, but it made the room feel cozy despite the lack of walls. "Why bother? You never sleep there. Hell, you never sleep."

"I sleep."

"You really don't." Books lined the built-in stone shelves surrounding a massive fireplace. Jenna let her fingers drift over the spines and plucked the most recent from the shelf. "Is this the new one? When's it due to hit stores?"

"Next week," Gillian said and tugged her t-shirt straight over the gentle curve of her hips. "Take it if you like."

"You know I can't stand being scared."

"It's a first edition."

"Sign it and I'll consider reading it."

"Read it and I'll consider signing it." Gillian blew a lock of dark auburn hair from her face. Eyes of polished moss scoured the room, seeking out anything she had forgotten. Moving to the far side of the cabin, she grabbed her laptop from the granite-topped kitchen peninsula.

"Does that even work without Wi-Fi?" Jenna asked and wandered through the small galley.

Gillian unplugged the computer from an aging ethernet cable. "It does what I need it to do. And I'm connected. I get email."

"Your phone is still attached to the wall," Jenna said dryly. "But the kitchen looks fabulous, and that bistro table in the nook is gorgeous."

A soft glow brightened Gillian's eyes as she looked over the room. "I do love it here."

"I won't say it doesn't suit you, but I still wish you'd moved closer to the city."

"I know." Gillian ducked into the bathroom to finish packing. Toothpaste and brush thrown into her make-up bag, she opened a drawer and pulled out a bottle of caffeine pills.

"No way," Jenna said and snatched the pills from Gillian's hand. "You'll be back on that fucking Provigil in days if you start this shit again. I thought you had it under control."

"I do."

"Then why do you have these?"

Shrugging, Gillian studied the freshly grouted tiles, fingernails playing the faded lines of scar tissue on her right cheek as if they were guitar strings. "I just . . . it was a safety net, all right? New house. Renovations. I got worried. And lately . . . "

Brow furrowed in concern, Jenna set the pills on the counter and inspected her friend closely. No amount of make-up could hide the dark bags under Gillian's eyes. Her favorite jeans hung loose on her hips, hands trembling from the multiple Diet Cokes coursing through her system.

"Lately what?" Jenna asked.

"Lately, the dreams have been getting stronger."

"Stronger how?"

"I don't know. I feel like . . . " Gillian shook her head. "Like sooner or later I won't wake up."

Softening, Jenna took Gillian's hands in her own. "They're just dreams, Gill. They can't hurt you."

"I know," Gillian muttered.

Snatching the pills, Jenna turned her attention to something more easily fixed. "How often have you been taking these?"

"I haven't touched them, I swear."

"Prove it."

"Open the bottle."

Lips pursed, Jenna twisted the child-proof cap, the seal beneath unbroken. It did little to appease her. "You shouldn't even have these in the house."

Gillian chewed her lower lip, cheeks glowing a shameful shade of pink.

Brushing a hand over Gillian's forehead to tuck a stray piece of hair behind her ear, Jenna offered her a smile. "You've got this, Gill. You know all the techniques, all the drills. You don't need this shit anymore, capiche?"

"I got it."

"Good, because you're not taking them with you."

"I just thought . . . "

"No arguments! You want me to watch the dog in your nightmare cabin in the woods, then dump the pills." Jenna held the bottle out to Gillian, who opened it again, peeled back the safety layer and dumped the contents in the toilet.

"Satisfied?"

"Son of a bitch," Jenna said and grinned. "The toilet works."

"Ye of little faith." Gillian caught her friend in a tight hug. "Thanks."

"You're welcome."

"I'll see about getting you a television when I get back."

"A little one with a DVD player would be fine. They still make those, don't they?"

Gillian finally smiled. "I'll find one for you. Retro is in these days."

"Deal. Now get your butt to the station before I change my mind about camping in your haunted-ass woods."

With a kiss to the little black and white mutt and a hug for her friend, Gillian grabbed her bags and stepped out into the dark.

CHAPTER TWO

"**NATHAN KELLER,** my man! What's going on!"

Nathan glanced up from his book to find layers of disheveled clothing hiding the scrawny body of a young man. Declan 'Dex' Cooper stood at the edge of his chair, mocking the quiet library with his garish presence.

"Dex," Nathan rumbled in a rusty baritone that both welcomed and dismissed the boy.

Beaming at the simple recognition, Dex slapped his hands together, fingers forming a two-gun salute. "Coming to dinner? Macho Nacho is all about the taco mania. Can't miss that."

"Not tonight."

"Suit yourself, my man, suit yourself." Dex slid into the chair across from Nathan, a furtive glance cast over his shoulder. He didn't need to be concerned. Hardly anyone other than Nathan ever used Somnium's employee library. Books, after all, had lost their luster years ago, just after Somnium had introduced its first virtual reading experience allowing a person to become a character in any work of fiction put on film. "You heard?"

Paper rustled as Nathan flipped the page. "Heard what?"

"Corridor's buzzing, man. They're saying Markway's dead. That he arced." Dex lowered his voice, as though the hushed tones would keep his news from being true. "They're saying 8924 took him down."

Nathan froze, muscles rigid beneath the light cloth of his dark gray MCL uniform. "It's a rumor. Nothing more. Corridor's full of them."

Dex ruffled his unruly mop of reddish-blond hair. "This one feels different, you know? Sleep Subject 8924 was under 10,000, man. One of the last of the Elite dreamers. If it's true, then there's only 24 Elite left. Twenty-four out of ten grand." Dex clucked a sympathetic tongue. "What the hell happened? All those people just—gone."

Feet shifted beneath him, Nathan laid his book on the table, leaned over and pretended to read. He knew 8924. On Markway's days off, he'd been the one to jump with the kid. Markway always called him "little man" although there had been nothing little about him. Now well over 30, 8924 had topped out at just this side of doughboy the last Nathan had seen him. "That's all you've got?"

"Blake's prepping on 9425. Makes two calls for the Elite tonight already. Fucking strange if you ask me."

Nathan suppressed the urge to remind Dex he hadn't asked. "Is it night somewhere in the world?"

"Yeah."

"Do people sleep at night?"

"Well, yeah."

"Then I'm guessing it's not so strange. Even for the Elite."

Dex stood and shoved his hands in his pockets, rubber wristbands bunching up against the strips of cloth he'd tied in place untold weeks ago. Nathan wondered briefly how the kid showered, but then again, judging by the smell, he didn't do it all that often. "Thought you should know."

"Now I know."

"Right." Dex clapped his hands again. "Tacos! You're always welcome to join the fun, my man. Corridor's a-buzzing and the Weavers are out on the town this dee-light-ful summer evening. Should be a lady or two with my name on her ass by morning!"

Nathan lifted a hand in farewell as the Dream Jump Operator departed. Gathering his things, he moved into the busy Somnium Corridor. The social heart of the company town, the thoroughfare provided an array of food and entertainment options, including the ever-present Somnium 'rooms'—each offering a variety of immersive virtual reality experiences designed by specialized programmers known as Weavers. All anyone had to do to enjoy a virtual life was subject themselves to a series of rapid images to prep their minds, the 'induction technology' similar to the subliminal messaging of old, when pictures of sex had been hidden in ice cubes to covertly promote liquor sales. In just minutes a customer could be standing in Paris with all the sights, sounds and tastes available at the touch of a hand. "Live your dreams" was a motto everyone at Somnium took seriously.

Nathan eyed the rooms and the people within, with disdain as he passed. Even after five years, he'd yet to set foot in one, and if he had anything to say about it, he never would.

Instead, he passed through an unnoticeable side door into the main office building. Alone in a concrete hallway that brought back too many memories of high school, he picked up his pace. It still took several minutes to reach the two elevators at the far end. Stepping inside, he punched the button for Sub-Level Two: MCL Housing.

Like company towns of old, Somnium offered a variety of living options to employees, most of whom were expected to live onsite. Executives could choose from an array of opulent single-family homes, while the mid-level peons made do with luxury townhouses and condos.

After his ascension to Fifth-Level MCL, Nathan had been offered his choice of condo or townhome, each with a coveted view of the mountains. He'd turned down both, choosing instead to remain in the basement housing where most of the other single male MCLs were stored like unwanted stepchildren. Nathan didn't mind. He preferred the small space of his two-room apartment and had given up the larger option to an Operator with a wife and two kids. The grateful family had invited him to dinner every Sunday since, and he had nearly run out of excuses for not attending.

If what Dex had said was true, he'd be offered Markway's house soon enough. Offered Markway's paycheck as well, and likely the coveted role of Head MCL.

But Nathan didn't want any of it. Not if it meant his friend was dead.

Door shut safely behind him, Nathan heaved out a breath and ran both hands across the amber depths of his messy crew cut. He moved quickly through the book-filled rooms to the bathroom. A splash of cold water across his deeply scarred cheek and forehead brought some life back to a face not even a mother could call handsome.

Despite his tall, well-muscled body, Nathan's fierce countenance more often brought shudders of revulsion than shivers of pleasure. A well-placed piece of shrapnel had impaled itself just deep enough in the boney cartilage of his nose to create a gash across his face that functioned like a culvert when it rained. Over the years he had found a few women who had been drawn to the brooding ill-grace of his looks. Women who misconstrued dangerous as sexy. But once they discovered the man beneath, they never stayed. No one, it seemed, liked to wake up with a gentleman when they thought they'd gone to bed with a son of a bitch.

Years before, he had trained at Annapolis, been tested and found more than capable in the desert heat. After a few short years of intense training the likes of which few would ever choose to endure, he'd been deployed as the head of a team whom he had trusted with his life, but whose ultimate leadership he'd found wanting. The corruption that started somewhere near the top had trickled down to leave a bad taste in his mouth he couldn't spit out. In the end, a private military corporation had summoned him, and despite reservations that it was more of the same, the money called and he had gone, only to find himself more disgusted than ever.

The call from Jon Markway had been a welcome relief, his old mentor a bright spot in the darkness he had come to believe ruled the world.

"There's shit you don't even know, my friend," Markway said over dark beers in a dark corner of a dark bar. "Shit you don't ever want to know. And the heart of that shit is this place. The bastards-that-be call it Somnium. Now I know you've had it with the PMCs, and this ain't much better. But the work. The work's different, Nate."

"Different how?"

"I'm not going to lie to you. The place is like living in an old-time mining camp buried deep in the fucking Appalachians. Nothing that don't belong to Somnium for miles around. No one gets in without a non-disclosure agreement, and nothing gets out that Somnium hasn't had eyes on. They make it so you don't want to leave. Offices, tech shops, housing, a world-class shopping mall they call the Corridor running right down the middle of town. You name it, it's there. But when you jump . . . " Markway shook his head, eyes bright. "It's like nothing you've ever done before and it's everything you've ever wanted to do. No limits, Nate. No limits at all."

Two weeks later Nathan had signed an airtight confidentiality agreement and moved in. For the past five years, he had jumped into the dreams of Somnium Sleep Subjects alongside Markway and a small company of men Somnium had recruited thanks to talents similar to his own. He put his life on the line every night and had never loved his job more.

Except now his friend might be dead and a second MCL was about to go to work on a night that felt strange from the moment he'd woken up.

Another Elite dreamer gone.

Markway gone.

He stared into the mirror as the clock turned over eight p.m. and wondered if tonight was the night he'd be gone as well.

CHAPTER THREE

CLAYTON MILLER STOOD at the head of a small but opulent conference room as he concluded his one, and usually only, pitch. Handsome features held a stony confidence, sharp brown eyes bouncing from person to person to ensnare an audience that included senior executives from several of the world's top companies and a handful of government officials.

"Say goodnight to your struggles," Clayton said, hands spread in invitation. "It's time to live your dreams."

A smattering of applause followed from all but one CEO, who scowled from the head of the table. "How the hell do we know this so-called immersion technology of yours actually works?"

Clayton raised an eyebrow. "How do you know it doesn't?"

"What do you mean?

"How do you know you're not sitting in one of my virtual realities right now?"

A murmur of disbelief circled the room.

"We know where we are," said one of the officials, unfazed.

"Do you?" Clayton snapped his dark fingers and the conference room disappeared, replaced by a Hawaiian luau, complete with the smell of cooked pork emanating from the slowly rotating spit where the conference table had been. Fragrant leis draped the necks of his vibrantly dressed guests. Products lined the walls, each picture advertising the purchase of an actual Hawaiian getaway with the simple touch of a finger.

Startled laughter greeted the change.

"It's like the holodeck from Star Trek, isn't it?" one of the executives asked.

"Or the Danger Room," said another.

"It's not like either," Clayton said with a smug smile. "But it's a reasonable comparison."

Someone leaned forward and touched the pig, only to whip his fingers away with a grin. "It's hot! How in the hell did you do that?"

"I won't be giving away my secrets," Clayton said. "Suffice it to say that thanks to the talents of my Weavers and Somnium's patented artificial intelligence technology, you are currently immersed in a variety of 'waves' designed to interact with your body's bioelectric signature to ensure that every sense is triggered in the virtual world. The waves read you and the room to ensure a safe experience. Move out of the room and the world you've created will go with you. Ask for a drink and you'll find it in your hand. Virtual reality without borders and without fear." Clayton gestured to the brightly colored drinks in their hands. "Go on. Taste it."

More nervous laughter followed as one executive chanced a sip. "That tastes like real orange juice."

"It is real, to your senses," Clayton said. "Anything you dream, my Weavers can create. And anything they create will feel as real as if it were happening in the real world. All you have to do is tell me your dreams, and Somnium will make them come true."

A second snap and they were back in the conference room.

This time the crowd gave an enthusiastic round of applause, even the angry CEO smiling broadly as he approached Clayton. "You've certainly got my attention, Dr. Miller. But what about the risks?"

"Risks?" Clayton asked.

"To the audience."

"I can assure you no one will fall off a cliff, if that's what you're thinking. The tech reads any imminent dangers—stairs, furniture, even other people—and either blocks or incorporates it into the visual field to guarantee customer safety. The immersion tech has cleared every safety test with absolute perfection."

"I understand there may have been some issues associated with the original programming—the induction tech—or whatever it is you call it."

"The general populace is not at risk from the tech," Clayton said, hands dipping into his pockets. "The platform is safe. Statistics have shown that less than one-one-millionth of a percent of the target population reject the induction programming."

"And what happens to that one-one-millionth of a percent?"

Before Clayton could answer, the slim, pale figure of his personal assistant emerged from the group. "Gentlemen, there will be plenty of time for questions after dinner," Evan James said. "Somnium would like to invite you all to spend the night in the complex. Our Weavers have created a very special demonstration I'm certain will satisfy."

The CEO didn't move. "Are you really going to tell me your technology, what I just experienced, doesn't mess with a person's mind?"

Clayton took a step closer to the man. "Do you believe we could've come this far if even a single person had suffered anything more than a few bad dreams after agreeing to our programming?"

"You'd be out of business by morning."

Lips curling, Clayton relaxed. "Exactly. No other company can provide the experience I offer, and no other company can guarantee successful influence over your buyers. You came to me because I can make your dreams come true. Literally. So cut the bullshit, and let's talk numbers, shall we?"

The CEO broke into a grin and offered Clayton a hand. "I'd still like to see the latest data on your safety protocols."

"My assistant will provide anything you need."

"Of course." Evan smiled, blue eyes sharp in the dimly lit room. "But first, do enjoy your dinner." Sweeping out a thin hand, Evan escorted their guests into the dining room and shut the double doors before returning to his boss.

"There's one in every pitch." Clayton said and eyed his assistant. "Why are you here?"

"Your presence has been requested by Dr. Braun. There's been an issue with Sleep Subject 8924."

"Walk with me."

Two quick turns down the immaculate glass and stone corridor found them at the double-doored entrance to Clayton's office. Modern low-profile furniture ensured a magnificent view of the Appalachians from floor to ceiling windows. Italian leather couches matched the chairs before Clayton's desk, where a Dream Jump Operator sat slumped over, head in his hands. An impeccably dressed man paced the floor, skin pale from a lack of sun. To see the hard lines of Elijah Braun's prematurely aged face in the CEO's office meant only one thing—something had gone horribly wrong with one of the MCL's dream jumps. Clayton had only a second to wonder what happened this time—and if it would finally afford him the opportunity he'd been waiting for—when the Operator hopped to attention and swayed dangerously, the last bit of blood draining from his cheeks.

"Dr. Braun," Clayton said, ignoring the boy. "What can I do for you?"

"We've had an issue with one of the Elite Sleep Subjects."

Clayton eyed the Operator. "Speak."

"My name's Wilson, sir. Eric Wilson. Jump Operator for the MCL division."

Clayton rounded his desk and sat down in a plush leather chair, fingers tented beneath his chin. "Go on."

Hands shaking, Wilson glanced at Dr. Braun for reassurance before he spoke again. "Sleep Subject 8924 is dead sir. He arced at the 18-minute mark."

Beneath the desk, Clayton felt his leg muscles spasm with excitement and kept his knees silent by sheer force of will. *Steady*, he thought to himself, the need for a calm, calculated veneer never more vital than it was in the next few minutes. He arranged his features into an indifferent mask. "It happens, particularly with Sleep Subjects under the care of the nightmare division. Why should this be my concern?"

Wilson shifted his weight. "MCL Markway died as well, sir."

Clayton spun his chair to the window, lips twitching with barely restrained glee. "The MCLs know the risks when they sign on."

Running a hand across the back of his neck, Wilson shook a nest of loose brown curls. "I couldn't get him out, sir. I tried but . . . "

Clayton stood. "Then it was Markway's choice."

"That's the thing, sir. I don't think it was."

Whirling to face the boy, Clayton pressed both hands to his desk. "The subject is dead, is he not?"

Trembling, Wilson nodded. "Yes sir. But I don't think that was his choice either."

"Hear him out, Clayton," Braun said.

"There was something different about the wave. Something . . . strange."

"There is no 'something strange,'" Clayton said. "There is just the wave."

"This wave killed Markway a full 30 seconds before the subject died."

Clayton shot his gaze to his assistant, who immediately closed the doors on the outer rooms. An eerie stillness filled the room while Clayton considered the petrified Operator's words. "Thirty seconds you say?"

"Yes sir," Wilson said.

"How long was he under?"

"Eighteen minutes, sir."

"Then he was within range?"

"Yes sir."

Braun put a hand on Eric's arm. "That's enough." Eric's head swiveled from Braun to Clayton, the tension palpable until Braun spoke again. "I'm sure you did your best for Markway. I'll expect a full report as soon as possible. You're dismissed."

Clayton felt the muscles in the back of his jaw tighten and he crossed to the sideboard to pour himself a brandy. He waited until the Operator had gone before he spoke again. "Always so careful to keep me at arm's length, aren't you, Eli?"

"There's a good reason for that."

"Then why are you still here?"

"We have to consider the possibility of another glitch in the induction technology."

"Always the induction technology." Bemused, Clayton tossed back the drink and poured a second. "Tell me, did you even consider that it might be a flaw in the dream jump software? In your own platform? That perhaps, if you let one of my Weavers examine your work . . . "

"That'll never happen, Clayton."

" . . . we might've been able to fix this before you lost yet another Elite?" Clayton shook his head and answered his own question. "Of course you didn't. You wouldn't. Far easier to blame the source instead of the savior, isn't it? But it's apparent your software is failing, Doctor. Despite all the money, time and technology you and Alistair Wilcox have poured into the MCL program, you've yet to save even one of the Elite. Seems to me all you're really doing is prolonging their misery."

"And if I gave you access to my tech? What would you do? Would you help them, Clayton? Or would you shut down the program? Take away their only hope?"

Clayton dropped his chin to his chest and hit Braun with a glare. "Why did you come to me with this?

"Something is wrong with the waves. The nightmares, they're different . . . "

"Different how?"

"The waves have shifted. It's subtle but every time one of the Elite goes under, it looks . . . " Braun paused, searching for the right word but failing to find it before Clayton grew antsy.

"It looks like what?"

"Like they're entering a conscious reality."

Clayton scoffed. "For god's sake, Braun . . . "

"You said it yourself. There is only the wave. And every time one of the Elite goes under, those waves edge closer to normal, cognitive function. Reality, as we know it, right here, right now. Only it's happening within the dream state, and that puts not only the Elite but also the MCL at risk."

"What are you suggesting we do?"

"Shut down the platform."

Clayton cast an annoyed glare over his shoulder. "Be sensible, Braun!"

"I am being sensible. With the induction tech offline, the Elite might have a chance."

"And just how long do you propose we stay offline?"

"As long as it takes."

"Absolutely not." Setting his empty glass back on the bar, Clayton buttoned his jacket and headed for the door, intent on rejoining his guests. "We've shut down before and nothing changed for the Elite. I won't stop everything for 24 people."

"Just how many do you intend to kill, Clayton?"

The words hung on the air, frozen in the hushed silence.

"Markway made a mistake and it cost him his life," Clayton said carefully. "Much as we try to avoid them, attachments can and do happen, even with men like the MCLs. He stayed too long. This was a bad call from a man who should've known better."

"I hope you're right," Braun said and crossed the floor to stand before Clayton, shoulders stiff. "Because if you're wrong, his death is on you. They're all on you." Spinning on his heel, he shoved through the double doors and stalked down the hall.

"Dr. Braun!" Evan called, catching him before the turn. "MCL Blake is prepping on Sleep Subject 9425. Should I stop him?"

"If we stop him, one of the Elite might die," Braun said.

Shifting gracefully to stand to his full and considerable height, Evan laid his impassive, deep blue gaze on Braun. "If we don't, they both might die."

"I appreciate your concern, Mr. James. But the MCLs know what they signed on for."

"Do they?"

Braun said nothing and Evan James dropped his gaze to his ever-present tablet before changing the subject. "Shall I arrange the usual package for Mrs. Markway?"

"Double it. That man was worth every penny."

CHAPTER FOUR

BY THE TIME Gillian hurried in to collect her ticket, Philadelphia's 30th Street Station seemed more like the hushed halls of a high school long after the students had gone than a major railway hub. Earbuds firmly in place, she printed her pass with barely a glance at the display, found an empty bench by the staircase to the platform and tucked her nose in a book.

Checking her watch, Gillian applauded her timing. The wait wouldn't be long, the danger of having to interact with society culled to a minimum. While her books had been relatively successful, the jackets didn't carry her picture, and she was certain she wouldn't be recognized. But as the conductor called them to line up before the escalator, her hands began to tremble. She let her fingers stray to the pendant around her neck and clutched the smooth face of the stone.

An overhead voice barked out the station stops for the long-haul train, the last Charleston, South Carolina. The ride would be difficult, but not as painful as the airport. It had taken only two flights, the ensuing nightmares so bad she hadn't slept for three days afterward, for Gillian to determine air travel was a monster she didn't need in her life. Buses were slow, and the risk of falling asleep behind the wheel was too great to drive herself, so when she traveled any distance, she used the rails. Most trips were reasonably enjoyable, and despite the anxiety of her mother's illness, Gillian looked forward to seeing her father at the other end of the line.

The line shuffled toward the staircase, the woman in front of her preoccupied with a whining child who wanted something no one seemed to have. Face buried in her book, Gillian didn't notice the errant piece of luggage until it was too late, and she lay sprawled across the tiles, book and earbuds flying as the mother looked on in frank dismay.

"Are you all right?" the young mother asked and shifted her cranky son from left hip to right.

"Fine," Gillian said and tried to ignore the blooming soreness in her hip.

"Let me help you up."

Gillian held up a hand. "No really. It's nothing."

She had made it to her knees when the kid sent a small foot flying, sneaker connecting solidly with Gillian's cheek.

The mother let out a startled cry. "Benny! I'm so sorry! He's never like this. It's just so late. Here, let me help." The moment the child's feet hit the ground, he pounced on the wayward bag and pulled clothing from the pockets until he screeched in delight. Electronic music assaulted Gillian's ears and a tablet shaped like a frog landed directly in front of her eyes.

"Froggie!" Benny cried and slapped his young hand to the screen.

"That's nice," Gillian said and averted her gaze.

"Is that what you wanted?" the mother asked. "Geeze Louise, you could've said froggie."

"Froggie!" Benny giggled.

Benny's mother helped Gillian to her feet with a shake of her head. "He loves that thing. He'll be a computer whiz one day, just like that Clayton Miller, I guess."

Gillian touched her cheek. "Or a kick boxing champion."

"Maybe so," the mother said with a laugh. She picked up Gillian's book and Discman. "A Discman! I haven't seen one of these in years! Are they coming back? I guess everything is these days. Retro." She handed it back to Gillian. "Can I get you anything? Some ice?"

"No, no, I'm fine."

"All right then. Guess we'd better get on board."

"Safe trip." Gillian disappeared down the stairs, feet carrying her as far from the hovering crowd as possible. Cheek throbbing and heart racing, she hid her face from the other priority boarding passengers waiting at the front of the platform. Back against one of the dirty tile walls, she clutched her elbows and rocked slightly forward. A cold sweat formed over her body, breath coming hard and fast. She searched for something to focus on, the urge to vomit barely suppressed.

"Five things," she whispered in the hopes of calming her overwrought nerves. "Find five things."

SOMNIUM

The printed platform sign. Tiles. Tracks. Luggage. The headlamps as the Amtrak Viewliner engine pulled into view. As she spelled out each five times, her heart began to slow. But she knew the tightness of her chest, the tingling in the back of her skull, the hum of her nerves against her skin. All sure signs of bad dreams to come.

Further down the platform, a conductor assigned seats to waiting passengers, while those with priority accommodations marched past Gillian. By the time she caught her breath, she was one of only a few people still waiting to board. The sleeper car conductor stepped off the train to collect her, concern furrowing his brow.

"All right, miss?" he asked.

"I'm fine. I'll be fine. I . . . Fine."

"You'll need to head to the passenger cars for a seat assignment."

"I have . . . " Gillian held out her ticket. "Private . . . "

"Ah." The conductor nodded in approval. "Right this way."

Smiling her thanks, Gillian breathed deeply, nerves singing like a tea kettle as she gathered her things and scurried onto the train. The attendant showed her to a small two-seat compartment, and she shut herself inside with a grateful sigh.

The train rolled forward and she tucked her bag onto the extra seat, kicked off her shoes and curled herself into a ball, eyes scouring the darkness beyond the window for any familiar sights. Twelve hours on a south-bound train. Delays were almost guaranteed, just as the news of her mother's condition on the other end was bound to be dismal. But as she sank into the leather, Gillian was certain of only one thing.

It was going to be a very long night.

CHAPTER FIVE

THE CORRIDOR BUZZED with activity and Dex navigated the stream of people as if he wore roller skates. Around him, Somnium's employees began, continued or ended their day at the multitude of shops, restaurants and bars located on the town's main thoroughfare. Weavers poured out of the Neuroscience Programming Center and joined the throng of office staff as second shift rolled over to third.

Threading his way to his favorite restaurant, Dex joined his friends at a table the small group laid claim to every Friday night.

"They say he seized up and two giant red marks popped up on his neck," said Laura Taylor, one of the company's top Weavers. Her knowledge of—and skill at creating—neural sensory projection programming was unrivaled, her ambition to be a vice president before she turned 30, never challenged.

Dex still marveled at the idea he even knew Laura, let alone that she would deign to sit with him every Friday night. A pretty young woman with dark hair and bright blue eyes, Dex had attempted to sweet talk her when he'd first arrived. Laura had rebuffed him, gently at first, before finally resorting to telling him flat out he was a pain in her ass and if he would just stop pestering her, she'd be happy enough to be his friend.

Since then, the fondness between them had grown into a strong friendship, and he now considered her a big sister and mentor. The newcomer she brought to the table, however, was no sister of his. Young and beautiful, she looked around the restaurant with a wide-eyed, captivated expression Dex had long associated with new Somnium employees. Aware of his slack-jawed enthusiasm for the pretty new recruit, Laura gave him an encouraging smile, and he slid into the seat beside the blonde.

"Hello beautiful, I don't believe we've met?" Dex said.

Laura rolled her eyes. Apparently, he had chosen the wrong approach, so he tried again.

"Declan Cooper. Dex to my friends, of which I very much hope you will be one."

Laura winced and shook her head in warning.

"Amanda Smith," the blonde said and offered Dex her hand.

Bowing, Dex placed a gallant kiss on the back of her knuckles. Laura slapped a hand to her forehead in defeat as a group of MCLs entered the restaurant.

"Who are they?" Amanda asked, eyes alight as she ripped her hand from Dex to dig through her purse. She came up with lip gloss, attention never leaving the trio in gray as she added an extra rose-colored layer to the one already in place.

"MCLs," Laura said with an indifferent shrug. "You don't want to go there. Trust me on this if nothing else."

"MC what?" Amanda asked.

"Mearan-Cadail Laoch," Dex said. "Or if you prefer to be grammatically correct, Laoch na Mearan-Cadail."

Amanda blinked.

"Loosely translated it's Scottish-Gaelic for nightmare warriors," Dex said.

"Nightmare . . . what?"

"Warriors."

"I don't get it. What do they do?"

Dex leaned over and lowered his voice. "Have you ever had a dream where you thought you were about to die?" He hooked a thumb at the trio of men. "They're the reason you didn't."

Amanda shuddered and took out her phone to check her lipstick with the camera. "I thought that was an old wives' tale."

"It used to be." Dex shook his head. "It used to be."

Holding her phone high in an attempt to get a signal, Amanda cursed under her breath. "You'd think the most innovative technology company in the world would have decent Wi-Fi."

Dex grinned. "You didn't read your contract, did you?"

"What do you mean?"

"You're on the Somnium system now, my dear. Contact with the outside world is strictly monitored, social media is forbidden and every message you send will be read by prying eyes."

"Seriously?"

"In exchange you get all this." Dex spread his arms to indicate the Corridor. "A self-contained little world that can be tailored to your liking. Great paycheck, outstanding housing, and the benefits . . . " Dex waggled his eyebrows and took Amanda's hand once more. "The benefits are very easy on the eyes."

Amanda giggled, and flipped her hair as she caught an MCL's eye.

"Dex," Laura said and drew his attention away from Amanda's primping. "If you have a few minutes after dinner, I want to talk to you about MCL Keller."

"What about him?"

Shifting her bag to her lap, Laura extracted a small disc coated in a bright, fiery red. She placed it on the table and tapped it twice.

"Whoa," Dex muttered and inspected the disc with interest and more than a hint of jealousy. "When did you get that?"

"I've been working on a special project," Laura said, lips twitching with pride.

"Is it true you can access all the mainframes with one of those?"

"Any Weaver worth their paycheck has access to the image libraries, servers and mainframes. They need them to create the sensory experience for the immersion rooms. Don't you have Weavers in the MCL?"

"We don't need them." Dex walked his fingers across the table to stroke the disc, only to have Laura slap his hand away. He leaned in to whisper his next thought in her ear. "We both know you're not just any Weaver, and I'm guessing not more than five people in this whole company have one of those. Am I right?"

"Maybe," Laura said and tapped in a passcode.

Curiosity piqued, Dex watched her closely. He was surprised by the disc's lack of security. The thought that it wouldn't take much to hack it prickled his skin with excitement. Sitting back, he adjusted the band at his wrist. Every MCL Operator wore one of the virtually unhackable devices, which was activated based on the individual's body chemistry. The bands allowed access to restricted MCL files, and enabled calls and communication with any of the other members of the division. It seemed strange that Somnium's money-making side wouldn't have the same standards for the secretive and highly coveted discs, but Dex knew better than to get into a device security argument with Laura when her face was set in work mode. Instead, he asked if she'd been promoted.

"If this project works out the way I hope." Laura shrugged. "MCL Keller is assigned to Sleep Subject 831, right?

"Always has been, always will be."

"I was doing a little research into the neurological patterns associated with persistent nightmare disorder, and I wondered if you've noticed . . . "

Laura trailed off as a hush fell over the crowd. She flashed her eyes to Dex, who took the hint and rose from his seat to make his way to Eric Wilson. All three MCLs followed Wilson's path with hard stares, jaws set tight. They rose in a single fluid motion as the Operator passed.

"Guess it's true," Dex said and caught hold of Eric before he crumpled. A quick nod to Laura sent the two women to the bar as Eric slumped forward into a chair, face in his hands.

The MCLs gave a solemn salute, a fist pressed to their hearts followed by a double slap to the patch on the shoulder of their uniform. It resonated throughout the restaurant, the soft murmurs starting again when the trio returned to their seats.

"You all right?" Dex asked.

Eric nodded and then slowly shook his head. "I lost him, Dex. I just lost him."

Dex put a hand to his friend's shoulder. "It wasn't your fault. If they know that," he chucked his chin at the MCLs, "then everyone else will too."

"Had to be." Eric stared at the table in the hope it might swallow him whole. "He died first. So it musta been my fault, right?"

"Who died first?"

"Markway. He died almost half a minute before 8924. I must've missed the return trigger. Missed something. But everything was so strange, Dex. The waves . . . " Eric shoved his hands into his hair. "Miller said it was Markway's choice, but I don't think it could've been, could it?"

Dex's eyebrows shot up. "You talked to Miller?"

"Had to. Had to tell him about . . . "

Dex jumped as his wristband vibrated. With a quick tap, the summons expanded before him, the biometric lock showing him the "for his eyes only" message. Eric saw nothing, only watched as Dex scanned the air.

"Who is it?" Eric asked.

"Keller's been tapped," Dex said and shut down the notice. "Has to be an Elite."

Eric grabbed his arm tight enough to hurt. "Who?"

"Won't know 'til I get there."

"Don't take your eyes off the waves. You hear me?"

"We'll talk later," Dex said and pried his arm loose. "I've got to meet Keller."

"Don't let him go the full 20 minutes. Pull him out at 18, no matter what. You hear me? No matter what!"

Hand raised in farewell, Dex hurried away.

"Dex! Dex wait!" Laura caught up to him as a large group of Weavers jostled their way into the crowded bar. "I wanted to ask you . . . "

"Keller's waiting. I've gotta run."

"It's just I wanted to know about the waves. You can see the nightmares in those lines better than any Operator I know." An excited young woman bounced over to Laura's elbow and asked to borrow some lipstick as a group of Marketing Executives waded into the lively fray. Laura dug in her purse, the item quickly passed to her friend before she focused on Dex again. "Sorry about that."

Dex shifted, impatient to be on his way. "What did you want to know?"

"Call me when you have a chance, all right? We can talk weaves and waves while your Sleep Subject dreams."

"I don't know shit about weaves, and you know it. Talk to your neuroscientist friends if you want . . . "

"I want to talk to you," Laura insisted as his wristband buzzed again. "But since that won't be happening for a while, just call me, all right?"

Rising on her toes, she pressed her lips to his cheek and dashed into the crowd. Dex blushed and glanced down at his feet. The red work disc leaned against his shoe. He picked it up and searched for Laura's lithe figure, but she had disappeared, engulfed by the cluster of Weavers and execs.

Another buzz and Dex tucked the disc into his pocket before he hurried away, mind on Eric's warning and the strange timing of Markway's death. He boarded the basement elevator, ready to seek out Keller, only to find him already on the move when the doors opened on Sub-level 2.

"We're up," Dex said.

"And?"

"It's true."

SOMNIUM

Ice blue eyes locked on Dex, who normally wouldn't have been able to hold such a look from a man like Nathan Keller, but in that moment, he had nothing to hide. Markway's death, strange as it was, was the truth. Cursing softly, Nathan stepped into the elevator and hit the button for Sub-level 5.

CHAPTER SIX

THE TRAIN FILLED to capacity after the first three stops at major cities. Behind Gillian's private compartment, the dining car had been a noisy nuisance most of the evening. She hadn't minded. The chatter kept her mind occupied picturing the people and the conversations behind the laughter rolling down the corridor. When the talk died down, Gillian settled into her book, only to find it didn't captivate her the way she'd hoped.

Eyes drooping, she pulled herself back to full consciousness, the worry over her mother, the tension of the panic attack and the long night catching up with her as the gentle rock of the train lulled her toward sleep.

Sleep. She'd never liked it much. Even as a baby her mother had difficulty getting Gillian to lie down. Back then, her dreams hadn't been quite so troubled.

Shifting to wake up her muddy limbs, she thought about the panic attack on the platform. It had been the worst she'd felt in years. Minor tremors happened all the time. A snatch of a streaming television show here, a glimpse at a smartphone there, almost any snippet of technology could trip her up, sometimes to the point where she'd missed appointments while curled up in a ball of cold sweat. Eliminating all technology but the essentials from her life had helped, but not much.

When the nightmares began, her father blamed it on Gillian's penchant for spooky books, her mother on the horror movies she loved. Both had been wrong, and despite their insistence on scrubbing her young world of everything more frightening than puppies and flowers, the nightmares had never gone away.

It had started on an uneventful Friday evening, the night spent watching *Aliens* with her brother, Toby, while their parents had been out to dinner. Ordered to bed when Liam and Amy Beth

SOMNIUM

Hardie arrived home, Toby had chased her up the stairs, 'jaws' snapping as she emulated Ripley and tried to blow him away. The pair quoted the old movie verbatim, Gillian going so far as to deliver Ripley's famous line before her brother had tackled her, a pillow fight ensuing before Amy Beth scolded them to bed.

It had been the last night Gillian ever wanted to dream.

Toby heard the screams a few hours later, the fight to wake Gillian proving disastrous when she'd punched her brother and slapped her mother hard enough to leave an angry red welt. She remembered nothing when they finally snapped her out of it. All that remained was an unshakable, lingering fear. She hadn't gone back to sleep that night. She'd barely gone back to sleep for the rest of her life.

Sporadic at first, the night terrors zeroed in on her psyche with a powerful punch that left her with more than an average fear of the dark. Each nightmare seemed as real to Gillian as daylight. Her life revolved around avoiding the dreams, and nothing anyone—not her mother, father, nor the multitude of psychologists—could say or do helped. The only spark of hope anyone had been able to offer was that she would one day grow out of them, the same way children grow out of their clothes.

Still, the nightmares persisted, and as she entered her teens, Gillian began to consume caffeine at alarming rates. It wasn't long before she found her way to more powerful stimulants. The slight tremors in her hands had gone unnoticed by those who worried more about the bags under her eyes and the dramatic weight loss she'd suffered than anything else. Whispers of anorexia circulated in the girls' locker rooms, replaced by bulimia when her appetite proved insatiable. Gillian didn't acknowledge or deny any of it. She'd simply gone on as if nothing had changed.

Dreams of an old hag, whose pus-riddled face and bone-crunching jaws plagued her youth, gave way to more imaginative visions. Each night her mind served up ever more violent deaths of family members or incorporated elements of gothic novels that ended badly when the crazed Bertha of *Jane Eyre's* world didn't die, or worse, came back to life after a skull-splitting plunge off a fiery roof.

Unable to sleep yet forced to function, Gillian suffered in scared silence until the day she stumbled upon the concept of lucid dreaming. Grabbing hold of the idea, she studied the phenomena, hoping to learn how to consciously behave within her dreams.

DEIRDRE SWINDEN

While she could never control what the actual dreams were, with practice, she gained enough awareness to recognize she was dreaming, and then to act with conscious decision within the dream reality. She learned her body's signs, the signals of the impending nightmares never varying from a tell-tale tingle that ran the length of her body, as if someone had activated her spinal network with a touch of a button. Later, she developed the ability to remain on the edges of REM sleep, going just deep enough to rest. Any night where she felt the tingle of her nerves, she did her best to stay awake, taking her rest on nights not plagued by darker dreams.

By the time she graduated college, she had cultivated a rather rare talent—the ability to consciously alter her actions within a dream. Each night she put her skills to the test, playing Ripley as she attempted to vanquish the aliens living in the recesses of her own mind.

Thoughts of suicide and depression inevitably accompanied her insomnia. As she aged, Gillian found her intentions growing darker every year, nothing but her mother's strong religious beliefs keeping her from severing ties with her own existence. She had nearly resolved to do it—condemning herself to an eternal hell couldn't be any worse than the one she lived on a nightly basis—when a fierce-looking stranger wandered into her realm.

At first he'd been merely a face in the crowd, watching her combat devils and demons. The idea of a handsome savior had never occurred to Gillian, which was likely why her mind had made his face so hideous—at least she thought it so at first. But when he finally waded into the fray, she discovered he was as capable of manipulating the dream state as she was. Together, they fought and won, his aggression and lack of charm comforting her as no handsome hero ever could.

But each time she went deep, the dreams seemed to grow stronger, forcing her into ever more intense situations, almost as if the nightmares had been studying her fears. Lately she had the irrational feeling that it wouldn't be long before she lost all control, and when she did, she'd be trapped in the nightmare forever.

The thought brought her out of a doze, and she shifted in her seat. Refocusing on her book, she tried to immerse herself in prose, but her attention waned. Before long, the train's gentle rock overwhelmed her, and the book toppled to the floor as at last Gillian succumbed to sleep.

CHAPTER SEVEN

NAVIGATING THE SECURITY to Somnium's dream jump suites seemed to Nathan like trying to get from New York to China by diving into a well. The first impediment included several large, armed men who knew every name they asked, but never deviated from the script of "Name" when the MCLs and Operators approached. Biometric eye and hand scans were followed by cursory pat downs before they passed into an airlock, only to be stopped again for a full body scan.

The extent of the technology Somnium held sacred was known to only a select few, and neither Nathan nor Dex would ever advance to that list. While Dex understood the inner workings of the dream link software, Nathan had never asked more than he needed to know. He simply didn't care. What was done was done. Every person who'd ever shopped the virtual rooms, attempted to play a video game developed using Somnium's base technology, talked on a 3D capable smartphone or learned how to speak and spell from a technical gadget had been caught in Somnium's virtual web. When the company had joined forces with online retailers to present an immersive virtual shopping experience, Clayton Miller and Somnium had damn near conquered the world.

Every day, more and more people chose to enter Somnium's worlds. For those who accepted the induction technology, the virtual rooms were nothing more than what they had always been—a mostly pleasant place for the mind to play. When Clayton Miller discovered a way to direct that play even when eyes were closed, eager industries lined up to toss around the ball. Porn mavens stood shoulder to shoulder with federal agencies to salivate over initial concepts and test runs. It had only been a matter of time and money before Miller directed both the waking and sleeping dreams of nearly every major population, the "I accept" button at the end of a long legal disclaimer no one ever read exponentially expanding his company's reach.

Every night, Somnium put products on display. For most, the dreams were simple enough—a barely remembered essence that helped to direct their hand when they shopped. As an MCL, Nathan knew for certain there were a finite number of dreams in the world, and most of the time, you weren't the only one dreaming them. But none of that mattered to him. He wasn't here to create the soporific fantasies that filled the days and nights of the lucky.

He was here to clean up the mess.

Entering their jump suite, Nathan veered into a small dressing room while Dex continued through a second airlock. Nathan suited up, his thoughts still on Markway, and he wondered if perhaps the old man hadn't been more than a little influenced by his own dreams when he'd first signed on to fight for those whose minds had rejected induction.

No one was sure when the deaths had started. People died in their sleep all the time. Most should be so lucky. But as more young people passed away in the absence of any known sleeping sickness, the foremost expert in nightmares, Elijah Braun, created the MCL from a handful of Somnium's own lucid dreamers. Using a new branch of sleep tech, the MCLs connected to and entered the dreams of those Dr. Braun had identified as potential Sleep Subjects. Those first few ventures were enough to discover a small glitch in the induction programming had shifted the way the Subjects experienced their dreams. Bodies reacted as if they were within the waking reality—a sleeping consciousness that had turned the threat of nightmares real.

The first years had been rough. Although the MCLs had fought diligently to save the dreamers, many were lost due to a lack of basic combat experience. New recruits were brought in with military backgrounds in addition to the required talents on the dream fields.

As the numbers of those affected by the glitch dwindled—either through acceptance of upgraded induction tech, or by other, more permanent means—the MCLs started calling the remaining Sleep Subjects the Elite. They were the last to be sacrificed "for the greater technological good" on the altar of virtual reality, and 8924's passing had dropped that number to a meager 24.

Kevin Davis's loss lay heavy on Nathan's mind as he joined Dex in the suite's inner chamber. He ran through all three of his assigned Elites' profiles, prepared to face the worst for any of them, yet knowing in his heart he would choose to die for only one.

"Who's on tap?" Nathan asked.

"8-3-1. Your dream girl got herself bitch slapped. Hard."

Adrenaline surged through Nathan's limbs. 831. The lowest number of the remaining Elite, and perhaps the best dreamer he'd ever had the privilege of serving. The challenges 831's mind offered were always vivid and frightening, and her talents in the dream reality were the stuff of MCL legend. Nathan had never let another MCL take his place once he'd established a link. For five years 831 had been his domain and his alone, and if he were forced to say why, his explanation had always been simple: 831's mind was too much damned fun.

Blue light from the tech infused the cool air. The skintight suit Nathan wore picked up the color in the metallic runners that lined his body. As he stood by the console where Dex worked, his suit reflected the pulsing light on wave screens that climbed wire netting like vines. The effect had earned Dex Cooper's desk the name "Chicken Coop" but it was far from a feathered mess. While less than concerned with his own personal hygiene, Dex had always been meticulous about his workspace. Currently the spotless console held nothing more than a handful of tablets and folders in a variety of colors, Dr. Braun one of the only heads of division left who insisted on paper backups. The largest folder stood open, Dex's careful printing labeling the inside of the tattered cover with the numbers 8-3-1.

In the center of the room, the link tank waited. Nathan fancied he could hear the gentle slush of the substance he climbed into every night, the material thin as water and yet stronger than rubber. It served to isolate his senses, depriving his mind of input from the real world and leaving him free to function at will in the subject's dream reality. Every time he climbed into the chamber, he had the sense of being swallowed by mud.

On screen, the waves danced, and Dex grinned. "Must not be looking forward to seeing you. Resisting the urge."

Nathan shrugged. "Always does. Prediction?"

"Down in less than 20."

"You sure about that?"

"It's all right here in the waves," Dex said and nodded to the bioelectric patterns flashing like heart rhythms across the left side of his screens. Nathan watched his own waves flow on the right, the mix a cocktail of his vital statistics, metabolic activity and neurological impulses. In the middle, a single row of monitors showed both Nathan and 831's waves crashing and mingling like tsunamis from opposite shores. A good Operator could monitor the movement with sufficient accuracy to predict the timing of the dream cycles. A highly skilled Operator could read a Sleep Subject's unique patterns and interpret the action as the dreams occurred—as if the waves were captions for the nightmare. Dex had shocked Nathan more than once with his uncannily accurate analyses of the dreams.

"831's holding tight to the delta," Dex said. "But she's slipped to NREM three times now. Won't be long."

NREM—the five-to-fifteen-minute pre-dream state of non-rapid eye movement. If Nathan was lucky, she'd go one more round, and he'd be able to slip in before she hit pure REM.

"Almost there," Dex said. "Wonder what she'll dream tonight."

"She dreams what they taught her to dream." Nathan tapped his code into a keypad next to the tank and then matched his palm to the glowing print of the biometric lock. The surface responded by undulating slightly, revealing the shimmering blue chamber that would hold his body, the substance pulsing in time with 831's waves. When Nathan settled in, the material would enhance connection, combining his energy and mind with hers in a single, unified pulse on Dex's center screens.

"Not true," Dex said. "She dreams the antithesis of what they taught her. If the dream advertising tech had worked, she'd be dreaming of milkshakes and fries and waking up to fight the urge to go to Mickey D's, just like the rest of the suckers out there. Poor schmucks. Never even know what hits 'em. She's one of the only real dreamers left." He slid his chair to the wall, flipped a few switches, then rolled back to the console. "She's holding out on you, my man. Snapped back to a doze. Damn this girl is good. Never seen anybody who can drop in and out like that."

Disappointment slugged Nathan across the jaw. If the trigger tech had been a mere snippet, 831 would be able to stay on the edge of the dreamscape rather than fall full force into REM. If she stayed on the outskirts, she wouldn't need him. "What'd she catch?"

"I'm just guessing but I think she got suckered into initial tech. If she goes all the way under, it'll be bad."

Nathan muttered a curse, strapped down his gloves and fitted a hood over his hair. Once in the tank, only his eyes, nose and mouth would stay above the surface. "Woman's damn creative when it comes to initials. Last week it was a full-blown zombie apocalypse. Week before that she was back at the beach."

"*Jaws?*"

Nathan's scowl was all the answer Dex needed to chuckle.

"I hate playing Quint."

Dex contained his amusement with difficulty. "Porn Weavers are on duty tonight. Maybe you'll get lucky, and she'll go for a sex dream."

Nathan glared at him.

"Easiest way to wake her up in a pinch."

"Not a whole lot of time for sweet talk when you're being burned at the stake."

"If she makes it to N3 . . . "

"Deep sleep? 831?" Nathan shook his head. "Never happen."

"But if she does, there's time enough for a good roll in the hay. And anyway, the number of times you've been in 831's head? Hell, you two might as well be married."

Nathan couldn't argue. In a way, it was true. They were more intimate than lovers. He and 831 had shared more nightmares than he cared to count, more than Markway had shared with Davis and more than any other MCL had shared with a single subject.

"Ahhh. There she goes. Can't resist it forever, can you darling?" Dex glanced up at Nathan. "She's moving down. You ready for this?"

"Let's do it. Link me in before she hits pure REM, will you? I need to be prepared for the shit that comes out of the walls."

"Red," Dex muttered with a shake of his head. "That woman dreams things covered in blood and then some. Initiating link. You'll be under in five assuming she goes all the way."

Nathan settled into the tank, the gel surrounding his frame until he couldn't feel his body. Dex bustled around him. The rest of the technology that would jump him into 831's dreams a confusion Nathan had little or no need to understand. When he'd asked on his first jump, the Operator shook his head and told him it'd be easier to teach a donkey to climb to the moon than teach a jarhead dream jump tech. Nathan hadn't much liked the comparison.

Set-up complete, Dex returned to his station and settled in behind the console. Music played in Nathan's head, a soothing requiem to the hell that lay ahead. "Two minutes."

Moving deeper into a slow-breath meditation, Nathan fixed his eyes on a large crystal of danburite, the material a bioelectric conductor that not only helped focus his mind but aided in the lucidity of the dream.

"Sixty seconds. She's hooked in and going down right before midnight." Dex's voice seemed to emanate from inside Nathan's head. "'*All that we see or seem is but a dream within a dream.*' Sleep well, my friend, and bring her home in one piece. See you in less than 20."

Nathan's chest hummed, the last link in his connection to 831 about to take place. He prepared himself for the feeling of falling, the kind that made most people surge awake to stop the plummet. When it hit, his well-trained limbs resisted the urge to save his spiraling psyche. Instead, he let himself fly, ribbons of light guiding him into Gillian Hardie's mind as she at last succumbed to sleep.

CHAPTER EIGHT

"BLOODY HELL." Gillian stood on what appeared to be an English moor. Purple heather swayed in a frigid breeze that tore through her jeans. Strands of auburn whipped her cheeks, and she tucked them behind her ears before she pictured herself in a thick pea coat, leather gloves and a fisherman's cap. With a second breath, she held a brilliant blade—a near perfect replica of the legendary Masamune Japanese samurai sword. The sheen danced in the light of a full moon painted red by approaching dawn.

The sun would never shine on such a landscape. Of that, Gillian was certain.

Black clouds thick with thunder swept away the moonlight, drenching Gillian in ominous darkness as a spray of sea foam kissed her cheek. She scanned the horizon and paused. A lone chair, large enough to be a throne but barren of the expected gilt sat on the edge of the cliff. A simple creation, it boasted nothing more than a ladder of wooden slats at its back and two thick arms. The seat lacked any contours to cradle the human body, comfort the last thing on the minds of its creators.

A piercing cry from an unseen gull forced Gillian's eyes to the sky. Beneath her feet a wetland of slick green moss placed her at the edge of a sharp cliff. At sea, a growing storm. On the bluff, the ghosts of Heathcliff and Catherine lurked without form.

At the sound of a cough, she spun, the clash of steel on steel sparking blue in the night and illuminating a war-torn face. Smirking, the newcomer dropped his ice-blue gaze to her outfit without letting go of the pressure on her sword.

"If we're going for *Wuthering Heights* again, perhaps a dress would be more fitting? Maybe something with a bustle? A silk corset to make your assets, shall we say, pop?"

"In your dreams, pretty boy, not mine." Gillian let her defenses drop. "It's good to see you, Nathan."

"The same, my lady," he said and bowed over her hand before straightening to look toward the horizon. Gillian followed his gaze, not surprised to find an ancient stone castle awaiting them.

"The Abbey." Nathan sighed as he prepared to face a host of religious zealots who asked relentless questions to which there were no right answers. Gillian would try to appease them. She always tried. And she nearly always woke when the flames started to sear her skin. "At least we're not already tied to the stake."

Brow furrowed, Gillian turned in a full circle. "Where did the chair go?"

"The chair?"

"I saw . . . " She shook her head at the barren landscape. "Never mind."

Nathan chucked his chin to the ruins. "Shall we?"

"Let's get the inquisition over with."

Stuffing her right hand in her coat pocket, Gillian exhaled a bit of tension as her fingers found a small coil of rope, a lighter and a serrated blade. Nathan exchanged his sword for a rifle. Ammunition lay draped over his chest and a pair of handguns rode leather holsters on thighs covered in loose fitting black pants tucked into combat boots.

"Damn ruin is two miles away," Nathan said. "Couldn't have dropped us a little closer?"

"Felt like going for a walk."

"Which is usually when the mutant hawks show up."

"It's night. No winged nemeses allowed."

"Never stopped them before," Nathan said and nodded to her sword. "That won't help if they do. Change out."

Instantly, Gillian strung an arrow where the sword had been, a compound bow held out before her.

"Better," Nathan said and once again scanned the horizon.

Gillian followed his gaze and then stomped a boot on the turf. "At least we're on solid ground."

"Anything's better than those damned sharks."

"It's a moor, Nathan. Usually find them east of oh, I don't know, an ocean. And my friend, you're here to help, not criticize. If I'm feeling the need for a tan, we'll head to Hawaii. No questions asked and none of your smart-ass remarks."

"When have you ever felt the need for a tan?"

"What did I just say about smart-ass remarks?"

Nathan grinned. "Ready?"

"As I'll ever be."

They moved slowly across the slippery slope, Gillian choosing her steps cautiously as they headed toward an outcropping of rock. Stopping short, Nathan knelt, a hand to the spongy surface.

"You feel that?" he asked.

"Feel what?"

"Tremor."

"I didn't feel any . . . shit." Gillian shifted her stance as he stood and placed his back to hers, the soft rise of the ground beneath her feet just enough to unhinge her balance.

"I think it's breathing," Nathan said.

"It?"

"The moor."

"That's new."

Nathan aimed his rifle at the ground. "If it swallows us . . . "

Ahead of him, Gillian pulled the rope from her pocket, the length uncoiling in waves around her feet. She tied one end to the arrow, then looped it through a quickdraw at her waist. Passing the coil, Nathan followed suit.

"We're going to need a strong anchor if we have to rappel," he said.

Barren landscape mocked them with a lack of anything suitable. Beneath their feet, the ground shifted in a slow, waking stretch. Fear flooded Gillian's limbs, Nathan's steady presence all that kept her from stumbling to her knees.

"Head for the rocks," he said. Gillian followed, feet moving slowly and carefully over the increasingly slime-coated stone. She had nearly reached the slick white surface of the outcropping when Nathan put a hand on her arm.

"Gill," he said, eyes wide with warning.

Her mind finally registered what she was seeing, the crisp white jutting somehow familiar, yet completely out of place on the moor. Mouth dry, she slid her tongue over her own much smaller versions of the glossy rocks. "You don't think those are . . . "

"Teeth," Nathan said and pushed her backward as the ground trembled again. "Move!"

Beneath their feet the monster rose, spilling them down slick scales toward the raging shoreline as the sleeping moor awakened.

"Dex, you got a minute?"

Dex dragged his gaze from the waves as Eric Wilson's head appeared on his console screen. "Whatever you got to say, say it fast. Keller's under and the action's getting good."

"Let me see the waves."

Dex transferred Eric's feed to observe the joined lines in the center screens. Practiced eyes watched the action in silence before Eric sighed with relief. "Normal."

"Hell yeah," Dex said, addressing Eric face-to-face once more. "Everything's going according to Somnium's master plan. In a minute or two we'll get the muah-ha-ha from the big bad, Keller will vanquish the evil and kiss the girl, and I will look upon that scowling, angry face I love so much once again. All's well that ends well."

"Let's hope it stays that way."

"It will."

"Dex—do you think—" Eric stopped short in his thought, eyes over Dex's shoulder. "What's that?"

"What's what?" Dex glanced back to find the fire-red work disc in view. "Oh right. Laura dropped it on my foot."

"You shouldn't have . . . " Eric jumped and held his wristband up to his face to check the display. "Son of a bitch."

"What is it?"

"Billings is on deck. Could be another Elite."

A tingle of apprehension crept up Dex's spine. "What's that, number four tonight?"

Eric's fingers tapped the air as he checked the feeds. "Blake went under a few minutes ago. That's three Elite under and another possibly triggered."

Stunned, Dex sat back. It wasn't unheard of to have four Elite under at once. Certainly not uncommon to have more than a few succumb to sleep each night. Nearly all of the Elite were on American soil, which cast a broad net of optimal dream time over the eastern hemisphere. But the Elite were all skilled in avoiding dreams and the triggers that brought about the worst of them.

"Go," Dex said. "Find out who it is."

"You should bring Keller out. Now. Before it's too late."

"He'd kill me."

"Worth the risk."

"Not to him. You know how he feels about 831. And besides, it's only too late if she flatlines, and even then I have three minutes to pull him before brain death occurs."

"Three minutes is a very long time to spend in an oxygen deprived brain," Eric said.

"Clinical death doesn't happen until the brain's energy ceases and the neurons stop firing. As long as there's electricity, there's always a chance she'll come back. He'd want me to leave him if it means she lives."

"Don't even think about that." Eric rubbed his temples. "Look, I know he'd die for her, for any of the Elite. But ask yourself this— is he willing to die with her?"

Slapping the connection closed, Dex pondered the answer as the waves jumped again.

"Hold on to me!"

Gillian reached toward Nathan, fingers clinging to a rock, the moss threatening to release her with a single wrong move. A taut rope bound them together, Nathan's feet right above her head. Stretch as she might, Gillian couldn't reach his hand.

"I can't," she said as her fingers slipped again. The weight of her body shifted dangerously, rope slicing against rock. Beneath her, hungry white creatures circled in black water. Above, the roaring menace leaned forward, powerful jaws hovering over Nathan's head. The edge of the moor crumbled like cheese beneath its weight.

"Control it," Nathan said, voice strong and stern over the roar of wind and waves. "You've done it before, you can do it now. Breathe, woman. Just. Breathe."

Clinging to the cliff, Gillian put her cheek against the moss and inhaled. A touch of sun landed soft as a feather on her skin. The roar of the moor slowed to the gentle gurgle of a mountain stream. At her back, Gillian rested on the downy green grass of a forest meadow.

"That's my girl," Nathan said, the reassuring presence of his leg a warm pillow against her cheek. "We're out."

Gillian fought back tears. "Not for long. Never for long."

A rough hand brushed hair from her forehead. "But for now."

With a nod, Gillian pushed up on her elbows and blinked at an all-too-familiar landscape. She groaned. "Bloody hell."

"You say that every time."

"And you know why."

Nathan eyed the Redwoods before inspecting the picnic lunch before them. "At least it always starts nice enough, although I would've preferred brie to gouda."

"Didn't realize you had such refined tastes," Gillian said in a voice that clearly told him where he could shove his cheese preferences.

"Try harder next time."

Fear ebbing as it always did when Nathan was with her, Gillian grinned. "Shut up and pour me a glass of that wine. If I'm facing down man-eating trees again, I need a drink. Damn you Steven Spielberg for making *Poltergeist* too good to forget."

Wary of the forest, Gillian watched the shifting shadows with a keen eye, a prickle of fear crawling up her arms. Nathan reached for the bottle. She caught his hand and pointed to the edge of the forest.

"Tell me you see it," she said.

"See what?" Nathan asked and spun to follow her gaze.

"The chair."

"What chair?"

The sky darkened, the wooden slats lost in the shadows. Boiling thunder clouds prepared to unleash a torrent of wind and rain. In minutes, powerful lightning strikes aimed directly at the clearing would send them scurrying for shelter among carnivorous limbs. Nathan watched the sky with apprehension.

"Something's different," he said.

Blood red clouds followed the black, sucking the heat of the day from the earth. Beside him, Gillian tensed and slipped her hand into the basket. The familiar ensemble of rope, knife and lighter reassured her. Beneath them, the ground shifted and rolled, the picnic blanket a rowboat adrift in a hurricane.

"What is that?" she asked.

Nathan shook his head at the crackling sky. "You tell me."

She gripped his arm. "Nate . . . "

Before she could utter another word, the ground dropped away and a black void swallowed them whole.

The engineer saw the fast-moving tanker truck in his mirror just before it plowed into the side of the Viewliner's third passenger car. At 12:03 a.m. a fireball shot 30 feet into the sky, consuming the truck and tossing the Viewliner from the tracks as if it were a child's toy. Metal twisted, the passengers who survived the initial impact screaming in a blinding inferno. Several more cars derailed, toppling the entire train as fiery bodies leapt from broken windows and stumbled forward to burn quietly among the trees.

In the sleeper car, Gillian Hardie's body flopped with the ease of a rag doll. The sudden movement of her head shattered the safety glass into spider webs. Later, the doctors would say that if she had been awake and able to hold herself stiff, the abrupt jarring would've snapped her neck. Broken couplings released the engine and two forward cars from the bulk of the wreck, and they careened into silence hundreds of yards from the fire.

It wouldn't be long before Gillian's unconscious body was found.

But time moves slowly in dreams.

CHAPTER NINE

ALONE BUT FOR his dreamer, Dex lingered on the waves. It was rare to lose an MCL, especially one as skilled as Markway. They were good fighters and strong dreamers. Many had been lucid dreamers long before ever joining whatever branch of service they had come from. Those who weren't developed the skill quickly enough thanks to Dr. Braun's training. Nightmares. Dreamscapes. Virtual reality. Dex wasn't sure any of it was worth it, and he didn't like the way Eric Wilson's warning kept rattling around in his head.

Not one to enjoy feeling unprepared, Dex swung from the waves to a second set of screens. With a few keystrokes he pulled up the histories of Keller's three assigned Elite and perused the last jumps. A quick skim of the link files showed nothing disturbing in the lines until he reached 831's history. At first he didn't see much of anything, but as he looked closer, he found several subtle changes. Starting just over three months ago, 831's dream activity had increased. Not so much that anyone would notice, after all, she suffered from persistent nightmare disorder—which was nothing if not "*persistent.*" But when taken as a whole, the increased frequency, coupled with an uptick in time spent within the dream reality was troubling. Add in the slight changes in the neuroscans from each jump and it was enough to make Dex's skin prickle with unease.

Sitting back, he let his eyes fall on the bright mystery of Laura's work disc. A check of the clock told him he had plenty of time left before 831's dream cycle would complete. He could call Laura and tell her he had it. He had just picked up the disc when a change in the hum of machinery caught his attention.

"What the hell?"

On the middle screens a jumble of light danced in unusual patterns. Confused, Dex tried to decipher their meaning.

"Not an arc. Okay. Not a fucking arc. Think Dex. Think. You didn't graduate at 16 with two degrees from MIT to sit on your ass when something goes wrong."

An alarm blared, and Dex swiveled in his chair to check 831's pulse. Something had forced 831's waves into a steep decline. Moments later, Keller descended at the same breakneck speed.

"No, no, no. This can't be happening. This cannot be happening."

Precious seconds ticked by as Dex silenced the squawking alarm, hands in motion to prep the emergency expulsion codes, eyes never straying from the screen as he waited for the signature arc that would confirm his worst fears.

"Come back to me, big guy," Dex said as the last numbers flew from his fingers. On the screen before him, the wretched computer asked if he really intended to initiate expulsion. "You're not going down if I can help it."

And yet, Dex hesitated.

If he pressed confirm, Keller's conscious would careen back from whatever hell 831 suffered in the dream reality and land hard in his own body. The repercussions of such a move might leave the MCL in shock, not to mention give him one hell of a headache for about three weeks, but shock was better than dead any day.

"Stabilizing," Dex said, awed gaze on the waves. "Jesus, she's stabilizing. You got her, big guy!"

Dex punched the air in victory, but the expected return to normal didn't come. Instead, the lines looked more like small, unsettled blips, connoting activity on a level deeper than sleep. Celebration abruptly halted, Dex sat forward, nose nearly touching the screens. "Not N3. Not this soon in the sleep cycle. So what am I seeing?"

An old memory surfaced. One his conscious mind discarded years ago, but his subconscious clung to, filing it away for just this moment when a singular, sterile note played in his mind.

"Not a flatline. Definitely not a flatline. But . . . oh hell no . . . "

The remembered scent of stale urine filled his nose, the little boy he had been, standing next to his mother while they waited by the bedside of his once lively grandmother. She had collapsed from a stroke the week before he turned six. The presents she had for him sat at home, unopened, while they hoped and waited, and waited and hoped, but neither had done any good.

That day his mother whispered a sweet goodbye in Gram's ear while Dex had fidgeted at the edge of the bed, watching the screens, fascinated by lines that spoke of what went on inside. Aside from the heart pump, the waves passing across the screen had been nothing more than small tremors. The doctor said it meant his Gram was no longer aware of anyone or anything, not even little Dex, who loved her so. When the lines shifted, the doctor ruffled his hair and said she was dreaming of heaven.

"Holy shit." Dex swung back to the keyboard, fingers flying to call up a similar pattern and he sat back, fist to his mouth, to compare the two. "Sweet Jesus, this can't be right."

It was a near perfect match: 831's statistics and the electroencephalogram of a comatose patient.

"Alive. She's alive," he said, relieved. But he wasn't sure what to make of the new pattern. The conclusion he wanted to draw was not one his logical mind could readily accept.

"If she's that far down, she can't possibly still be dreaming—can she?"

Nathan hit the linoleum with a grunt, shoulder taking the brunt of both his and Gillian's weight when she landed on top of him. In a flash he rolled her to the side, angling his back to whatever stood ready to attack, eyes racing around the hazy gray space until Gillian smacked her hands to his shoulders.

"I like you, my friend, but this is no place to get cozy," she said.

A crimson blush filled Nathan's cheeks. Nothing more than two layers of clothing kept them from being more intimate than even Dex could have imagined.

A wicked grin sparkled in his direction. "You're cute when you blush."

Nathan released her. "No one has ever called this face cute."

Gillian sat up and brushed dirt from her t-shirt. "Tell you what, we ever meet in the daylight, you take me to dinner and we'll see about me making us breakfast."

"Deal," Nathan said and helped her to her feet. He held her gaze, the feel of her pulse against his hand strong and steady, but she seemed to be losing heat. "Conjure yourself a sweatshirt or something, this place is fucking freez . . . " He stopped short, suddenly focused on their surroundings. "Where the hell are we?"

Ash covered the walls. Broken and burned furniture was piled in a discarded heap in a corner. Eyes wide, Gillian took in the nightmare dreamscape that had been all too real more than 20 years before, whole body quivering as she circled the room.

"No," she said, skin rippling in revolt. "Not here. Anywhere but here."

Nathan took her weight before she crumbled to the floor. Fear lurched through his limbs. In all the dreams they shared, she had never caved, never refused to keep going. She'd had her moments when the terror got hold of her, but she'd always come back to him. To watch her collapse, reduced to a mess of weeping flesh, was more than unsettling. "Where is here?"

Tears swam on the edge of her lashes, a long moment passing before she managed to gain her knees and lock them in place once again. Backing away from Nathan, she gripped her elbows and put her back to a piece of crumbling concrete. She stood before him nearly transformed, the child she had been easily seen beneath the woman's veneer.

"Home," she said and then spelled the word. "H-O-M-E."

Nathan cocked an eyebrow at their surroundings, the pile of ripped mattresses and rusty bedsprings a haven for rats and roaches. Against one wall, a line of old washing machines and dryers flanked a dilapidated change machine resting precariously on its three remaining feet. A dented dryer with a dark smear of rust like an angry arrow pointing at the lint trap caught Nathan's eye. The machine stood several feet forward from the others, as if it had stepped out of line. Only a single wooden chair with a slatted back seemed intact. "If this is where you're cooking me breakfast, no offense but I ain't eating it."

Gillian slid down the wall, knees pulled to her chest. "Not my home now. My home then."

"Then?"

She pressed her forehead to her knees. "The misspent years of my youth. My home. For five very long years."

Nathan knelt before her and gripped her hands. "Talk to me. Where are we?"

Tucking herself deeper into a ball, Gillian silently pointed at a copper plate next to a set of light switches on the wall. Concerned,

DEIRDRE SWINDEN

Nathan brushed away years of dust and ash, the scent of burnt wood still heavy in the air. The letters he revealed were simple and black, but a shrill note of warning rang in Nathan's head as he read the words:

Laundry Room 3-B. Davidson State Mental Institution.

CHAPTER TEN

T HE EVENING HAD been going well, a fine dinner served and consumed, French wine still flowing as the midnight hour arrived. Clayton Miller's guests were enjoying themselves immensely. As he prepared to wrap up the festivities with a reminder of the next morning's facilities tour, his assistant appeared in the corner, Evan James's face paler than usual. Dark eyes signaled Clayton, and after a few more minutes of smiles and answers, he pulled away to join Evan by the door.

"What is it?" Clayton asked.

Evan merely held out the ever-present tablet, MCL Blake's latest—and last—jump moving smoothly before his eyes until the last two minutes, when the signature arc left both Blake and 9425 in flatline. As Clayton read the report, he felt a cold sweat break out around his balls and looked up sharply at Evan.

"Any others?"

"Keller is under on 831. Billings is prepping now for another Elite."

"Tell me about Blake."

"Dr. Braun is still examining the body. He has yet to post the results. All we know is that it was an arc the likes of which none of our Operators have seen in years. Not since the first losses."

"Jesus," Clayton muttered. Much as he had denied it to Braun's face, he couldn't help thinking the doctor may have been right about the waves. And if it were another glitch in the induction tech, everything Clayton had built would fall, and he would never get his hands on what he really wanted.

"There's something else, sir. Senator Wilcox called. Seems he heard about Markway."

"How the hell . . . " Clayton stopped himself as his voice rose, a glance tossed over his shoulder at his guests. He ran a hand over his lips and nodded to Evan. Manufacturing a smile, he let his voice boom across the room.

"My friends, Mr. James will show you to your rooms for the evening, and of course, your money is no good at any of the game rooms or bars on the Corridor tonight. Please excuse me, business calls. I'll see you all for the tour in the morning."

Cooing in happy delight, his guests released him.

"Get me Braun as soon as possible," Clayton said. Leaving his assistant to manage the horde, he strode down the hall to his office.

How long had it been since he'd spoken to Alistair Wilcox? Clayton couldn't be sure. Long enough that a call from his old business partner on a night like this seemed at once precipitous and dangerous. While it was possible the Senator's intention might be a simple "duty" call in the wake of Markway's death, Clayton didn't delude himself it would be.

Alistair had oversight of the U.S. Government's dealing with Somnium. When the time had come to ensure Somnium's mission would be allowed to continue, Alistair had been the natural choice to run for office. Amiable when he needed to be, he had a way with people Clayton could only marvel at. He'd been elected immediately, wormed his way onto the proper committees, and then paved the way for Somnium's rise. By agreement, Alistair had never once returned, choosing instead to receive confidential updates on Somnium's activities. That he had heard about Markway so quickly was troubling, and Clayton wondered just who had given Alistair this particular update.

Safe inside his office, Clayton poured himself a large glass of bourbon, sat down at his desk and faced the window. Outside, the night lay deep and silent, the furor of the Corridor relegated to the far side of the immense building. He vaguely registered the majestic view of the rising quarter moon over the mountains, but his mind drifted to a conversation that had taken place nearly 30 years before, when the Somnium technology had been in its infancy. He and Alistair had been the only people who had believed in the possibilities. Like Gates and Allen, they had spent a lifetime in a make-shift laboratory before they'd turned 25, perfecting the tech and developing the induction program. Delivery had been an issue, until Alistair made a simple suggestion.

"Treat it like a virus."

The outcome had been a well-controlled program that required nothing more than the use of a satellite, streaming platforms and a few select placements via smartphones and tablets. With the increased acceptance of wireless technologies, Somnium had found its real footing, and the rest flowed naturally.

Until the first wave of sleeping death.

It had started slowly. Years passed before the statistics showed anything more than two or three hundred people dying in their sleep in the major cities. It had taken a wave of "sleeping sickness" for it to be called to Somnium's attention, and even then, the rising rates of night terrors in children across the globe were little more than a blip on the screen. Most blamed it on the increasing susceptibility of children to violence peddled through television, music and video games.

Alistair had been the one to make the connection. A friend's daughter suffered the sudden onset of night terrors after a night streaming old movies on Somnium's network. A night, Alistair discovered, that coincided with the initial induction programming wave. Looking back, it seemed so simple. A "glitch" Alistair called it. Something they'd fixed by the second round of live programming. But by then the damage had been done.

"Dr. Miller?"

Clayton looked up from the dark landscape and gulped down half his drink before he stood to face his assistant. "Yes?"

"I thought you'd like to know there's been another," Evan said.

"Another?"

"Trigger."

"Who?" Clayton asked.

"Deakins is on deck."

Clayton dropped his chin to his chest, hand over his eyes. "Another Elite?"

"Yes sir."

Clayton cursed softly and faced the window again. Contemplating his reflection for several long seconds, he tucked his hands in his pockets, suit jacket billowing out around his slim hips. "Where's Braun?"

"On his way."

"Keep me apprised of all MCL activity. If one of them so much as sneezes, I want to hear about it."

"Yes, sir." Evan paused at the door, eyes on his tablet as his brow furrowed.

"What is it?" Clayton asked.

"An accident on the northeast corridor railway. Not far from here. Perhaps we can offer our medical staff and services? The press would be invaluable."

"Absolutely not. Last thing we need tonight is a bunch of strangers on the premises."

Evan clenched his fist by his side and let his dispassionate stare linger on Clayton for several moments before he left the room. Clayton faced the darkness of his reflection once again, brown eyes focused on black irises, the windows, some said, to the soul. He touched a hand to the glass.

"Tonight," he said with a growing smile. "All of your dreams will finally come true."

"What the hell just happened?" Dex said to no one in particular as the lights in the jump suite flickered. Feet firmly on the floor, he inspected the controls. Everything seemed to be running smoothly, and if it didn't, instant back-ups would come on, the redundant generators set to ensure power to the rooms never went out.

But something had caused the lights to flicker, and the repercussions if Keller woke without a return trigger could be devastating. Dex and the other Operators had once asked about such a possibility. Dr. Braun's reply had involved a stern look, a warning that threatened treasured parts of their anatomy, and the implication that MCLs without a conscious mind would likely eat more than brains.

Of course, Dex wasn't exactly sure Keller would wake up. Ever.

Opening a connection, he called Laura. Drunken laughter, merry voices, all the happy sounds of the Corridor on a Friday careened into the quiet room as Laura's face bobbed into view.

"Dex! What's up?" she asked.

"What happened?"

"What do you mean?"

"My lights flickered."

Laura let her eyes roam the restaurant. "Nothing happened here."

"You didn't lose power?"

"Nope. You all right?"

"I'm fine. Just a little spooked. Is Eric around?"

"He took off. On deck with Billings."

"If you can get him before he goes through to the suites, tell him to stop in."

"You got it. And Dex . . . " She leaned closer to the phone, voice hard to hear among the chaos. "They're saying Blake arced."

A thousand-legged insect crawled down Dex's back.

Laura signed off before Dex could tell her he had her work disc. He checked the clock, the countdown nearing the last few minutes of a standard REM cycle. All MCLs were to be pulled after 20 minutes of dreaming, or so the Operators' manual said. Any dream lasting longer than that meant both dreamer and MCL were only two percent likely to make it out alive. Keller had pushed 831 to the limit before, and he had always won. But 831 was no longer in a standard cycle. Hell, Dex wasn't even sure she was still dreaming. Was it possible to dream in a coma?

The clock continued its inexorable march toward 20 minutes, while Dex stared at his screens.

He had a choice to make. If he pulled Keller out now, 831 would die.

And Keller would kill him.

If he didn't, Keller would follow Markway. And 831 would still die.

And Keller would kill him.

"What happens if I let you go?" Dex whispered. Nineteen minutes. In 60 seconds, Keller and 831 would go where no MCL had gone before. Behind him, the pod door released with a whoosh of air and Eric Wilson joined him.

"Laura said you . . . " Eric followed Dex's gaze to the slow tick of the clock. "What the hell are you doing?"

Dex didn't move, mind still attempting to make a choice whose repercussions he couldn't know. Eric shook him and when he got no response, headed for the controls. In a flash, Dex jumped to his feet and threw out a hand to cut him off. "Don't touch a goddamn thing!"

"You have to get him out!"

"I know! Please . . . I need to think."

"There isn't time to think. You're going to kill them both. Do you hear me? Dex!"

"Look at the waves! Fucking look and then tell me if I should pull him out."

The sound of Dex's panic was enough to stay Eric's hand. A quick glance at the screens made his knees crumble and he stumbled backward, a hand out to the desk to hold himself up. "This looks like she's . . . "

"Comatose."

"But those patterns . . . They're . . . Oh . . . Oh my god." Eric sat down hard, the wheels on Dex's chair carrying him away from the console, focus never leaving the middle screens. "831's still dreaming, isn't she?"

"Yes," Dex said and let out a breath he hadn't known he was holding.

"But if 831's comatose, then Keller's . . . "

"Trapped. If I pull him, 831'll die."

"Have you tried?" Eric asked. "To get him out?"

Dex shook his head. "And I'm not going to."

Anger balled Eric's hands into fists. "You can't just leave them! The manual explicitly says . . . "

"I know what it says! Show me the page where it details what to do if a Sleep Subject goes comatose while dreaming and I'll be happy to do whatever the goddamn guidelines suggest." Dex narrowed his eyes in warning. "But I won't pull Keller. Not if there's a chance 831's still dreaming."

"All right," Eric said and slowly relaxed his hands. "All right, I get it. But there's got to be something we can do."

"You got any bright ideas, I'm listening."

"Can we send someone else in?"

"And risk a second stuck MCL?" Dex shook his head. "We have no idea what that would do to 831. A second connection is always a risk, especially with the skilled dreamers. Even if it didn't override her system, she might take out any newcomer just because." Deep in thought, Dex looked over the tech, fingers dancing absently in time with the classical music Keller played to enhance his jump meditation. "There's got to be another way to reach him. Something . . . "

"You're taking too big a risk," Eric said. "We have no idea how long 831'll be like this. What if she never wakes up?"

"Then he never wakes up and they can live a long happy life together inside her vegetized head."

Galvanized, Eric headed for the door. "We need to bring Dr. Braun in on this. Now. Find out if he's really stuck."

"Don't," Dex said. "Please. Not yet. She's still following the normal dream patterns, so REM should be done soon. If she goes another full cycle, I'll have an hour at least to figure out what this is before she dreams again. Hell, if she makes it to N3 sleep, it may be the best night's rest she's had in years."

"If she gets there. We have no idea what will happen the further down she goes. What if she can't make it back? Even to the REM cycle?"

Dex held out his hands, palms up, pleading with his friend. "You know how Keller feels about 831. He wouldn't want us to let her go easy."

Eric's hollow eyes refocused for the first time that night. "All right," he said at last, and Dex nearly hugged him.

"Thank you."

Wristband humming, Eric shook his head. "I gotta go. But stay in touch. You see anything weird—weirder—call me. Better yet, call Braun. Promise me."

"Will do." Dex faced the screens as the jump clock rolled over 21 minutes. Reaching out, he reset it to zero.

"Jesus," Nathan muttered and looked at Gillian. "Why didn't you say something?"

"What was there to say?" she asked. "You don't know what it's like for me, even now. To admit to something like this? People don't look at those of us who have spent time in these places the same way. Hell, most of the staff wouldn't look at us while we were here. We're invisible to the world because they don't want to know it could happen to them, that they might somehow catch crazy just by breathing the same air."

"Gill . . ."

"So I'll ask you once and only once," she said, green eyes imploring. "Would you still have come to help me if you knew I was nuts?"

"Gillian." Nathan sank to a squat before her. With a soft hand he brushed hair from her face and cupped her chin. "I'll always come."

Reaching out, she encircled his neck, grip so fierce Nathan nearly lost his breath as he drew her to her feet.

"Thank you," she whispered.

"You're welcome." Overwhelming joy sparked in Nathan's stomach at the pressure of her lips on his cheek. Afraid he'd lose himself in a dream he would never actually get to live, he let her go. "Conjure yourself a sweater or something. Seems this floor isn't going to swallow us anytime soon. And where the hell are your shoes?"

Startled, Gillian looked down to find her feet bare as they had been when she'd taken off her boots on the train. Imagining the texture of leather encasing her feet, she took a few deep breaths as Nathan moved around the room, searching for a way out. When he came full circle, he found her standing before him wearing the same jeans and t-shirt she'd had on when she arrived and a baffled expression.

"I can't change it," she said. "And the kit's gone. The rope, knife and lighter. They're not in my pockets. They're always within reach. It's the first thing I learned." Gillian eyed him. "And why on Earth are you wearing that?"

Nathan glanced down at his attire to find he was in his link suit, something he never would have conjured in the dream reality, let alone in Gillian's presence. He stepped back and breathed deeply, his own image in real clothing mirrored in his mind. Opening his eyes, he found himself still sheathed in the slinky fabric.

"Nothing," he said. "I can't change it."

"This isn't right," Gillian said. "Everything we had with us in the last stage is gone. Like it was . . . "

"Erased."

Gillian reached out and Nathan slipped his hand in hers.

"You ever had that happen in a dream?" she asked.

"No. You?"

She shook her head. "I don't like this."

"Me neither." The room shifted, the ash gray walls replaced with gaudy yellow tile, the sounds of a living, breathing institution breaking the silence before it flashed back to gray.

"It's waking up."

"Like the moor," Nathan said. "At least it's a similar pattern. Gives us something to work with. What was it like when you were here?"

"Cleaner. Too clean. Sterile, like a morgue."

"Bad choice of words." Nathan yanked a set of dusty scrubs from a pile of old laundry and shook out the bug carcasses. With a glance back at Gillian, who politely turned away, he slipped out of his link suit and into the scrubs.

After a moment she said, "It was never this quiet."

Distant voices crept through the walls like ghosts. Tiles the color of sunshine filtered through smog fought to be seen before drifting back behind ash as the room shimmered. Further away, ominous screams careened along the linoleum hallways.

Gillian shuddered, the hair on her arms standing at attention. "That's more like it."

"Tell me what happened here."

"It burned."

"Before that."

"Nothing. Too much." Gillian's mind raced through the years and the fears she had hidden so deep she fought against remembering them even now. Down the hall, metal scraped over metal, the sound like a shower curtain dragged to the side. "This is where I learned."

"Learned what?"

"How to control the dreams. So why can't I now?"

"Just means we need to work with what we've got." Nathan sifted through the debris in the hopes of finding a weapon. "Why are we here, Gill? Why does this place frighten you?"

She shot him a look that clearly said, "Are you kidding?" and Nathan shrugged.

"Sorry. But if this place frightens you, why haven't you dreamed of it before?"

"My parents brought me here when I wouldn't sleep. They said it was to protect me. I'd grown addicted to stimulants and collapsed one day when I was 13. Officially, the docs labeled it as a psychotic break due to persistent nightmare disorder-induced insomnia. The dreams. They were bad."

"Who taught you lucid dreaming?" Nathan pounced on a broken chair, the nails like claws as he pried the wooden back from the seat.

"One of the doctors here. He gave me a book."

"That's it?"

"That's it."

"No other help?"

"Nothing that worked," Gillian muttered.

Nathan paused, a hand out to stroke her cheek. "It's a wonder you're still alive."

"No shit."

"Tell me everything you can remember."

Wrapping her arms around herself, Gillian set her back to the wall and forced her recollection to the surface. "I read the book in one night. Took me a month before it actually worked. Just recognizing when I was dreaming helped me wake myself up. I picked up on signals. No sense of smell. Not being able to read or not knowing how I got somewhere. That sort of thing. As I became more aware, more lucid during the dreams, it got easier. Of course, mastering the fear also meant that it got harder to wake myself up. All the usual techniques, screaming, slapping or hurting yourself, falling—they stopped working for me years ago. Even a surge of adrenaline couldn't wake me when I went deep."

"You think that's why the dreams are getting stronger?" Nathan asked.

"Christ. Now I'm a fear junkie?"

"Never said junkie."

"You implied it."

Nathan offered nothing more than a wry smile.

"I created the survival kit—the rope in case I found myself down a hole or in need of climbing, the lighter for fire and light, and the knife for obvious reasons. Manipulating myself and the environment came later. It took me years to master it."

"And you were here the whole time?"

"I earned my high school diploma here," Gillian said. "They let me out when I turned 18." She stood beside him, eyes on the shifting gray color of the door while Nathan broke down the chair. "I came to this room the night of the fire."

"Fire?"

"It started here. An orderly was killed. Michael Shearer."

Nathan eyed her trembling hands, uncertain why an orderly would frighten her so badly.

"Things happen in hospitals like this, Nathan." Gillian lifted a piece of broken wood and held it before her. "Things that go unreported, or if reported, not believed because of the state of our minds. Things we couldn't get away from. They were, after all, the ones with the keys to our rooms, and more often than not, we were tied down for our own protection." She spat out the last word as if it tasted foul.

Nathan stared at her. "Gill . . . "

"I don't need or want your pity," she said and faced the doorway, a far off look in her eye as she steeled herself for what might come through. "I don't deserve it."

Puzzled, he watched her carefully, but she wouldn't look at him.

Down the hall, a door creaked open, the slow whine of unoiled hinges dragged out for a maddeningly long three seconds. A hush followed, the sound like the rustle of leaves on concrete. A loud crack ripped through the room, and Nathan faced the door to find the solid, heavy wood had repaired itself from the floor all the way to the filmy glass window.

"Gill, we need to move."

"There's nowhere to go. Nowhere he won't find me. That's what he said. That night and so many others. Until the last time. After that he never spoke again." The flat timbre of her voice and simple resignation in her eyes was unnerving. "He's still here. Trapped in my nightmares. Just like I am. Maybe he's always been here. I watched that bastard die, and he didn't stop laughing. Not even when the whole fucking place started to burn."

The soft rustle moved toward them from an unseen spot down the hall. Nathan stood beside her, the wooden stake in his hand feeling woefully inadequate. He propped a piece of an old chair under the doorknob before he scanned the debris again.

"Sheets," Nathan said, but Gillian didn't move. He gripped her arm, the faraway look one he had seen on the battlefield. It frightened him more than what approached in the hall. "Gill! Stay with me."

With a gasp and a shudder, she came back to him. Relief slipped through Nathan's limbs. "Find sheets," he said. "As many as you can. Until you wake up we have two choices, fight or flight. And right now, flight seems like a very good option."

"Sheets." Gillian nodded. "On it."

As she moved about the scattered debris and checked the old dryers, Nathan tossed several rotting chair parts and mattresses away from the far wall. He uncovered a small window just as Gillian found her way back with an armload of potential rope.

Outside the door, the room shifted. Bustling noises of a busy hospital reached their ears. The lights overhead flickered, igniting the room's yellow walls as they surfaced from the dusty gray interior. Bars covered the window.

"We have to move fast," Nathan said as the laundry settled once again. The ominous shuffle came closer. A shadow passed in front of the milky glass window. Gillian tied the sheets together with strong knots. At the door, the knob rattled and turned, grunts of eager excitement from the thing beyond, enough to fray Nathan's nerves. He picked up the slack in the sheets and broke the window. They were three floors up and had enough sheeting to reach only two.

"Any more?" he asked. Gillian shook her head. "Then we're going to have to jump."

The room surged to life and a young woman rushed inside. She wore torn sweats and a coating of blood from a wound on the side of her head, ponytail askew. The deep, panicked green of her eyes was immediately recognizable as she searched for a place to hide.

Gillian caught her breath, trembling hands clutching her own head in pain. "Oh God, not again. Please not again."

Nathan hauled the sheet rope toward the window, only to have it pool at his feet. The hideous mustard yellow walls beamed with sparkling fluorescent light, the bars of a fully functioning mental institution firmly in place as both Gillians collapsed to the floor.

Sirens careened into the night air. The heat of the fire melted the tracks. Those who lived huddled in tight patches of human misery on the road, the moans and wails of the wounded mixing in eerie wolf-calls to the night sky. A broken moon overlooked the scene with smiling indifference.

Survivors helped the others escape the train cars, the bravest racing into the heat to see if any of those locked in the three most affected cars remained alive. Two more passenger lives were lost in the efforts. The news stations would later hail them as heroes, profiling their lives and capturing the grief of their spouses and children. Splinters in the skin of pain.

Bodies lay scattered around the site. Blood black against

concrete and grass, caramelized by the heat of flames that sucked air from the sky to feed hungry tongues. By the time the engines arrived, trees had been engulfed, the surrounding rocks scorched, grass charred.

News helicopters circled above, capturing the chaos and broadcasting it over the airwaves to the insatiable public, who digested the carnage and vomited it back to all they knew.

A searchlight lingered over a single corpse, pale skin glowing in the flames and searing heat despite the distance from the scene of impact. A bloody splotch on a rock nearby, the camera focused on a stuffed giraffe that had avoided decapitation by bare minimum of thread. Its tiny owner had not been so lucky.

In the overturned sleeper car, no one noticed Gillian Hardie still breathed.

CHAPTER ELEVEN

K NEE BOUNCING NONSTOP beneath the polished steel desk, Dex watched the waves. On his personal tablet, the projected feeds from Somnium's security cameras skipped among the offices and Corridor shops as if it were the evening news.

On a Friday night, anyone who wasn't working or preferred the company of family found their way to the Corridor and stayed long after midnight. Restaurants buzzed with the hum of voices, music, laughter and singing, the din strong enough to crowd out thoughts.

Flicking his way through the feeds, he landed in *Cliché*, a small bar frequented by Weavers and Operators who got the joke. It was his and Eric Wilson's favorite haunt, the discussions they'd gotten into over a plate of wings and pints of beer historic, or so they thought at the time. The ethics of Somnium's practices had been hotly debated, options for helping the Elite that seemed brilliant by the light of the jukebox always felt a shade too risky to mention during working hours.

Tonight, those discussions might have been relics from the stone age.

As he searched the cameras for MCLs and zoomed in on their conversation to eavesdrop on any news of Blake, Dex thought back to his recruitment, seeing it now for the clandestine bargain it had been. Honored to receive such treatment, he had been bewildered by the offered paycheck and then startled to discover that yes, he would indeed set aside some of his basic morals for a creative combination of science, money and dreams.

If anyone other than Eric knew he had let Keller go longer than the standard 20, he'd likely be fired on the spot. Dex had read his contract closely enough to know it would be years before he could land another tech job, and if he ever spoke of the MCL division, he'd lose absolutely everything that remained in his bank account.

SOMNIUM

But at that moment, the only thing that mattered were the waves.

Instead of the subtle manipulation of innocuous dreams, Dex saw them—perhaps for the first time—for what they truly were. Lives out of balance.

Markway's arc had been unsettling. If it were true that Blake had gone down, Dex had to admit he would no longer be able to find Somnium's mission as simple as he had when he signed on. After all, what was one more advertisement? They weren't manipulating someone's decision any more than a commercial on television. Parts of Somnium just functioned when the rest of the world had gone to sleep, playing commercials directly to the brain. It was no more harmful than sleeping with music or the television on—two things Dex had done all his life.

But as he followed the slight hitches in 831's waves, he considered things he'd taken for granted differently. The tech had become more than just a commercial. Somnium had become more than just a virtual reality company. And he had become more than just an Operator.

Two lives danced on his screens. Dex stood as a god before them. All it would take to become their executioner was a flip of a switch. He glanced at 831's file.

"I don't even know your name," he said and pulled the paperwork across the steel desk.

As he read, he thought about Markway's death, and about Keller and how he would be happy to forfeit his life for a woman he'd never actually met. He thought about 831, who never had a choice other than to give up. And he thought about himself, wondering how much he would be willing to sacrifice to help save just one.

"Fuck it," he muttered.

Biting down on his bottom lip, Dex put his hands in motion to do what he did best.

Yellow walls faded in and out. At the door, angry scratching intensified into a fierce pounding that reverberated along the empty halls like a jackhammer. Hinges groaned under the weight of whatever lay beyond.

Two Gillians—the teen she had been and the woman he knew—lay in a faint at Nathan's feet. One was a memory, an ephemeral actor in the dream, and while every instinct told him to protect the teen, it was the woman he needed to save.

"Gillian," Nathan said as loud as he dared. No response. He slipped the sheet rope around her waist and tied it tight. Lifting her into his arms, he turned for the window to find the bars once again in place as the door crashed open.

The putrid stench of an age-old bog cut off the air until Nathan felt as if he'd been coated in an algae-infested blanket. A slosh, like the sound of wet skin on linoleum, lurched slowly toward them as a low chuckle rumbled through the room. It was followed by a short and uneven staccato tap. Nathan chanced a glance over his shoulder as Gillian stirred.

"Hello, girlie."

What slithered through the door was a grotesque parody of a human. Its eyes glowed, livid with hatred, the sallow yellow of the room echoed in what little remained of his skin. The wooden tap proved to be an exposed and blackened heel bone. But its driving force lurked just beneath its crumbling hips. Gillian had buried this fear long ago, and what rose from the grave of her memory looked as if it had spent 20 years clawing its way out.

On the floor, Young Gillian scrambled to get away. Trapped against the wall, she curled herself into a ball against the dented dryer, heedless of the electric sparks erupting from the back of the faulty machine. "Stay away. Stay away from me. Don't you touch me!"

The thing dropped to its knees, curled dirty, talons around Young Gillian's ankle and pulled the girl forward. It tore the sweatpants from her hips, discolored nails leaving lines of burning red blood behind. A fist strike to the girl's temple sent her reeling, the floor undulating like an image in a fun-house mirror.

"Hold on," Nathan muttered and stumbled to the left. He lost his hold on Gillian who toppled onto a pile of debris.

The room shifted back to ash and soot, the vision of the past disappearing as quickly as it had come, nothing but the young girl and the monster left behind. Nathan put himself between Gillian and the thing in the corner, its lip-less grimace landing square on the window as it readied itself to pounce.

"Gonna eat you alive, little girlie."

"Get away from her, you bastard." Gillian emerged from behind Nathan, a chair leg in hand. She swung down with everything she had. Three nails embedded themselves in the monster's skull. The rotten cheekbone shattering as she struck again and again, the brunt force sending the slime-ridden filth to the floor.

"Glad to have you back," Nathan said. "Now haul your ass out the goddamn window before I throw you out."

Gillian hiked herself onto the sill as the room shimmered between past and present once more. "You always say the sweetest things."

Nathan climbed up behind her and stared down into an abyss. Mist swirled below, hiding whatever lay beyond. Inside, the hospital breathed, yellow walls resurfacing. Smoke rose from the dryer, and the heap in the corner began to laugh.

"You can't hide from me, girlie. You never could."

"Maybe not," Gillian said. "But I can still run."

Freeing herself from the sheet, Gillian held out her hand, green eyes landing on Nathan.

"Time to fly," she said.

Nathan felt his back straighten, the joy of being seen by those eyes enough to outweigh any fear of what lay beneath the mist as he took her hand in his.

A screech of anger tore through the room. Skeletal fingers stretched through the bars, a single claw sinking deep into Gillian's heel. She ripped her foot away, the action propelling them off the ledge and into the darkness beyond.

SSS 831: Gillian Hardie. Age 35. Occupation: Writer/Editor. Marital Status: Single. Diagnosis: Persistent nightmare disorder with multiple psychotic episodes; insomnia coupled with severe depression. Current Medication: Patient refused all therapeutic attempts at pharmaceutical intervention after succumbing to stimulant addiction and institutionalization. Survival Prognosis: Weak.

"Gillian Hardie," Dex said and sat back, eyes on the waves. "Nice to finally meet you."

The classified dossier on Somnium's longest surviving Sleep Subject had been enough to turn Dex's stomach. It hadn't taken much to find it, and he wondered how easy it would be to hack past some of Somnium's heavier security. Skin tingling with the thrill, he had to remind himself he'd been "recommended" to Somnium by the Department of Justice and warned not to fuck up again when they'd dropped him off.

Chewing on his lower lip, he considered the new information. Overhead, the lights flickered, and Dex mentally ran through the chain of failures that would need to occur for a full power loss in the suite. It was an array of impossible scenarios that had suddenly become real possibilities when the lights dimmed again. Preoccupied with his thoughts, he nearly missed it.

A dip in the center waves.

"Another stage," he muttered and glanced at the clock. He wondered vaguely if Guinness kept a record of the longest REM cycles. "At least you're not going any lower. What's happening to you, Gillian Hardie? And how can I help?"

A few quick taps to his tablet brought Laura onto his screen.

"What?" she said, annoyed at his disruption. She turned her camera just far enough to show off the handsome marketing executive sitting beside her.

"I need you to find someone for me."

"I'm busy, Dex . . . "

"I could hack the tracker myself, but you've got access. I need you to find Gillian Hardie."

Laura excused herself from the bar and ducked into the quiet of the Ladies' Room. "How the hell do you know that name?"

"Don't ask. Find her for me, will you?"

Laura pursed her lips in disapproval.

"Just do it, Laura."

"Don't you talk . . . "

Dex leaned in. "Keller's still under. And so is 831."

The screen tilted in a vertigo inducing tumble from Laura's hands. It hit the floor face down, a bold crack in the tiles filling Dex's screen. "Laura?"

"I'm here," she said and picked up the phone. "You went down over two hours ago."

"I did."

"And Keller's still under?"

"Plausible deniability. Find her. Please."

"I'm on it." She dug into her bag, panic moving her hands. "Where the hell is my . . . "

"Work disc? You dropped it," Dex said and held the disc up. For a moment, she looked ready to vomit. "You all right?"

"Yeah. Yeah, I'm fine. That's my personal project disc, Dex. Don't mess with it, all right?"

"I'll keep it safe for you. Call me when you've got her."

Dex severed the connection and checked the waves. "Hold on, 831." Picking up her file, he read quickly until he stumbled upon a section of Dr. Braun's personal notes.

' . . . similar to SSS 542, 831 displays an array of lucid dreaming capabilities. According to her MCL, her ability to manipulate herself within the dream environment is uncanny at times. However, she is unable to release or reset to a more normal dream state. When triggered, she is immediately immersed in a nightmare realm, and typically goes through a double cycle with a 60-minute lull between dreams—markedly faster than most sleep subjects. MCL Keller notes that her nightmares are increasing in intensity . . . '

Dex looked up the record. Somnium Sleep Subject 542 was before his time, but he knew the subject's fate. He wondered what he might learn, fingers flying as he once again breached Somnium's security only to be stopped by an even more difficult firewall.

"Shit just gets deeper," he muttered and cracked his knuckles. "But Dex Cooper always finds a way. Let's do this."

"What are you telling me?" Clayton Miller pressed two fingers to the bridge of his nose and shut his eyes, the data he'd been offered making little sense even to his structured mind. "Break it down in English."

Across the room, Eli Braun shook his head and fumbled again to find the right words. "He went down at the 18-minute mark. Before his Sleep Subject. Just like Markway. With an arc stronger than any on record."

"Are you telling me these MCL deaths have nothing to do with the Sleep Subject? How is that even possible? It's the subject's goddamn dream."

"Then there must be something else in the waves," Braun said.

"You haven't shown me proof of that."

"These people aren't dropping dead in the middle of breakfast. They're dying in the link. The MCLs are arcing in the link. And everything I've seen points to stronger and stronger realities. Even with the MCLs' help, the Subjects can't fight it off anymore. There has never been a case where the MCL could not get out. There's plenty of time for expulsion prior to brain death if the Subject's heart stops. It must be the programming." He jabbed an accusing finger at Clayton. "Your programming."

Tired of the argument, Clayton seized on an idea spawned by the doctor's words. "Have any of them died after the subject?"

Braun set his hands on his hips, chin sinking to his chest in defeat. "No."

"Then bring one of the MCLs out. We need to find out what's going on in the dreams."

"If we do that, one of the Elite will die."

"May die, Doctor, and it's a chance we have to take . . . unless . . . " Clayton sat forward. "When will the dream imaging prototype be ready?"

Braun blinked in surprise. "Dietrich's still working out the bugs. It won't be ready for another three months at least, although I hear marketing already dubbed it ImaDream, or something similarly stupid."

"We'll see about the name. Can it be used tonight?"

"Absolutely not. We need to test it on more than monkeys, and to date, we have no idea of the repercussions of a second tap into the MCL's subconscious while he's within the dream reality."

"Then we have no choice. Wake up one of the in-process MCLs." Clayton raised a hand before Braun opened his mouth to object. "We need to know what's happening, and this is the only way to be sure."

Braun hesitated. "All right," he said at last. "But we give them a full 15 minutes if needed. And I want to be there when he comes out."

"Fair enough."

"We'll wake the highest numbered Elite. Chances are greater

the expulsion will force an automatic wakefulness in the Sleep Subject, whereas the lower, more skilled dreamers would simply keep going."

"How long before you can get the MCL lucid?" Clayton asked.

"Depending on the severity of the expulsion, an hour, maybe more."

"Then get to it, Doctor."

Clayton followed Braun to the door, eyes on Evan James who sat primly at his desk despite the late hour. "Get me Phil Dietrich."

"It's nearly one a.m. sir," Evan said.

"I damn well know what time it is. There's a reason I house my people onsite. So wake Dietrich up and tell him to get his ass here. Now."

Twenty minutes later, the squat figure of Dr. Phillip Dietrich stood in the office in a pair of baggy pants and a sweat-stained t-shirt, hair standing out from his head as if it had been electrified. He blinked rapidly at Clayton behind a set of glasses that made his rheumy eyes look like shifting pools of uncooked egg.

"Tell me about the dream imaging tech," Clayton commanded. "How long before it's usable?"

"According to Braun, we're still months out and if he had his way, we'd never use it."

"And according to you?"

"It's ready for human testing. It's been ready. For months. A few mixed results with the chimps so Braun won't authorize any further clinicals. Man needs to unpucker his ass and let scientists be . . . "

Clayton cut him off. "Define mixed results."

"Three chimps dead, two damaged, ten positive results with no lingering side effects even after multiple links."

Clayton eyed him, not sure he wanted any further definition of what Dietrich considered "positive results" that didn't involve an image of a dancing banana. "Were you able to see anything?"

"Fuzzy at best, but Laura Taylor's been working on enhancing the effect."

Clayton faced the window. "If we go live tonight, what are the chances the programming will work? That we'll be able to see the dreams of an MCL?"

"The prototype is ready," Dietrich said, wide awake now. "I'd say we have a good chance of full view given the right frequency on the reverse weave and the strength of the dream."

"And the side effects on the human brain?"

"Impossible to tell for sure until I have a human test subject."

"Then give me your opinion."

"Based on the chimp tests, they should be minimal."

"Do it," Clayton said. "Recruit volunteers from the lower MCL division. I want results as soon as possible."

"Of course. I can have something to you by Wednesday."

"Tonight, Doctor. You have three hours."

"Hours?"

"You heard me. I'll observe the test personally. Ms. Taylor will assist you."

An unmistakable gleam lit Dietrich's eyes, and Clayton felt a sudden revulsion toward the little troll. "We're on it."

As Dietrich bustled out, Clayton noticed the shadow in the corner. "Don't look at me like that, Evan. I'm trying to save their lives."

"At the expense of the MCLs?" Evan let the thought linger before he drifted silently away.

At the window, Clayton wondered how Evan managed to chill the air so thoroughly on his way out.

Gillian opened her eyes and groaned.

"Don't say it," Nathan said.

"Why the hell not?"

"Because every time you say 'bloody hell' it kicks off whatever is going to happen, and right now, I'm happy to be right here."

Gillian pushed up on her elbows, the bed beneath her back squeaking under her weight. "I know this place."

"Where are we?"

"Home."

"You're going to have to be more specific."

"The place where I grew up."

The soft eggshell-white walls of her childhood room comforted Gillian only for a moment. Beside her, Nathan perused the multitude of rock and movie posters clinging to the walls, *The Sisters of Mercy* and *Bauhaus* riding the back wall beside images of *Lord Huron*, Barns Courtney and *The Airborne Toxic Event*. Sigourney Weaver's 'Ripley' dominated the right. On the left, a bay window looked out on a mist-covered drive.

"Never knew you had such eclectic taste," Nathan said.

"Smart ass comm . . . " She hissed in pain, the hole in her ankle bleeding freely over the comforter. Removing her sodden sock, she inspected the raw edges of flesh around the puncture, the skin plump and burning an infected red.

Brow furrowed, Nathan slid to the end of the bed. "You've never had an injury spill over before."

"First time for everything."

"We need a first aid kit."

"Bathroom," Gillian said. "Under the sink."

Nathan found the bandages, packed the hole and bound it. With gentle hands he flexed her foot, pausing when she sucked in air. "Can you put weight on it?"

Gillian swung her feet over the side of the bed and stood. Nathan caught her as she wobbled.

"Let's hope we don't have to run," he said.

"Optimism," Gillian muttered. "I think I prefer the smart-ass remarks."

Evening light bathed the dim room, the soft glow of a half-moon falling on the deep blue of a comforter decorated with brightly colored fish. It shone a cold silver on the dresser and light green on the rug. Gillian's skin remained pale, but her hair danced red in the beams. She gave Nathan a puzzled look.

"What?" he asked.

"You're still wearing the scrubs. You've tried to change it?"

"Nothing works."

"Something's different, Nate. I don't know what it is or why, but I don't like it. Why can't I wake up?"

"Just a matter of time. Break it down for me. Where are we?"

"This is my parents' house."

"Why does it scare you?"

"It doesn't."

"Something about it must. Maybe not in the traditional sense."

"When have my nightmares ever been traditional?"

"You've tried to wake up?"

"Of course. But I haven't slept in days. I must've gone out hard." She eyed him. "You have any bright ideas, I'm open."

"I've heard sex works."

"What idiot told you that?"

Nathan grinned. "Demons it is."

Repressing a chuckle, she hobbled to the closet, pulled a pair of boots from the shelf, and returned to the bed. A light breeze tossed the hair from her shoulder, the scent of lilac wafting through the window. "I always loved that bush. Sat right outside my room. In the spring and summer, it perfumed the air while I tried to sleep. It made me feel safe." Looking out the window, she froze. "Nate . . . Do you see it? On the driveway."

Nathan cupped his hands around his eyes to cut the glare. "See what?"

"I thought I saw a chair."

"In the driveway?"

"I've been seeing it. The moor. The forest. The one you broke up at the asylum."

"A chair," Nathan said, brows raised in skepticism.

"You haven't seen it?" Gillian asked.

"Would I know it if I had?"

"I don't know," she said and relented with a shake of her head. "I guess I really am losing my mind. What was it you said about sex?"

"Supposedly a surefire way to wake up the body."

"Guess it is a different kind of adrenaline. Not so much fight or flight as it is stay and surrender. Not something I ever did in this room. My parents sold this place before I got out of Davidson. Moved south to reduce their bills after the institution claimed nearly everything they had. I visited their house there many times—in fact, I was on my way there. My mother . . . she's sick. But it was never my home again."

Nathan sat down beside her. "I never really had a home. My parents moved wherever the government sent them. Name a place, I've probably lived there."

"What was your favorite?"

"Glasgow."

"Scotland?"

"Kentucky."

Gillian chuffed. "Seriously?"

"Acres of land. Feel like you can breathe. Raise some horses maybe, or dogs. I miss having a dog."

A small smile played on Gillian's lips as she looked at him. "You surprise me."

"You shock the hell outta me every time I see you." Nathan glanced around at the bedroom and took her hand in his. "Why are we here, Gill?"

"I don't know, but I guess we're going to find out."

"How do you suggest we do that?"

Lifting her chin, she said, "Bloody hell."

"Got one!"

Peeling back an eyelid, the medic shined a light into the moss-green eyes of a woman she'd found crumpled against a broken window. The pupils barely reacted to the influx of light. A quick poke to her hand with a sharp object found the subject unresponsive. The medic's partner ducked his head into the little room.

"What the hell happened to her foot?" he asked. "That puncture looks infected."

"Must've happened before the crash," the medic said. "Tag her. Burns are our priority right now. This one's beyond our help. Get her on a bus and pray she comes around on her own."

Lifting the radio to her lips to call it in, the medic paused, watching the woman's eyes shift beneath her lids.

"What is it?" her partner asked.

"I don't know," the medic said. "But I swear I saw her eyes move. Like she's dreaming."

"She's unresponsive. She can't possibly be dreaming."

"I don't know," the medic said again and stared at the placid face for a moment before she shrugged. "I guess not."

Her partner put a hand on her shoulder. "We've done what we can for her. Come on, we got another one a few compartments ahead."

"Still breathing?"

"Talking."

"Thank god." Taking one last look at the woman, the medic stood, shrugged off the uneasy feeling and headed down the hall.

CHAPTER TWELVE

SOFT WHISPERS ANIMATED the house. A light came on in the hallway accompanied by chatter from a family dinner below. Gillian closed her eyes and listened, her father's laughter ringing up the stairs. He had always been one to bellow, where her mother tittered, often eclipsing her good humor behind a hand to ensure no one saw her teeth. As a girl, Gillian had never understood it, her mother's beauty singular in her mind, her father's reasonably good looks no match for the lovely deep brown eyes and well carved cheek bones of her mother's face.

It would be years before she would learn that her mother's front teeth had been capped thanks to damage sustained when she was 18 years old. The beating she took from her own father's hands on the night she'd lost her virginity had damaged her looks—a fact that had almost immediately ruined the relationship. But Gillian's father had looked beyond that funny smile and drew the beauty behind it into the light. The teeth had been repaired after Amy Beth McBride had foregone the more traditional ring in favor of Liam Hardie's engagement gift of a stunning smile.

"Movie night," Gillian said.

Nathan shifted his gaze to the hall. "Huh?"

"Saturday. Family movie night. Pizza. Toby making a run for ice cream when he wasn't on a date."

Nathan took her hand in his as more laughter spiraled upward and the house breathed again. In moments a young woman, gangly and awkward as any thirteen-year-old girl could be, rushed through the door, handsome brother chasing her into the bedroom. At seventeen, the older boy was the spitting image of his father, dark locks, blue eyes bright and intense under bushy eyebrows. In a year he would defy his grandfather's wish that he join the Lutheran clergy and instead enlist in the Army to earn money for college. He'd find he would enjoy the structure, rising quickly among the ranks and earning his way to Officer Candidate School. And in just five more years he would lose his life in an accident abroad.

"That's enough you two," Gillian's mother said. She collared her son and put a hand on Gillian's shoulder to keep the two of them apart. Young Gillian managed another swing despite the enforced distance. "You both have youth group in the morning. And you, young lady, have confirmation class. Now get to sleep."

"Not going," Toby said and grinned at Gillian.

Amy Beth sighed heavily. "It's your choice, although I wish you would."

"Not fair," Gillian said. "Why doesn't he have to go?"

"Because he's made his decision." Amy Beth fingered the cross at her neck. She glanced at her son, the muscles in his jaw tightening in preparation for an argument the whole family knew better than to start. "When you're confirmed, you can make your own decision about the church. Until then, you do as I say."

"Yes Mo-om," the two children answered together. With a kiss to them both, Amy Beth floated out of the room, leaving them to finish their game with one last swipe of claw-like hands and a mouthful of giggles.

The room settled into darkness, the young girl restless in her bed, a scruffy little dog curled up tight at her feet when she finally drifted off. As the clock on the dresser ticked over 1 a.m., Gillian tightened her grip on Nathan's hand, and he found himself holding his breath, skin prickling. The young woman sat up in bed, unseeing eyes glittering in the moonlight, mouth open. A sound like the screech of brakes erupted from her, continuing unabated even when the lights came on. Toby slammed into the room followed closely by Liam and Amy Beth. Amy reached her first, but the girl thrashed violently away, slapping her mother to the floor and kicking her brother when he tried to help. An instant later, she jumped to her feet, arms flailing to beat her skin as if she had caught fire.

"Gillian!" Liam launched at his daughter, only to take a fist across the cheek. He caught her arms on the second attempt and she reared back, cracking the drywall behind her head and dragging her father with her. A kick to his chest forced him to release his grip.

"I cracked his ribs that night," Gillian whispered. Nathan stared at her. Her skin had lost all color, the veins of her face visible in the moonlight, a deep sadness in her eyes that Nathan had never seen before. "Broke Toby's wrist and sent my mother to the dentist."

"This is not your fault," Nathan said, anger at Somnium clenching his fists. Heat rushed to his cheeks as the woman beside him faded.

"It was always my fault."

Nathan caught her chin. "No, Gill. It wasn't."

On the bed, Young Gillian finally snapped out of the dream, whole body quivering while the family stared at her in awkward awe, not one of them daring to comfort her. Amy Beth sobbed quietly on the floor, cradled in Toby's arms.

"This can't go on," Liam said as he held himself together on the window bench.

"Daddy, I'm sorry!" Young Gillian lunged toward him, wild with fear that had nothing to do with her dream, but Liam backed away from his daughter. "Daddy?"

Hand up to silence her, Liam collected his wife and son and left the room. Young Gillian curled into herself. Alone. Terrified for more reasons than the lingering dream, she put her back to the wall at the head of her bed, knees up to her chest and arms wrapped tight around her legs.

Nathan watched the family leave. "What the fuck?"

"Nate." Gillian reached out to stop him, but he moved swiftly into the hall to eavesdrop on the meeting beyond the door.

"It's getting worse," Liam said with a grimace.

"She hasn't slept through the night in months." Amy Beth reached into her robe pocket to withdraw a prescription bottle that didn't belong to the family. "I found these in her bag."

"Something has to be done." Liam looked back at his terrified daughter, who rocked herself on the bed, shivers visible even at a distance. "I'll make a few calls. It's time."

Gillian floated into the hall, vanishing body no longer beholden to gravity. "They left me that night. Called the men in the white coats and I disappeared for five long years."

Nathan found what remained of Gillian behind him, her skin translucent, the tract of blood beneath discernible. She had faded to near invisibility, the wall beyond in focus. Nathan drew in a sharp breath.

"Gillian . . . "

"My mother came to visit me once," she said. "Just once. She said she was sorry, but she couldn't stand to see me in there, with the shoes without laces and the clothes without belts, zippers or ties. My hair was always a mess because the rooms had no mirrors. The first night there my roommate spent the whole night screaming. Her name was Chloe, but I found out in the morning it was her other personality, Chelsey, doing the hollering. They had to tie Chloe to the bed at night so Chelsey wouldn't hurt her. They sent me there, Nate. To that place. To that hell."

Nathan caught her shoulders, seeing his own palms on the other side of her disintegrating bones. "I won't leave you."

"I disappeared like breath on a cold wind. Slipped out of their lives like I was nothing more than my family's bad dream."

Catching her fading cheeks in his hands, Nathan drew washed out green eyes to his. "I see you, Gillian Hardie. I will always see you."

She stared up at him, uncertain and frightened, eyes flicking to the frozen moment of her youth when she had discovered how easy it was to be abandoned.

"Look at me," Nathan said. "There's no changing what they've done. No fixing a wrong that never should have been. But you have to make the choice to stay, to fight. Here, now. Do you understand me?"

Beneath his fingers, pale flesh solidified, the color of her eyes deep and strong once more. She leaned into him, cold cheek pressed to the warmth of his chest. Wrapping his arms around her, Nathan buried his own fear in her hair, the strong steady beat of his heart moving in time with hers.

"Stay with me, Gill," he whispered. "Please. Stay."

"I'm with you." She lifted her face to his, only to be startled away from his gaze by a hitch of broken breath in the room behind.

The girl on the bed crawled backward, body pressed tight against the wall. Young Gillian was riveted on the closet door, mouth open in a silent scream. From the darkness, a single tendon-covered bone left a mark of fresh blood on the wall as it curled around the door frame.

"Hello, girlie."

"Shit shit shit! Pull her back, big guy, pull her back!" Dex sat at his desk, fingers clamped and sweaty on the edge of the stainless steel. Frantic eyes watched the downward drift of 831's waves, which seemed headed for the inevitable. But something was different this time. Keller held strong, his patterns staying low but not following 831's as they had before. Words banged against Dex's clenched teeth. "Please dear God, I will never hit on another woman with a cheesy line again if you . . . "

Dex rose to his feet and punched the air.

"Yes!"

Glancing around to be sure he was still alone, Dex dropped to his knees and clapped his hands together beneath his chin.

"Thank you, Mr. Almighty, for not making me finish that sentence. You're a class act."

With a cluck of his teeth and a quick firing of a hand-gun-finger at the ceiling, Dex collapsed back into his chair, heart pounding. But when he looked back at the center screen, his stomach dropped to his boots.

Something new had crept onto the middle screen, a blip in the waves that ran concurrently with 831's. It seemed to chase her patterns, an echo in her brain waves. If Dex hadn't known better, he would've said it looked almost like a third consciousness.

Overhead the lights dimmed, the hum of the machinery disintegrating around him. All nine of the Coop's screens flickered, a single image popping up in the static. Blink and he would've missed it, but Dex could've sworn it was there.

The lights returned with a pop, bright and normal, the screens back to their usual mix of waves. Dex stuck his hands in his hair, wondering if he had really seen it.

A chair. Stark and somber. A relic from his catholic grade school.

"I can't take much more of this, big guy," he said. The echo had disappeared, all systems within normal range, and Dex let out a sigh. "Okay. We got this. A little time and a shitload of luck is all we need."

SOMNIUM

As the rush of blood slowed, Dex realized with a jolt that he'd let 831's paperwork fall to the floor. Cursing, he bent to pick it up and stopped short.

"Oh hell." He lifted a sheet marked Pharmacological Intervention. "You weren't part of that mess, were you?"

Dex had heard the stories, told over drinks by drunken MCLs. A total of 50 Elite had still been on record at the time, the ranks dropping to 30 in less than three nights when a pharmacological attempt to quell the nightmares had gone badly wrong. Only the strongest of the Elite—or those who hadn't slept at all during the three days it took to clear their systems of the drug—had been able to survive. After that night, 831 had emerged as the lowest-numbered Elite, her rival for the honor gone before the first dawn.

A new trainee, Dex had listened with enthusiasm to the cautionary tale of a young MCL, who himself had been brand new that night and unprepared for the task ahead.

"I was scared shitless," the MCL said. "Markway went in with me, and damned if he wasn't the only reason the Elite lived the night. I got caught in the return trigger. They didn't send me back in for a month and my head ain't been quite right since." The MCL finished his beer in one long swallow. "But that's all right I guess. Hell, that Elite ain't been right all his life, has he?"

Dex made it a point to ask Dr. Braun about the drug involved. Research studies had shown nightmare relief from alpha blockers used to treat high blood pressure. Because many of the Elite were already on anti-psychotics or antidepressants, which were often thought to raise blood pressure, the medication should have had a soporific effect on those under the influence of the Somnium-induced dream reality. Instead, it backfired. The medication, initiated into the food and drink of the Elite through carefully placed watchers or therapists, increased blood flow, causing the racing nightmares to overwhelm the Elites' sensitive systems. The crash had taken only two MCLs but by the end of the week, 20 of the Elite succumbed to strokes, heart attacks and organ failures of all kinds. The remaining numbers had been immediately relieved of any medication and given stimulants to keep them awake until the drugs were out of their systems.

At the time, Dex thought medication a reasonable solution. Somnium offering hope for a decent night's rest. That the Elite had been medicated against their knowledge never crossed his mind. He thought, like most at Somnium, that it was for the best.

Five years later, he was no longer sure anything Somnium did *was* for the best. He'd seen proof enough of that.

His tablet pinged, the note from Laura a welcome relief from his thoughts.

Train wreck on SE corridor. Same coordinates as Hardie's tracker.

Beyond the doors, the hall came to life, but Dex's work with Keller would go on uninterrupted. The others in Keller's care would be taken care of by other Operators and junior MCLs, but the sudden flurry concerned him.

Stacking the paperwork back on the desk, Dex didn't notice Laura's disc remained on the floor, only the tip peeking out from beneath the console as the lights flickered again.

Gillian lunged for the bed as Shearer emerged from the darkness. The putrid stench he carried filled the room like a backed-up sewer. Her fingers glanced off the young girl's skin as time shifted, and she careened into the wall, shoulder marking the spot where her former self had ruptured the drywall. Stars swam before her eyes as the nightmare from the closet condensed into surreal form.

Shearer had changed.

Flakes of skin had congealed, the sallow yellow of death now a bleeding ruin of animated flesh. Muscle had formed over the bones. When he stepped into the shallow moonlight, he looked as if he'd been eaten by vermin, wounds still moist and oozing.

Nathan slammed into Shearer with the full force of a seasoned linebacker. They hit the armoire beside the closet, the collision leaving a streak of gore on the white surface and sending a stream of swimming trophies toppling from the shelves. In seconds Nathan had his arm wrapped around Shearer's neck, the satisfying snap of bone ringing loud in the quiet house. He let the body slide to the floor. Breath sharp in his chest, he held out his hand. "Let's go."

"Is he . . . " Gillian asked.

"I'm not sticking around to find out."

Gillian slipped her hand in his and hopped off the bed, carefully sidestepping the body. Nathan pushed her into the dark hallway, and they moved fast toward the stairs. Movement at the edge of her vision pulled her up short, and she clamped a hand over her mouth to stop the scream.

"Bloody hell," Nathan breathed and came to a halt behind her.

What remained of Toby waited on the landing, the colors of his desert uniform still visible beneath the coating of blood. The bomb had taken his lower limbs and one of his arms. The once brilliant blue eyes erased. With his remaining hand he pulled himself forward, torso sliding up the steps, the hinge of his jaw working silently.

Behind them, a distinct crunch of a bone reset, preceded a low and menacing rumble.

"Change it," Nathan said. "Do it, Gill. Change the scene."

"How?"

"You know how. Conquer it. Conquer this fear. Just this one."

"But that's . . . that's . . . "

Nathan forced her to focus. "Eyes on me. Breathe."

Nodding, Gillian pivoted and dashed forward into what should have been her parent's bedroom, only to find a concrete barrier in her way. She careened into the wall as Nathan slammed the wooden door, the lock clicking firmly in place from the outside. Whether it stood against the living or the dead remained to be seen. Moonlight streamed through cobalt glass, the name chiseled on the outside reflected backward on the floor before them, but Gillian read it easily enough.

McBride.

"Fuck me," Gill said.

"Not exactly the scenario I was hoping for the first time I heard you ask that," Nathan muttered with a wry smile. "Break it down. Where are we?"

"The final resting place of the one of the meanest men I've ever met."

"Who?"

"My grandfather."

"Why'd you bring us here?"

"I don't know."

As a girl, Gillian had been to the family mausoleum only twice. First when her grandmother had died of breast cancer. She'd been eight and had thought the little stone house behind her grandfather's church a grand place to play, but her mother had not let her go inside. When she was 20, her grandfather choked on a large piece of meat, his second bride unable or unwilling to save him and he'd slipped into a coma from which he'd never awoken. He'd been interred in the family crypt alongside his first wife and the long-dead ashes of his brother. Three empty shelves remained and likely always would. Liam Hardie refused to spend his afterlife with the man he called "that fucking prick." He'd bought Amy Beth and himself two plots on the hill overlooking the bay near their home. What little they'd been able to salvage of Toby had been enough for her mother to convert into a diamond—the thought so morbid Gillian shuddered every time she saw the necklace. Gillian hadn't given her final resting place much thought, and she hadn't thought about her mother's family crypt in years.

Her grandfather, on the other hand, had maintained a starring role in her nightmares. Cruel and emotionally abusive to the entire family, he had singled out Gillian for the bulk of his venom, her gender enough to secure his hatred. His passing had been like a warm spring rain that cleansed the hypersensitive air surrounding the family. The hateful bastard had not been missed.

Which apparently ticked him off.

On the concrete shelf before her, a coffin shifted, as if whatever rested within had suddenly sprung to life, hands and feet beating the dust from the wood. Behind them, an urn spilled its contents like a broken hourglass, an unseen wind whipping it into form.

Nathan caught Gillian's rigid shoulders. "You need to wake up."

"I can't," she said. "I've tried, but I can't."

"Then get us out of here."

Gillian slapped his hands away. "You find a way, you let me know."

Satisfied with her anger, Nathan searched the crypt for an option but found nothing as a second coffin dropped from its shelf with a crack and spilled its contents. A hand thin as a root and draped in flakes of desiccated skin landed near Gillian's feet, its ringed fingers groping forward like some awkward scene from a 1930s silent horror film.

On the right, her grandfather's coffin surged upward, standing on end, held by some unseen force. Mesmerized into silence,

Gillian watched the latch explode, the casket's lid squealing on unoiled hinges. Inside, her grandfather had barely aged a day, telltale moss the only indication of his rot. When his eyes snapped opened to reveal nothing but hollows of slithering shadows she let loose, crying out with all her might in the hope the act might free her from the vision.

A hand landed on her shoulder, and she struck out blindly, limbs flailing in the ash storm. Nathan caught her fist before she landed a blow and pulled her to his chest. Time slowed as he pressed his forehead to hers.

"Stay with me," he said.

Heart pounding, Gillian snapped her mouth shut and nodded.

"Breathe," Nathan commanded and Gillian's ragged breathing eased.

"Breathing," she whispered. "B-R-E-A-T-H-I-N-G."

"That's my girl. You with me?"

Another deep breath later, Gillian nodded. "I'm okay." A memory surfaced with her slowing pulse, and she knew what she had to do. "Let's get the hell out of here."

Spinning on her heel, she faced the coffin. Nathan looked on in horror as Gillian lunged forward, hand outstretched. A vise of bony fingers clamped down on her wrist and the stench of burning flesh filled the last remnants of air. An unnatural heat radiated up her arm and Gillian sent a frantic scream over her shoulder. "Help me!"

Unsure what Gill was doing but always willing to follow, Nathan grabbed the steel urn and smashed it against the old man's skull. Gillian reached inside the rotting shirt, a glimmer of silver flashing in the light. Wind swirled, ripping the air from their lungs. A high screech erupted from the corpse's thin mouth, and the body leaned toward Gillian's neck, teeth bared. Nathan grabbed a heavy vase filled with silk flowers, their bright coloring subdued with dust but still irreverent among the cold gray stone, and slammed it across the skeletal face. Bone broke and what few teeth remained skittered across the floor. The weight of the vase knocked both the body and Gillian to the dusty stone on the far side of the crypt, but she'd achieved her goal. A key dangled in the light.

"Fucking prick always had to have a way out. Even after he died."

Grinning, Nathan helped her up. Dust from the urn congealed

around them, the half-formed thing wrapped in a filmy gauze of near-humanity. They sprinted through the door and tumbled into the thick mist beyond.

***

"Dex? Dex!"

A quick tap to his tablet and Dex had Eric's face on the screen. His friend's skin had turned a new shade of corpse in the watery blue light of the pod. Dex nearly recoiled at the sight.

"What the hell is up with the lights?" Dex asked, eyes on the flashing bulbs. The power to Keller's pod held strong, only the lights in the suite dimming and rising in a strange pattern, almost like . . . Dex couldn't put his finger on it. The erratic flickering had served to do nothing more than drive him nuts.

"Dex, I need you to shut up and listen," Eric said. "They're going to wake up Billings."

Dex froze. "What?"

"Stay quiet. After Markway, I want someone else to witness this."

Dex's view dropped to the console's keyboard, only a sliver of the room visible as the whoosh of air from the jump suite door resounded. Moments later, a hip positioned itself behind Eric's chair and a familiar voice rang out.

"Wilson," Dr. Braun said, a hand on Eric's shoulder. "Why are you still on duty?"

"Billings is my MCL, sir."

"You should've been taken out of the rotation," Braun muttered. "No time to fix it now. Pull him at the 18-minute mark. We need to ask him a few questions."

Eric clenched his hands into pale balls on his thighs. "Sir?"

"I wouldn't ask if it weren't important."

"What about 9998, sir?"

Braun sighed heavily. "I'm afraid he'll have to fend for himself. I've a crash cart prepped. Trigger him at 18."

"Yes sir."

In his own suite with the mic muted, Dex let loose a string of irreverent curses. The consequences of the trigger would put both the MCL and the Sleep Subject in danger, one from a lack of protection and the other from a whiplash effect of being expulsed from the dream reality.

Expulsion was a last resort, a final means of defense for the MCLs, and many would rather go down fighting than face the death of one of their Sleep Subjects. When it came to the Elite, Markway and Blake had done what every MCL in the unit would do, no questions asked, no regrets.

In the five years Dex had been at Somnium, only one MCL had been pulled before the return trigger. Rumor had it Dr. Braun still spent several hours a month visiting the man, who did nothing but sit quietly in a corner of his room and breathe.

And yet, Dex thought Braun might be right to do it. If Billings was experiencing anything like what Dex was seeing with Keller and 831, he'd be happy to have a few answers no matter how hard they were to come by. Dex sucked in his bottom lip, teeth absently peeling chapped skin when the alarm sounded.

"Expulsion prepped," Eric said.

"Do it," Braun said, fingers contracting on Eric's shoulder. Eric hit confirm, and Dex started to count the seconds until he might hear Billings' voice.

A roar of pain startled them all. Eric's laptop hit the floor as Braun bolted toward the pod. From the vantage point under the console, Dex had a clear view of the action. Billings ripped himself out of the pod only to collapse on the floor, every muscle in his body twitching under latent electrical impulses.

Braun kneeled beside him, and Billings brought his limbs under control long enough to grab the man by the shirt and pull his face close.

"No . . . Matt . . . What . . . "

"Billings," Braun said and tried to soothe the MCL, who shifted his grip to his own head.

His back arched as if he'd been pierced by something large and sharp. A spray of blood erupted from his mouth, covering Braun's face just as the singular hum of a flatline rang in the space.

Overhead, the lights went out.

Nathan hit the ground and winced, the unforgiving surface rising too quickly to meet him. He'd just barely been able to ensure Gillian's safe landing as they once again slipped through the dream world. "Son of a . . ."

"What?" Gillian asked, concerned gaze floating over him.

"Rock."

"Oh, like that's supposed to make me feel sorry for . . ."

Nathan clamped a hand over Gillian's mouth and surveyed their surroundings. "If you say it, I'm not going to be responsible for what happens to you."

With a quick flick of her tongue against his palm, Gillian was free to offer him a stunning smile.

"Bold move considering you know where that hand has been," he said.

"Ahhh, but it's where we are that counts. Move."

"What if I'd rather stay put?"

"Then I will not make you breakfast. Come on, we're home."

She rolled away and Nathan heaved a sigh, the grass soft and cool against his skin, the earth comforting as a pillow to his tired body. "Is that supposed to make me feel better? We've been home twice tonight and all it's gotten me is a questionable batch of god knows what relative of yours stuck to my skin and a crappy pair of scrubs."

Gillian grinned. "You all right?"

"I'd be fine if you'd quit landing on me."

Crisp night air carried the scent of water and pine, filling Nathan's mind with nostalgia. Right away he knew something was different. A million stars shined overhead, another hundred lights rising from the grass in search of a mate as fireflies swayed in the breeze. It was a vista he had never seen before in any of Gillian's dreams. One that felt, if he could bring himself to actually use the word, safe.

But he hurt. Bruises from the battle rode the surface of his skin, his mind unable to control the exhaustion. He wondered briefly how long he'd been under, the stress of Gillian's dreams always taking a toll, but he couldn't remember the last time they'd moved through four different scenes in one night. She always managed to wake before they'd lasted much longer than three.

With a sigh he propped himself up on his elbows to get a better look around. Less than a hundred yards up the hill, a small cabin beckoned. Aside from the house there wasn't a light in sight, the building surrounded by trees and slopping hills. Azalea bushes lined a wrap-around porch, a swing its only occupant. A mild breeze moved among day lilies, irises, hostas, caladium and begonias, the mounds of color drained to mere hints in the moonlight.

"Nice place," Nathan said.

"Thanks." Gillian offered him a hand. "Now get off your ass and I'll see about getting you some real clothes."

Nathan gripped her outstretched hand. "This is yours?"

"Home now," Gillian said. "Come. I know I'm dreaming but I'm starving and for once, I actually feel safe, if only for a minute or two."

A tingle rumbled over his skin at her use of the word—the same he had been thinking moments before. "N3," he muttered.

"What did you say?"

"Nothing." Safe. And yet, not right. Still, he smiled at her enthusiasm, which he hoped to keep up by asking if she'd lived in the house long.

"Moved in a few months ago."

"Much history?"

"Ghosts a plenty," Gillian said. To Nathan's surprise she left her hand in his as they headed for the front porch. "The land once belonged to a master journeyman, who had begun building a stone house about half a mile deeper into the forest. Unfortunately, he didn't survive to see it finished. Crushed by a wall of rock when an apprentice mixed the cement improperly. They say he's buried at the edge of the wood and watches over the land. The second owner died while working on the summer kitchen. Hit by lightning."

"Lovely. Exactly the type of place I'd expect you to own."

"We're just getting warmed up. There's a creek that runs through the property about half a mile into the woods. Local legend says the third owner's daughter had an illegitimate child and he forced her to drown the baby. Sometimes at night you can hear crying in the woods—but I'd be willing to bet it's just foxes. I've seen plenty of those around."

"No demons in the laundry? Decayed bodies on the stairs? Dead relatives in the closet?"

"Just a few mice. And one witch who is thought to be buried head down, out by the summer kitchen. She was strung up after several children in the area were found dead three months after she moved in. Most likely she brought typhus with her, but hey, typhus and witchcraft are like bread and butter. Supposedly you can see blue fire in the trees on winter nights."

Chuckling at himself for scanning the woods, Nathan asked, "How much do you own?"

"Ten and a half acres altogether. But don't worry, only eight are actually haunted."

Impressed, Nathan scanned the clearing. "Definitely room for a paddock and some stables."

Gillian led him into the cabin and he wondered how long they would have before it started again. Before Shearer invaded this home too, or some other piece of Gillian's psyche leapt out of the closets of her traumatized mind.

"You're limping again," Nathan said and followed her into the kitchen. "Should probably take a look at that bandage. Take care of that burn on your wrist."

Gillian glanced down at the four red lines across her forearm. "Doesn't hurt."

"Still . . . "

"It's strange," she said and slumped down on a chair. "But everything about this nightmare is. I should've woken at the surge of adrenaline that came with the pain. But this dream, it just keeps going."

She kicked a second chair out from the table and set her foot on the dark wood seat. Nathan searched the drawers before pulling a large chef's knife from the butcher block. He handed it to Gillian and grabbed two smaller versions for himself.

"First aid kit?" he asked, and she nodded toward the cabinet beneath the sink. Moments later he laid out disinfectant, a box of gauze and a roll of tape on the table. He straddled the second chair and sank down, lifting her foot onto his thigh.

"I'm beginning to think this isn't a nightmare," she said.

"Stress dream?"

"My stress dreams usually involve the threat of exsanguination."

"No vampires. Right. So not a nightmare and not a stress dream. And we've been here far too long now for your normal dream cycle." Nathan untied her boot without looking up. "Theories?"

"A few, but first, I need to know something," she said, fingers wrapped around the hilt of the knife.

Removing her foot from his grasp she leaned forward, the knife's steel tip pointed directly at his gut. A single upward thrust would end his life. Nathan raised his eyes to hers, the look that held him sending a chill down his spine.

"Who the hell are you and why have you been invading my dreams?"

SSS 9998: Matthew Anderson. Age: 32. Occupation: Accountant. Marital Status: Never married. And now he never would be.

Dex sat back, a hand over his mouth, the other wrapped around his chest.

Eric's feed had cut off the moment the lights went out. The pod and console still had power thanks to the back-up generators. After what happened to Billings, Dex was fairly certain it'd be at least a decade before Braun tried to bring out anyone else, but the suite had never lost power before. He checked on Keller, wondering what the MCL was seeing as a slight frown pulled at the corner of his mouth. "Don't worry big guy. I won't let them expel you no matter how much the lights flicker."

On the center screens, the rhythms of 831 and Nathan's minds remained low but functioning. There'd been a lack of any significant activity for more than 30 minutes, but that was typical of dreams.

"Got yourself a break in the action," Dex muttered and checked his watch, noting the time at 2:00 a.m. to ensure he wouldn't miss the start of a second REM period at the culmination of a typical 90-minute sleep cycle. While most adults would follow a similar pattern four to six times per night, it was rare for an Elite to go more than one after a trigger like the one 831 received. But this was not a normal night, and 831 was not a normal dreamer.

Still, Dex was glad for a bit of quiet.

Checking on the Corridor, he found the jump suite lights weren't the only ones down. When Billings arced, the surge had hit the pods, each of which were contained by a closed electrical system. Dex had asked about it once, only to be told by Markway in a voice that shut down any further questions, that it had been done to "make damn sure the buggers don't get out." Lately Dex found himself wondering if Markway hadn't been hoping the "buggers" didn't get in while he was busy saving someone's ass.

In the jump suite hall, the emergency lights reflected off the sheet over Billings' body. Two lower MCLs wheeled it away, likely to be stored next to Markway's corpse on Sub-level 7 to await autopsy. Braun and Eric Wilson followed like mourners in a funeral procession. Dex said a silent prayer for Billings, and then slapped the feed off as Braun headed for his suite.

"Bugger," Dex muttered and glanced at the center screens with apprehension.

Moments later, the doctor stepped into the room, his face aged another few years since Dex had last seen him. He'd changed into a spare MCL uniform, but a splotch of blood still lingered behind his right ear.

"Cooper," Braun said with a nod of greeting.

"Sir," Dex said and got to his feet, back straight.

"Easy, Dex. This isn't an inspection." Braun crossed to the sleep pod. He let his hands rest on the edge of the bed and gazed on Keller's slumbering form with a mixture of distress and pity. "How long has he been under?"

Dex shifted his weight. "Just a few minutes sir."

Braun nodded as he watched the slight twitches in Keller's face, a grimace crossing the man's lips "Who's he with?"

"831."

Braun looked up, startled. "I thought she went down over an hour ago."

"She did. Second cycle."

"Unusual for her."

"Everything about her is unusual. Especially tonight."

Tucking his hands in his pockets, Braun shifted his gaze to the wall and stared hard at the tech. Shoulders slumped, he let his head drop as if a difficult decision had leapt like an acrobat onto his back only to lay there unmoving. Uttering a soft curse, he returned to the straight-backed posture Dex had always admired, yet never felt a need to emulate. He drilled Dex with a look that made the Operator feel like a penitent child. "Dex, you should know that Markway, Blake, and Billings are gone. I won't lose Keller. And whatever we have to do to keep 831 safe, do it. Do you understand?"

"Yes sir."

Nodding, Braun stared at the suite as if he were seeing it for the first time. "We'll figure out the power surge. Generators are holding strong. In the meantime, you have my permission to exceed any protocols. And Declan . . . "

"Doc?" Dex said, surprised Braun knew his actual first name, let alone used it.

"Do not pull him out. I don't care who asks or how long it takes. Keller stays with 831 until she wakes herself or you get a return trigger."

The directive went against everything Dex had trained for. To hear it come from Braun scared the hell out of him while at the same time sending a surge of relief through his limbs. "Yes sir."

"Something's going extremely wrong tonight. But I won't let 831 pay the price for this company's mistakes." Braun prepared to leave and then paused, a puzzled glance at the waves on Dex's middle screens. "How long did you say he's been under?"

"Only a few seconds, probably still establishing the link."

"All right. Find me if anything happens. Anything at all."

With a whoosh of air Braun left the room and Dex crumpled into his chair.

Nathan lifted his hands, holding them palms up without dropping Gillian's gaze. "How'd you know?"

"Your clothing when we landed in the hospital," she said. "You've never worn anything like that before and I've never even seen anything like it, so there is no way my imagination would conjure it on you. So tell me what the hell, and who the hell, you are. Because I know you're not what I always thought you were."

"What did you think I was?"

"My hero," Gillian said. "And by 'my' I mean literally mine. A fractured piece of my own psyche conjured to help when the dream reality got stronger. But you're not, are you?"

Nathan dropped her gaze. "I'm nobody's hero."

"I need the truth, Nathan. You owe me that. We lost everything but the clothes on our backs when we moved from the forest. My kit was gone, and neither of us could manipulate a damn thing. So this isn't a dream. Which means you're not part of my mind, even though every place we've traveled tonight has belonged to me and, I'm assuming, exclusively to my memory. So what are you?"

Nathan hesitated, eyes firmly on the knife in her hand.

Huffing in annoyance, she tossed it to the table. Cool fingers lifted his chin. "I know you're not here to hurt me," she said and something feral in Nathan's chest relaxed. "So please, talk to me. The least you can do is tell me your name."

"You know my name."

"Your full name."

"Nathan Keller," he said. "Commander Nathan Keller, United States Navy, retired. I currently work for Somnium Corporation, where I hold the designation of Fifth-Level Mearan-Cadail Laoch."

Gillian mulled over the term. "Fitting."

"You know what it means?" Nathan asked, surprised.

"Loosely defined, you're a nightmare warrior." She stood and crossed to the oven, taking an omelet pan from the drawer beneath. He followed and leaned against the peninsula while she gathered onion, pepper, eggs, milk, bread and butter from various spots in the small kitchen and then turned on the oven. "Key to a good omelet is to let it finish in the broiler. That way you don't get any runny parts."

A long-fought tension eased out of Nathan's shoulders, the truth simpler than he had ever hoped it would be. "You're taking this really well."

"Don't get me wrong." She found the chef's knife and sliced into the onion. "I'm not sure I could be much angrier at you right now. You've invaded my dreams for what, five years?"

"About that," Nathan confirmed.

"So I'll repeat. What, exactly, are you?"

"A man."

"How is that possible?"

"Story usually goes that a guy meets a girl . . . "

The chef's knife hovered under his chin. "Damn it, Nate, don't fuck around. You know what I'm asking."

Gently, he shifted the knife away from his skin. "The doc calls it consensual dreaming."

"I never consented to any of this," Gillian snapped and returned to the cutting board to dice the peppers. "Not that it appears to have mattered. But how are you here? Why are you in my dream?"

"You've heard of Somnium?"

"Of course. But what does that company have to do with me?"

"You were triggered tonight."

"Triggered?"

"Someone showed you something or you caught a commercial. Some technology based on Somnium's platform. I don't know where you were or what you were doing. Do you remember?"

Nodding slowly, Gillian sliced a pad of butter and let it melt in the pan before she slid the onions and peppers onto the hot surface. "A child showed me a tablet. Some sort of game he liked. I was on my way to see my mother. I must've fallen asleep on the train."

"That'd do it." Nathan leaned over the onions and inhaled deeply. "That smells delicious."

"Don't change the subject."

"I'm not. I'm pointing out that I can smell. Have been able to, in almost every stage."

Gillian stopped whisking and looked at the pan. "I'll be damned."

"You just may be, but trust me when I say it ain't my fault. You were exposed to Somnium's sleep induction technology years ago. When your mind rejected it, your body changed its response to dreams. The neurons that turn off reality when a normal person dreams backfired, and your dream reality became more or less real."

Eyes wide, she faced him, the bowl trembling in her hands. "Then the nightmares. They're real?"

"They're dreams," he said and took the mixture from her to pour it into the sizzling pan. "But your body reacts to them as if they were real."

"Then I really can die in my dreams?" Gillian asked. "How close have I been?"

"Very."

Gillian backed against the cabinets and dropped to the floor, knees to her chin before she looked up at him. "Every time I've seen you?"

"Yes."

"Then my books . . . "

"I've read them."

Startled, Gillian allowed herself a moment's vanity. "What'd you think?"

"Highly instructive. Far more useful than the MCL training manual."

Gillian huffed and then sobered again. "I never told anyone they were inspired by my dreams."

"I know."

"Then how . . . "

"Because I know you, Gill. I've shared those dreams. You know it too."

A blush crept into Gillian's cheeks. He had recognized himself in her latest character's smart-ass remarks and defining facial characteristic. "True enough."

He clasped her hands to draw her back to her feet. "You know, I didn't like the way the last one ended."

"Why not?"

"Your Nicholas got the girl," Nathan said with a wry smile and a soft squeeze of her hands. "Somehow I never do."

Blush deepening, Gillian shifted her attention back to the eggs. She ran a rubber spatula around the edge of the mix. "Why wasn't I told about this?"

"I don't know, Gill, and that's the truth. But they've been watching you for years."

"How did you know I was . . . what did you call it? Triggered?"

"You wear a pendant."

Gillian's fingers darted to her neck. "My friend Jenna gave it to me. Green chrysoprase. She said it was to draw out my creativity and balance my dreams."

"It has some sort of metal in it?" Nathan asked.

"A vein of nickel." She transferred the pan to the broiler. "Are you saying Jenna knew? About all this?"

"If she gave you that pendant, she knows."

Tears welled in Gillian's eyes as she leaned against the refrigerator. "I don't understand any of this. I have one friend, Nathan. Just one. And you're telling me she's done this to me?"

"No, Gill," Nathan said and cupped her cheeks. "She's trying to help you. Same as me. And you have two."

"Two?"

"Friends."

Gillian put a hand to her mouth to stop the sob. "She never believed me. When I said the dreams were getting stronger. She said they couldn't hurt me. Why did she lie?"

"I've been with you every time. I know they're getting stronger, but I don't know why any more than you do."

She pushed away to check on her eggs. "And this one? Why can't we change this one? Why can't I wake up?"

"Did you take anything? Before you fell asleep?"

"No. Nothing. Jenna won't even let me have caffeine pills."

"I meant to help you sleep."

"For god's sake, Nathan. You of all people should know I never actually want to sleep."

"Sorry."

"Damn well better be." She pulled the eggs from the oven and slid the omelet onto a plate for them to share. "So what do we do?"

"Ride it out," Nathan said. "Best we can do is fight until someone either figures it out or you wake up. We've gone through at least one dream cycle. The average adult goes through . . . "

" . . . four to six," Gillian said. "I know the patterns. And if we've only been through the first, then our odds aren't looking so good. Especially if we can't do anything but try to survive them."

"We won't give up."

"Can you wake me up?"

Nathan shook his head. "No. Your body is under your control, not ours. I can influence your thoughts and actions in the dream reality, but I can't wake you. You're the only one who can do that."

Hands on the counter to hold herself up, Gillian swallowed hard. Lifting her chin, she eyed her reflection in the glass. "Can you get out?"

"I don't know. But I'm not going to try if that's what you're asking."

"What happens to you if I don't wake up?"

Nathan caught her gaze in the window pane and gently placed his hands on her shoulders, Adam's apple bobbing in his throat. "You sleep, I jump. That's the way this works. You start to wake up and I get ejected from your head."

"You can't get out before that?"

"Only if I shoot myself in the foot."

"Why the foot?"

"I'm a soldier, Gill. To shoot myself in the foot triggers a very specific reaction in my brain. My operator spots it and initiates separation."

"Operator," Gillian muttered. "Christ."

"Dex, actually. Bit of a dork, really, but just about the smartest kid I've ever met."

Gillian huffed, a smile tugging her lips. "You like him."

"He's got a good heart. Not that I'd tell him that. Would go right to his rather scruffy head."

"Nate, you don't think I did this to myself, do you? Trapped us here somehow?"

"No," he said. "I don't. Whatever this is, we'll figure it out."

She ducked her chin, stroking her cheek against his fingers. "Eat," she said softly, tears slowing until she finally faced him with a sad smile. "Seems I'm not waking up anytime soon, so we need some strength. Because the next REM cycle is coming. And it'll be here sooner than we think, sooner than we want, whether I say it or not."

"Load her up!"

A team of medics lifted the stretcher into the ambulance, where an EMT waited to peel back the woman's eyelid once more. Confirming the diagnosis scratched on a piece of paper attached to the body, the medic looked over the woman as the conveyor tossed a backpack into the ambulance. The EMT applied a quick salve to the burn marks on the woman's wrist and checked her ankle only to stop short. She read the paper once more, confused.

"Hey wait!" the EMT yelled.

The conveyor slammed the first of the ambulance doors. "What?"

"You missed the burn on her arm," the EMT said.

"She's lucky that's all that burned."

The EMT tried again. "This note says something about a puncture on her ankle."

"So?"

"So there's nothing there," the EMT said and rolled both of the woman's feet to show the man perfectly smooth, unblemished skin. "You sure you got the right slip?"

SOMNIUM

"It was stapled to her clothes. It's the right slip." He slammed the door and the EMT shrugged, moving quickly to attach a drip to the woman's arm as her partner drove over the bumpy ground toward the highway.

CHAPTER THIRTEEN

"**L**AURA, THANK GOD."** Dex opened the feed and Laura offered him a simple wave of greeting. "Talk to me. What's happening outside?"

"You have to see this."

A video popped up in the middle of Dex's screen, and he felt the hair on the back of his neck prickle. "Holy . . . "

Intense carnage surrounded the train. Multiple firetrucks, ambulances and other emergency personnel had been summoned to the scene. Fires burned, water rained down from hoses perched on ladders. News helicopters didn't hesitate to show the burned corpses lying in scorched grass. The scene cut to an on-the-ground interviewer and Laura stopped the show.

"It's bad, Dex. They're saying hundreds dead."

"Hardie's alive. I know that much for sure."

"She's going to be hard to find. The tracker hasn't moved. She might've lost it."

"Then check the hospitals, will you? I need to know what's happening to her."

"You got it. You all right?"

"I don't know," Dex said and ran a hand over his eyes. "Braun was here. He gave me permission to let Keller go long."

Laura gasped. "You're kidding. Have you told him? About her?"

"No."

"It's too dangerous, Dex. You need to . . . "

"Ms. Taylor?"

Laura looked up over her shoulder and flashed a quick, uncomfortable smile. "Mr. James! I didn't think you frequented the . . . "

"Mr. Miller requested you join him in his office."

"Of course," Laura said. "I'll be right there."

Laura waited until Evan James slunk away before she spoke. "That guy gives me the creeps."

"Something just off about him," Dex agreed.

"I need my work disc, Dex. Now," she said. "Do you have it? I can come get it."

"You know you're not allowed in the MCL corridor."

"Then I'll give you my password and you can transfer the files. Do you have it?"

"It's right . . . " Dex glanced around. "It was right here."

"Dammit Declan!"

Startled, Dex held up his hands in mock surrender. "Easy. I'll find it."

"My personal project is on that. You don't know what it means to me."

"I'm getting an idea."

Laura dropped her forehead to her hand. "I'm sorry. It's just . . . it's important, all right. And that guy just freaks me out. Always watching." She shuddered. "You know he posted for an MCL position? They say he failed the psych evaluation."

"Makes sense. Not sure I've ever seen him sleep. Spends more time with his tablet than actual humans. Be careful."

"Always am." She gave him her password, the numbered sequence easily committed to Dex's memory. "Transfer the files to my band when you find it, all right?"

"No problem."

Laura severed the link and Dex looked around, feeling the isolation of the jump suite. Shuffling 831's paperwork, he searched the mess for the disc Laura had dropped.

"Where did you go?" he muttered.

Standing, he circled the desk, wondering what had happened to the damn thing when the waves jumped, the echo he had seen previously dancing across the middle screen once again.

Dex leaned close. "What the hell is that?"

He had nearly resolved to call Braun when the waves sputtered to life, marking the start of another dream cycle.

"Here we go." He reset the clock for the full 20-minute REM stage, wondering how long it would last this time, and if he'd still have both Subject and MCL at the end of it.

"You should have your back to the wall."

"I've had my back to a wall my whole life," Gillian said as Nathan joined her on the porch. "It hasn't helped much, has it?"

"Guess not," he said with a wry smile.

Gillian suppressed a laugh as she gazed at his new attire.

"Don't," he warned.

"Can't . . . help . . . it . . . ," she burst out, laughter ringing in the trees.

Nathan rolled his eyes and gazed down at the too-short jeans and loose t-shirt, a whirling dervish pictured on the front. Little brown hands and fangs were the only visible attributes of the cartoon character. Still, the laughter was a welcome change from the suppressed anger of the kitchen. "The scrubs were better, weren't they?"

Attempting to control herself, Gillian pressed her lips together and nodded. She had changed as well, a pair of fresh jeans hugging the curves of her hips and a black v-neck tee that made her hair look darker in the half-light from the moon.

"I'm changing back."

"I'm sorry." Gillian patted the spot beside her on the porch swing. "You just don't look like you."

"Your ex had god-awful taste," Nathan muttered and sat down beside her.

"Just one of the many reasons he's my ex."

"What were the other reasons?"

"Same old story. He wants to stay the night. I tell him no. He asks again. I tell him why. He says it's all right, he's not afraid of a bad dream. And then one morning, usually about a week later, I get the look from at least one black eye, more likely two, and he says the classic line."

Huffing, Nathan pondered the trees. "It's not you, it's me."

Gillian laced her fingers with his. "You've heard it."

"With this face? They never ask to stay the night."

"Idiots."

"Every last one." Nathan squeezed her hand. He couldn't remember the last time he'd found her so beautiful. The moonlight caught her hair, red strands igniting like spiderwebs in the dew of an early fall morning. In the trees, mists had overtaken the grounds, dancing blue lights flitting among the undergrowth.

Gillian followed his gaze. "We don't have much time, do we?"

"Nope," he said. "What've we got?"

A small arsenal sat on the porch railing. Along with the butcher and chef's knives, she'd found several smaller serrated blades, a mini-axe, two cans of hairspray and a lighter to round out their options.

"Not much," she said. "Have you tried to change anything?"

"Would I be wearing a Tasmanian devil right now if I could?"

"Always preferred Dumbo myself."

"Would've pegged you for a Mad Hatter kind of girl."

Gillian grinned. "The teacups made me ill when I was a little. But that doesn't explain this." Reaching down she slipped her foot out of the boot and drew her sock aside. She'd removed the bandages when she'd changed, finding the skin beneath nearly healed.

"Really doesn't," Nathan said.

"So what's the plan? Gotta be some way out of this, no?"

"I sure as hell hope so. What do we know?"

"We started off in a dream."

"The Inquisition at the Abbey," Nathan said, as familiar with Gillian's regular stable of nightmares as she was. "But we never made it to the torture. Hell, we never made it to the Abbey."

"No," Gillian agreed. "The sky was different at the picnic. I've tried every technique I know to wake up and I can't. You got any ideas?"

"This is your mind. I'm just along for the ride. I can help you fight, but I can't control your body."

"Feels like I got stuck in the middle of a fight or flight response."

"Deer in the headlights."

"Yep."

"So how do we get you unstuck?"

"You'd think being trapped in a crypt with your dead grandfather would do the trick, but . . . " She shrugged. "I really want to see my mother again."

"You will. We're only here until you work up enough adrenaline to trigger awareness."

"Unless . . . " Gillian glanced at their surroundings. "My house.

My childhood home. My past. My life. My fears and sins. All adds up to another less optimistic option, doesn't it?"

"You think this is some sort of near-death experience?"

"The life review fits. We've been to a few pivotal moments in my youth. Places where I could've—should've—made a different choice. Maybe I flatlined?"

Nathan shook his head. "There's only one place I can't follow. You're not dead yet."

"Everything I've read about NDEs says it's a peaceful experience. Long tunnels of light where the dead relatives come to greet you, not eat you. Unless we go to the other end of the spectrum."

"Which is?"

"A weighing of sins before being cast into the inferno. Tell me something, Nathan. Do you believe in God? Hell? Purgatory?"

"Like I said, it's your mind. Doesn't matter what I believe."

"Humor me."

Wary eyes on the dancing blue lights edging closer to the tree line, Nathan shrugged. "I believe life *is*. Squash a bug, life is *no more*. And we're all bugs."

"Then when I die, if I've done something horrible, I get off scot-free? Go to sleep and never wake up?"

"We've all done horrible things," Nathan said. "And not one of us gets off scot-free. That's the power of our conscious minds. We pay for our crimes while we're still alive."

"Then all of my guilt shows up in my mind?"

"As you have nightly proof."

"I'm not sure I believe it's just guilt swimming at the bottom of those cliffs," she said with a heavy sigh. "But if it's true it can kill us, then why do you do it?"

"Do what?"

"Come into my dreams. You don't know me. There's no reason to help me."

"Your mind is too damn much fun," he said, the automatic answer leaving his mouth before he could stop it.

"Right. Try again."

Nathan dropped his chin and stared at his hands.

"Is it so hard to answer?" Gillian asked.

Shifting his gaze to the trees, he watched her from the corner of his eye. "The best days of my life have been spent dreaming of you."

"You mean dreaming with me?"

"No," Nathan said and faced her. "I mean dreaming of you. And if this is the only way I can be with you, then I will keep dreaming of you, with you, and for you."

"Nathan . . . "

He rose to his feet and leaned heavy on the railing to avoid her gaze. "Don't say it."

"You don't know what I was going to say."

Nathan huffed and glanced back over his shoulder. "Yes, I do."

"What was it?" Gillian rose to join him.

"Something about how you appreciate the sentiment but . . . " He faced the trees. "When it comes to me and women, there's always a but."

Gillian glanced at his rear. "It is a rather attractive ass."

"Gill . . . "

"Are you going to let me talk?"

"No."

"Why not?"

"Where in the hell are the mutant hawks when I need them?"

"Don't change the subject."

Nathan rolled his chin to the sky. "I'm afraid to hear what you have to say."

"Because you're not handsome," she said, and he looked away again. She pressed her butt to the railing, the soft touch of her fingers on his cheek drawing his eyes back to hers. "What if I said you are?"

"You'd be a liar."

"Then what if I said you're the only hero I ever want to get this girl?"

"You mean get the girl."

"No," she said with a soft smile. "I mean this girl."

Nathan felt his chest rise, back straightening. "Don't tease me."

Gillian caressed his cheek. "You know that place between sleep and awake, that place where you still remember dreaming? That's where you're always waiting for me. And I have been happy to find you there."

"J.M. Barrie said that. *Peter Pan*, I think." Nathan slipped his arms around her waist, forehead to hers.

"More or less. Promise me something?"

"Anything."

"Promise you'll look for me. When we're awake. When all this is over. That you'll find me in the real world."

"I'll be waiting at your door."

"Then we'll save what happens next until I see you there."

Mist encroached on the house and with it, three dark figures arranged themselves in an arc a few hundred feet away. On the wind, the gurgling scream of a drowning child.

"Round two," she whispered.

Nathan followed her gaze. "How many ghosts did you say this property has?"

"Two men, a baby and . . . "

"One witch," Nathan said, eyes on the apparition that stood at the height of the semi-circle. Dark hair cascaded over her face, pale limbs jutting out at unnatural angles from a simple white gown, and he found himself grinning as he picked up a knife. "Just had to go with the the woman in white. Are we talking *Ringu* or *La Lorna*?

"More *Autopsy of Jane Doe.*"

"Fucking hell. That movie scared the shit out of me. What possessed you to watch it?"

"Thought the whole 'learn to fight a dead witch' thing would come in handy one day."

"You didn't finish it, did you?"

"I finished it. Not my best choice of educational film," she said and picked up the lighter and a can of hairspray. The trio floated silently toward the porch. "I had to stop it three times to go pee. That bell on the toe of a moving corpse thing really got me."

Nathan chuckled. "We're going to have a long talk about your choice in entertainment when we meet."

"I think you mean *if*. If we meet."

"When," he said firmly, and caught Gillian's smile from the corner of his eye. "I don't get invited over by many beautiful women, you know."

"Me neither." She grinned up at him. "Shame there doesn't seem to be time to work up some of that stay and surrender adrenaline."

"Get through this cycle. If we're still alive, we'll consider it."

"There's some proper motivation."

The wraith let loose a scream that shattered the windows. Nathan put his back to hers. "Let's do this."

SOMNIUM

Clayton Miller looked up as Evan opened the door to his office and encouraged a pretty young woman to enter. With a nod to his assistant, Clayton beckoned the newcomer forward.

"Ms. Taylor, come in. Can I get you something? A drink?"

"No, thank you. I'm fine."

"Of course." Clayton invited Laura to sit down, rounded the edge of his desk and leaned against it, hands clasped before him. "I imagine you're wondering why I've called you here. Especially at such an hour."

"It is a little awkward," Laura said with a slight blush.

"Mr. James tells me you're one of the best Weavers we have, capable of ensuring a full sensory experience in the virtual world. I understand you've been instrumental in the building of the sleep commercials. Your work in neural networks and natural image processing has been, and I don't say this lightly, outstanding."

"Thank you."

"Ms. Taylor, you should know it has also come to my attention you've been doing some—shall we call it extracurricular?—work with Dr. Dietrich on the dream imaging prototype."

Laura squared her shoulders, chin up. "I have."

"Have you been able to establish a clear image?"

"I'm very close."

"Then I need your help with—what does marketing call it?"

"ImaDream," Laura said.

"Yes. Well, we'll see about that. I've asked Dr. Dietrich to bring the technology online. You've been assisting him?"

Laura clamped her teeth together with an angry click. "Assisting? Is that what he told you?"

"I'm aware that Dr. Dietrich is not a hands-on developer, Ms. Taylor. Nevertheless, he is in charge of the program. At least for now." Clayton looked pointedly at Laura. "I've ordered the first human testing to be done tonight."

"Tonight? But Dr. Braun hasn't . . . "

Clayton held up a hand. "I've authorized the test. As of this moment, you will report directly and solely to me. Assist Dr. Dietrich. I want eyes on him at all times."

"And in return?"

"A successful test of the prototype will result in a new division," Clayton said and rose to his feet. Laura mirrored the gesture, and Clayton felt a subtle hint of her ambition echo in his bones. "One that will need a leader I can trust. Can I trust you, Ms. Taylor?"

"Absolutely, Dr. Miller."

"Good. Call me Clayton."

Laura flushed pink once again. "Thank you, Clayton. I won't let you down."

"I'm counting on it. Dietrich's in the labs." Clayton handed her a card. "My personal cell number is on the back. I want reports every half hour."

Scanning the image with her wristband, Laura waited a moment while Clayton busied himself at his desk. Satisfied that the conversation was over, she spun on her heel and headed for the door, a haughty swagger in her hips. As he watched her leave, Clayton wondered idly if he hadn't just let a viper loose on the rats.

"This doesn't seem fair," Gillian said and lifted a hand to the back of her head. Beside her, Nathan crashed into the fireplace hard enough to crack the stone.

"How so?" he asked with a groan.

"The wraith gets all the power, and we can't even arm ourselves. Why is that?"

"Damn fine question."

"It's my goddamn head. I should be calling the shots."

"So call them." Nathan launched toward the door. In a swift move, he buried one of the final knives in the eye of a rotting corpse, the smell of ozone emanating from blackened flakes of skin. Reaching down, he pulled Gillian to her feet and ducked into the kitchen where he put their backs to the peninsula. "What've you got left?"

Gillian lifted empty hands. "Nothing. You?"

Cursing, Nathan chanced a glance around the edge of the cabinets. "How'd we get out before?"

"Swallowed. After that we jumped into the mist."

"Anyplace around here to do that?"

"There's a cliff edge by the creek. It's not very high."

"How far?"

"Half a mile."

"Through the blue fire." Muttering a stream of obscenities under his breath, Nathan darted out to grab a poker from the fireplace before the dark-haired wraith crossed the window. "What about the crypt?"

"Key to the door."

A screech tore across the room. Gillian's eyes bulged as she stared at the wraith's pale skin, the waves of black not revealing a face but something registered familiar. It held its distended hands by its thighs, claws cupped as if to clutch cannon balls, the swirling mists of blue flame coalescing at its command. A keening emanated from its mouth, the scream rising as color congealed into a ball before its hips. Four dark lines appeared across its forearm.

"Nate, do you see . . . "

"I see it," he said. "But we have to move. Now." Nathan shoved her hard to the left and pushed her through the door as the peninsula exploded.

Expecting a step down, Gillian stumbled. Nathan caught her by the waist only to find plush dark blue carpet beneath his feet. A shining mahogany desk crowned a room dressed in bookshelves and academic accomplishments.

"Whoa," Nathan muttered, and glanced over his shoulder to be certain nothing had followed. Tremors of blue lightning receded as the room took shape. "Where are we?"

Recognition drained the color from Gillian's face. In the far corner, an old school chair, stark and simple, its laddered back out of place in the opulent office. "Bloody hell."

"Talk to me," Nathan said.

"College."

"Why?"

"I don't know."

"You must. Why does this frighten you?"

"Nathan, I . . . "

The door opened and a young student was ushered into the room by an imposing woman in a red suit. A second girl, a buxom blond with a streak of bright blue in her hair, caught Gillian's hand and gave it a squeeze before the woman in red closed the door in her face.

Nathan recognized 20-year-old Gillian, who took a seat before the large desk.

"Oh God, it's the day . . . " Gillian choked on the words.

"What day?" he asked.

"Ms. Hardie," the red-suited woman said and settled into a deep leather chair. "This is not the first time you've been in this office."

"No, Dean Abbott."

"Based on your academic achievements, we were willing to offer you a second chance after the sustained disruptions you caused in the dorms. While your move off campus has been an acceptable alternative, it seems to have spawned other issues. The committee debated the claims on both sides. To recap . . . "

Young Gillian's eyes found her feet while Dean Abbott perched a pair of purple spectacles at the end of her aquiline nose and withdrew a single sheet of paper from Gillian's file.

"The complaint was made by one Shawn Burke. The young man suffered a broken toe, fractured ribs, and a dislocated nose, not to mention substantial bruising to a rather more sensitive area. Do you deny that you caused these issues?"

"I didn't mean . . . "

Dean Abbott glared down her nose at Gillian. "Yes or no, Ms. Hardie."

"Yes. I mean no. I don't deny that I hit him."

"Although the local magistrate has seen fit to drop the charges against you, it is my duty to inform you that the committee rendered its own verdict in the matter." Dean Abbott closed the file and settled her most unnerving stare on Gillian. "This is your third strike, Ms. Hardie. And while your scholarship has been exemplary, our moral code requires a certain standard of conduct from all students, even those living off campus."

"Yes, Dean Abbott."

"Ms. Hardie," Dean Abbott said more kindly. "Can you give me any reason for your conduct?"

"I have bad dreams."

"That can't have been all there was to this complaint." The older woman rounded the desk. "Give me a reason, Gillian. Just one good reason and I'll find a way to let you stay."

Gillian wiped her cheeks, pursed her lips and looked away.

After a prolonged silence, Dean Abbott returned to her plush leather chair, a firm tap of the paperwork on the mahogany surface before she tucked it back in the file. "I am sorry to do this, Ms. Hardie, but if you cannot provide any additional defense, I am forced to abide by the committee's decision and revoke your scholarship."

Mind racing as her future circled the drain, Gillian swallowed hard. "Will I be permitted to come back if I can pay full tuition?"

"You think your family can come up with it?" Dean Abbott said with a frank look.

"There are loans," Gillian muttered, well aware her family's circumstances wouldn't provide much of anything. Even qualifying for financial aid would be difficult given the outstanding sums her father still owed Davidson Institution.

"I'm afraid we won't be able to readmit you even if you could come up with the money. But if you withdraw, I will refrain from filing a formal dismissal. You can reapply elsewhere, including for financial aid. It's the best I can do for you, Gillian."

"Thank you, Dean Abbott."

"You may go."

Young Gillian rose to her feet, squared her shoulders and lifted her chin as she left the office behind. Confused, Nathan followed Gillian and her younger self out the door and onto the quad where Jenna found her.

"Well?" Jenna asked.

"I'm out."

"It's not fair! You didn't do this. Not on purpose."

"It's done, Jenna. That's all there is to it."

"Gill . . ."

"I'll see you." The two girls embraced before Gillian left the scene alone, mist creeping up to shroud the red-brick path where they stood.

"I finished my degree at UNC," Gillian said to Nathan with a sad smile. "They accepted me on partial scholarship on the condition that I allow them to study me in their 'Neurodiagnostics and Sleep Science' program. I haven't lived with anyone for more than a week since."

Loneliness emanated off Gillian in waves of pungent regret, Nathan's own life mirrored in hers. With a wry smile, he shook his head. "I'm not buying it."

Startled, Gillian faced him. "Buying what?"

"The broken toe. You missed his instep. And you don't miss. Solar plexus, instep, nose, groin. Classic defense technique. You want to tell me what that jerk actually did?"

"He was Jenna's boyfriend. Stumbled into my room one night. Just a drunken mistake."

"Was it?"

Gillian bristled. "Does it matter? When he touched me, I hit him so hard he lost a testicle. He filed assault charges and when I told my side to my court-appointed lawyer, he cut a deal."

"A deal? Why the hell . . . "

She cut him off. "Who do you think the jury would've believed? Me? The ex-drug addict with a five-year stint in Davidson on her record? Or the star forward on the basketball team with the stellar, down-home smile? Shawn claimed he was drunk. Turned left when he should've turned right, and I clobbered him. How does a jury decide what was real? His word? Mine?" She shook her head. "What was real was a broken nose, cracked ribs, and a ruptured testicle. That's what the jury would've seen. I got off easy."

"You were defending yourself. He deserved whatever he got."

Blue lightning flickered in the mist, and Nathan's skin crawled as the stench of the bog drifted over his shoulder. Gillian glanced down at her stomach as if she expected something to emerge.

"I don't feel right," she said and reached out a hand to Nathan. He had barely grasped her fingers when she slipped backward, sucked into the mist as a low chuckle filled the diminishing air.

Dex stared at the center screen and shook his head in denial. The waves shifted apart, running nearly parallel instead of intertwined. "That's not possible."

Nothing tonight is, he thought and sat forward, uncertain what to do.

On his right, 831's heartbeat spiked, rising to dangerous and rapid levels that seemed incongruent with her mental activity. Dex felt a surge of hope, the rise more than enough to trigger wakefulness in even the deepest sleepers. On his left, Keller continued strong and steady. And in the middle . . .

Dex jumped backward, the light so intense it forced his eyes closed. Gripping the desk, he found his breath somewhere on the floor behind him and blinked, trying to make sense of the latent image.

The split-second flash had shown him something unbelievable. The same chair as before and yet different. The additions simple but coarse. A single steel panel added to the slatted back. At its peak, a crown no one ever fought to wear. On the seat, a steel plate held in place with raised rivets, the discomfort minimal to those forced to feel leather straps tighten across chest, wrist and ankles.

Dex had caught snippets in the waves before. Little flashes of color or a hint of scenery when the dreams were strong. His reports had been the impetus for the dream imaging prototype, Laura's interest in the patterns insatiable, her attention when he spoke of them rapt and more than a little flattering. But he'd never seen anything like this. Nothing so precise. He was out of his depth, and he knew it. He hailed Laura once again.

"Not now, Dex."

"Find Braun. Do it. I don't give a shit what happens to me. Tell him . . . " He looked directly at the camera. "Tell him 831 needs him."

Laura paused in her work long enough to huff in annoyance. "I'll do my best, but I can't talk to you now."

"Where are you?"

"Labs."

"What the hell are you doing there at this hour?"

She finally looked at him. "You okay?"

"No. I'm spooked. Bad. There are things happening here. Strange fucking things. I can read most waves, but these aren't normal. And . . . "

"And what?"

"I keep seeing a chair. It's on the screens. Almost looks like the kind inmates used to refer to when they said 'ride the lightning' and I don't know if I'm going crazy or if the virtual shit is leaking into the sleep tech. And there's something else in the waves. Almost like a third consciousness."

Laura's face filled the screen. "Tell me what you're seeing."

"There's this extra wave. It's not even really a wave." Dex cradled his head in his hands. "Hell, I'm not even sure it's actually there."

"Dex . . . " Laura put a finger to her lips and turned off the camera. The mic remained open, and Dex instantly muted his side. Fingers in motion, he searched the security feeds for the lab cameras. In moments he had a complete view of the room, and the handsome MCL who slipped his arms around Laura's waist.

"McDonough," she said.

"Been a long time," the MCL said.

Laura slapped his hands away. "There's a good reason for that."

"Come on, Laura. You weren't always this stiff."

"Maybe not," she said with a cruel smile. "But I always had my sights set higher than a third-level MCL."

Chuckling, the MCL withdrew his arms. "Here I thought that was why we worked. What the hell is it I volunteered for anyway?"

"ImaDream," Laura said, and Dex felt his balls retreat toward his stomach. "We're testing it. Tonight."

Unconcerned, McDonough draped himself over a chair. "What do you need me to do?"

"Sleep," Laura said. "And try not to die."

The hitch of her breath cut through darkness vibrating on its own wavelength. Flat on her back, Gillian lay on firm but soft ground. The oppression of the tight space weighed down on her as she waited for her eyes to adjust. When it didn't happen, a familiar tingle of panic started in her toes and crawled up her limbs.

"Nathan?"

The word traveled only a few inches before it bounced back.

Reaching out, she found a palm's width of room on either side of her hips. Material soft as silk brushed her fingers. In front of her face, she had about a forearm's worth of space before she touched, puffing.

"Bloody hell."

Fingers traced the head panel, finding it tapered just over her forehead.

"This can't be."

Tucking her hands close to her body, she ran them down her chest and to the end of her shirt. Fumbling at the edge of her jeans, she dug inside her pockets.

Nothing.

No lighter. No rope. No knife. No Nathan.

Lifting her head, she tried to see her hands in the dark. The only sound was the slight scuffle of her movement.

"Wake the fuck up, Gillian. Wake the fuck up."

Shaking violently, she shut her eyes and tried to focus.

"Light. L-I-G . . . L-I-Fuck me. L . . . L . . . L . . . "

Sweat broke out over her body, the urge to evacuate her bladder overwhelming as she slammed her fists to the head panel, tearing at the silk until her fingernails were bloody. The rending of the fabric screamed in the silence.

Cold metal met her tortured skin and she sensed the immense weight of the earth pressing down on the coffin's lid.

Terror struck with the force of a pile driver. A shriek erupted from her mouth, two decades' worth of fear forcing its way out of her throat and into the limited air as she lost all conscious thought.

Nathan hit the dirt with breath-taking velocity, the moist ground sinking as the mist expelled him like a particularly virulent bolt of lightning. His bones ached, the subtle cold of the damp soil working its way inside his skin, and he found himself at the edge of the summer kitchen on Gillian's property. His fingers sank into the churned earth when he sat up.

"Gillian?"

Silence. Nothing but the sound of his own breath disturbed the night air. The stars he had seen when he first arrived were gone, the lightning bugs dispersed into the forest. And while the mists lingered at the edge of the trees, the dense thickets seemed mere imitations behind the shifting gray curtain. Instead, his sole focus lay on the house and the summer kitchen, the blue lights of a small pool shining between them.

Stillness. Profound as a calm ocean at night.

Until she—until it—stepped forward out of the mist.

Scrambling to his feet, Nathan eyed the wraith. It stood at the edge of the trees, but came no closer, distended fingers hanging loose by her thighs. On one wrist, four dark lines formed an awkward tattoo of burnt flesh. On its ankle, a mark swollen and dark. Even from the distance he recognized it.

"Gillian."

It said nothing and made no other move, dark eyes glistening behind a curtain of hair.

"Representative," he whispered. "What are you trying to tell me?"

Nathan thought back to their arrival, to the stroll up the hill to the cabin and the stories Gillian had told him of the property. His memory clutched at something about the summer kitchen and the tale of a 'Typhoid Mary' buried head down.

Buried.

Beneath him a sound, so faint he wouldn't have heard it if so much as a cricket chirped. It rose up from the earth, finding its way through crevices of dirt to whisper into the stiff air with all the exuberance of a popping soap bubble. Nathan took one last look at the wraith, who stood silent as a stone bust at the periphery of the visible grass, and then put his ear to the earth.

The cry came soft as a bird taking flight, but to hear it through the dirt meant she must've been screaming at the top of her lungs.

For a single moment, relief flowed through him. It had to be enough to wake her, but he felt none of the usual triggers that would signify the simple and swift ejection from her dream when she woke—the feeling like a swimmer who'd held his breath too long finally coming up for air. The connection between them remained strong, deepening even as darkness consumed the landscape until there was nearly nothing left of the scene.

On his knees, he scooped fragrant earth with both hands before a soft whistle passed his ear. A shovel appeared propped against the crumbling corner of the kitchen. *A change. But how? Had Nathan done it himself?* In his mind he saw the earth move, lifting up as one piece and landing in a heap five feet away, but there was no changing what lay before him. Grabbing the shovel, he sent up a silent prayer that she wasn't too deep.

Time passed. In dreams, it moved either too slow or too fast, or sometimes not at all, but just as his arms were about to give out, a ping sounded beneath the tip of the blade. Sliding the shovel to the left, he found the edge and dug a gap. The hinge appeared, and he shifted his attention to the far side, all the while listening for any sign of life, but his breathing and the persistent slough of the shovel unloading soil were all that remained.

In moments he had the lock exposed, and he slammed the

shovel against it, breaking into the casket on the third try. Dropping to his knees, he wrenched open the lid. She lay quiet within, skin tinged blue against the white backdrop of bloodied silk overlays. He slipped his hands beneath her shoulders and lifted her out. Around them, nothing remained of the world but the casket, the dirt and the hole. Pale mist covered the ground right up to the edge of the grave.

"Gillian, dammit, don't you do this."

Laying her on the dirt, he pressed his ear to her chest, the faintest hint of a beat reaching toward him with a feeble thud.

"Please," he begged. "Stay with me." Tilting her head back, he pressed his lips to hers and pinched off her nose. Her chest rose with his breath, once, twice, three times before he sat back, hoping for more. "Come back to me."

Taking a second deep breath, he leaned over again.

"She's crashing!"

"Almost there," the ambulance driver called. He swerved around a slow-moving Prius, the lights of the hospital just ahead. The emergency lane was crowded with other buses discharging patients into the hands of the orderlies.

"She's not going to make it," the EMT said and fitted an oxygen mask over her patient's face. She readied the automated external defibrillator and positioned the paddles over the woman's chest, waiting for full charge, when a gasp of breath condensed on the plastic mask. Poised over the heart, the EMT watched carefully as the meager beat strengthened once more, the blue pallor of skin moving back to pale, a hint of pink in the woman's cheeks.

"Jesus," the EMT muttered, heart racing. "She's stabilizing."

"We're here," the driver said. "Good work."

"I'm not sure I had anything to do with it."

The rear doors swung open, and an orderly inspected the human cargo. "What've we got?"

"Head trauma, burns on the wrist," the EMT said. She piled tubing on her patient's stomach and touched a hand to the woman's forehead as the orderly pulled the stretcher forward. "Good luck."

"Burns?" the orderly asked. "Where?"

"Right wrist."

"You sure about that?"

The EMT paused, a sense of déjà vu causing the hair on her arms to stand at attention. She looked at the wrist, the salve she had used glistening in the lights, but the marks had disappeared. "What the hell?"

"We'll check her," the orderly said. "Get your asses back to the site."

The gurney sailed into the bright lights and clean white walls of the hospital.

"Let's go," the driver said.

Shaking her head, the EMT climbed back into the bus, uncertain why she felt so uncomfortable, fingers absently rubbing together as if she were trying to clean off clinging oil. When the ambulance moved, she felt better, her focus back on the task at hand.

Gillian Hardie was someone else's problem now.

CHAPTER FOURTEEN

GILLIAN HEAVED IN a breath of her own, body slumped until a rasping cough brought her back to full awareness. Nathan caught her in his arms, the mist receding to reveal the cabin as she sat up and clutched him.

"I don't . . . ever want . . . to do . . . again . . . " she said between coughs.

Nathan put his lips to her forehead to suppress a laugh and blinked rapidly to hold back tears. "Then wake the fuck up, my lady."

"You think it's so easy? You try it."

"Not before you." He lifted her chin to catch her eye. "Never before you."

"Is it done?" she asked and looked up to find a sky full of stars.

The sense of safety returned as Nathan got to his feet. He scanned the edge of the forest, but the wraith was gone. "For now. Come," he said and helped her out of the hole. He stroked the plastered hair from her sweat-drenched forehead, her skin colder than the last time he'd touched her. The stench of her fear drifted into his nose, but he breathed it in with joy. "Let's get you cleaned up."

"Nathan."

He faced her, the look in her eyes causing something deep in his gut to shift with fear and longing. Leaning forward, she pressed her lips softly to his, breath warm as she hovered close in anticipation of a response.

"Thank you," she said.

"Thank me when you wake up. That'll be enough."

Moving quickly to put some distance between them, he caught her hand and half dragged her back to the house in an effort to focus on anything other than the desire threatening to overwhelm his good judgement. He left her by the bed and stepped into the bathroom to start the shower.

"We need to get you warm," he said when he returned. Taking her hands in his, Nathan rubbed them vigorously. "You're losing too much heat."

"Nathan . . . "

"You can get cleaned up first. I'll keep watch."

"Nathan!"

He looked up to find her begging him to answer a question he couldn't let himself entertain, not now. Not here.

"Don't . . . don't ask me to . . . "

The soft touch of her hands as she enfolded his, triggered a yearning that ran the length of his body. Every nerve screamed at him to do what she wanted, what he wanted. Extracting himself, he ducked back to the shower to check the temperature. A fine spray hit his arm as she stepped up behind him and ran tentative hands over his shoulders.

"Am I that repulsive?" she asked.

Nathan chanced a glance at her. "Of course not."

"Then why won't you kiss me back?"

He said nothing. She stepped around him and placed his hands on her hips as she drifted into the steam, clothes clinging to soft curves a moment later. Lifting a hand, she traced the lines of his scar with her thumb, and he pressed his cheek into her palm.

"Someone told me sex was a surefire way to wake up," she said.

"What idiot said that?" Nathan muttered.

"Tell me you don't want to. Tell me I'm too ugly. Tell me you'll never love me. Tell me to go to hell and I won't ask again."

"You know I can't do any of that."

"Then kiss me back."

"We're not safe." His arms betrayed his words and slid around her waist to pull her closer. "And I can't do something that would leave you so vulnerable no matter how much I may want to. Don't you understand?"

"Explain it to me."

Nathan pressed his forehead to hers. "I can't watch you die."

"I'm not dead yet, thanks to you." She lifted her chin, breath dancing on his lips. "And if being buried alive wasn't enough to wake me, I'm willing to give even stupid ideas a try."

"It's not safe."

SOMNIUM

"We're never safe."

"Gillian . . . "

She cut him off, lips to his. The hunger for her touch surfaced with a force that shook his skin. Heat spread down his torso, awakening desire with a strength he had only known in his private dreams. He pressed his lips to hers and took her to the tiles, an arm out to cushion her, breathing almost forgotten as the water caressed them.

"Tell me I'm not dreaming," he whispered.

"Can't do it." She kissed him again. "But it's a damn good dream."

"Bit of a change for you."

"What have I told you about smart-ass remarks?"

With a laugh he pulled back to catch her face in his hands. "This is the part where you always disappear."

"I'm not going anywhere." Her fingers found his skin and she slipped the jeans from his hips. "Do you think we'll remember this? In the morning?"

"I will always remember this," he said, and cast his misgivings aside as he swept her into his arms.

Outside, the electrified mists drifted closer.

Dex's brow furrowed as he watched the fluctuations in the waves couple with rising heart rates before a sudden, silly grin broke out across his face. "Hot damn. If that doesn't do it, I don't know what will."

Embarrassed, he dropped his eyes to the floor to discover the edge of a red disc peeking out from beneath the console. "There you are."

Overhead, the lights popped, flickered and then held steady. Punching Laura's password into the disc, he was about to transfer access to her wristband when he inadvertently opened the only file it contained. A cursor blinked at the end of a numbered list next to a recommendation for testing. It read like a roll call of the Elite's finest dreamers: 0831, 5987, 7128, 8924, 9103, 9425, 9579, 9620, 9909 and 9998.

Intrigued by more than the thought that four of those dreamers had been called that night, and of those under, only one remained alive, Dex scrolled to the beginning of the document.

The more he read, the more uncomfortable he became. As an Operator, he hadn't ever fully considered the impact the programming might have on the mind. All the tech really did was prepare the brain for the sensory virtual reality experience. Like biologic drugs, it simply switched on and enhanced a person's natural abilities. Laura told him it wasn't harmful, and while the long-term effects were still being studied, he, like the rest of the world, had opted to live in the moment instead of worry about the future. It was a theory that left most people relying on advances in medicine to cure the ills associated with the passions of their youth.

But as Laura's theories on reverse imagery unfolded, a primal revulsion formed in his belly, his instinct for self-preservation rising like sickness. For the first time since he'd blown apart a zombie in a virtual gameroom, he felt the urge to scrub his brain clean of all Somnium had ever done. Bile climbed his throat as he reread the list of recommended test subjects.

"What did you do, Laura?"

As if the thought had brought it on, his tablet buzzed, a note from Laura advising him to "tune in."

Checking the time, he glanced at the waves. Satisfied the next dream cycle had yet to start, he popped open the virtual screen. In a few quick moves, he had the labs' security cameras focused. Laura was busy attaching electrodes to the MCL's head in the lab bedroom. When she returned to the control room, he clicked open his mic.

"How's it work?" he asked. "The reverse dream imaging?

"Basically, the computer reads the electronic impulses of the brain during the sleep cycle and then develops the visual based on pattern recognition. It feeds those patterns into Somnium's deep learning data banks to recognize the complex neural activity of the dream. Then it draws from the graphic database to develop the image and out pops the dream. Your deepest, darkest desires on screen for all to see."

"No fucking way," Dex muttered, and Laura grinned.

"You're too smart to think it can't be done."

"I meant there'd be no fucking way I'd ever volunteer for that shit."

She chuckled. "No one should. Not yet, at any rate. Most

dreams are like cotton candy. They dissolve at a single touch. To be seen, the dream needs to create a strong bioelectric impression on the brain."

"Like a nightmare."

Laura nodded. "Something strong enough to see, but not so strong that it triggers the adrenal response."

"So bad enough to wake someone, without actually waking them?"

"Most people wake from the fear of a nightmare. But the MCLs and the Elites have trained themselves to withstand fear that would cause the average dreamer to wet the bed. It takes a lot to wake them. They were a natural choice for the ImaDream tests."

"You developed this?"

"The weave connection," Laura said. "Took a good deal of work and some trial and error at first. Particularly when only the strongest dreams showed even a hint of an image reversal. But I think with a little fine-tuning, we'll be able to broadcast it to a virtual room. Think about it, Dex. The MCLs could be inside the dream without having to jump. What are you listening to, by the way?"

Dex froze as Mondo Cozmo's "Plastic Soul" filled the room in a slow building crescendo. "Stay there."

Moving quickly, Dex checked every possible audio option, shutting off speakers until he was down to nothing more than the Chicken Coop's vital systems and his own computer. As he approached the pod, the source slowly became clear.

"Where's it coming from?" Laura asked.

Dex looked back, eyes wide. "Keller."

Gillian slipped a brush through her hair, tied it back with a purple rubber band and checked her look in the mirror to see the happiness she felt reflected. Her skin remained pale, the bags under her eyes an almost permanent addition, but a pleasant flush and a simple smile had found their way to her face. It had been a long time since she'd felt even mildly happy in a dream. It had been a long time since she'd felt mildly happy anywhere.

Pinching some extra color into her cheeks, she looked at the rumpled sheets of her bed, Nathan no longer among them as a song that reminded Gillian of lazy Sunday mornings filtered into the air. She found Nathan in front of her sound system, dressed once again in the scrubs from the asylum. The antique turntable was in mint condition, and he'd perused her extensive collection of vinyl while she'd dressed, finding among the records a gem she didn't remember purchasing. Music washed over them and she slipped her arms around his waist. Catching her hands, he lifted them to his lips, closed his eyes and smiled.

"What has you smiling?" she asked and kissed his neck.

He spun her to the end of his arm, drawing her back to sway in time with the music. "This song always reminds me of you. 'Every time I shapeshift into form, I'm standing there right next to you.' Defines my nights with you in a single line."

Gillian smiled and kissed him again.

"Amazes me that it's here."

"It isn't," she said.

"What?"

"I have absolutely no idea where this came from." She slipped out of his arms. "I don't even know this song. But I like it."

"Mine," Nathan muttered, thoughts on the shovel and how it had appeared when he needed it. "It must be mine."

"I would imagine you'd bring a little something with you into my dreams." She headed for the kitchen, Nathan on her heels, and inspected the damaged peninsula. Sighing, she dug into the refrigerator for a bottle of water. "I hope this doesn't carry over into the real world. I just finished remodeling this kitchen."

"Gill . . . " Nathan said and caught her hand, eyes bright as she sat down at the bistro table. "If this song is mine, it must mean I changed it."

She froze. "Do it again."

Nathan hummed softly, and the song shifted, a new tune emanating from the speakers.

Gillian clutched his fingers in excitement. "Try your clothing."

Nathan pictured himself in his own clothing—black cargo pants, a black t-shirt, black leather boots on his feet—but nothing shifted. "Dammit."

"We'll take what we can get," she said as mist crowded the windows. "It's coming soon."

"Remind me to tell Dex his suggestion was bullshit."

"Still a damn good suggestion."

"Wanna try it again?" Nathan asked with a squeeze of her hand.

"Love to, assuming we make it through this cycle."

"Proper motivation. Dream. Reality. Fear. How do we solve a problem like a never-ending nightmare?"

"Interpret it," Gillian said and blinked. The man across from her was no longer Nathan and she knew instantly the dream cycle had started again. Thin hands trembled by gaunt cheeks, fingers moving as if to play piano in midair. "Patrick?"

"That's right, Gilly. If we translate the monster to what it represents, we stop dreaming that particular dream. You get me?"

Gasping, Gillian looked around the crowded asylum lounge, the stale urine tiles welcoming her back with stalwart indifference.

"I'm telling you. Interpretation is the key," Patrick said. "That's the way to solve the riddles. Find the shit that doesn't belong. You figure out what the dream represents and it disappears, leaving nothing but the stuff they're beaming into our heads behind. Savvy?"

"I got it," Gillian muttered. Across from her, Patrick Dolan had his manifesto open, the tiny black print covering the page in circles of ambiguous thought. Craning her neck, she searched the room. "Where's . . . "

"Where's what?" Patrick asked and pushed his glasses over the rather awkward bump in his abundant nose. The frames appeared large on his thin face. Dark brown hair floated in unwashed waves around his tense shoulders. "You just have a microsleep? You slipped into neutral there for a minute."

"No, I'm all right."

Patrick put a bony hand over hers, concern in his deep blue eyes. "How long's it been?"

"Two days."

"Watch out for hallucinations." He shifted his chair closer to hers. "I'm telling you, Gilly, these dreams of ours aren't real dreams."

Tears welling in her eyes, Gillian caressed his cheek. "I know, Patrick."

He seemed not to hear. "They're beaming them straight to our fucking brains. Straight into our brains!" Letting go of her hand, he smacked his neck at the base of his skull three times in succession, as if he were trying to dislodge water from his ear.

"You were right," she whispered.

"Right about what?"

Gillian searched the crowded lounge. "Where's Shearer?"

Bristling, Patrick's lips twitched into a sneer. He reached out and snatched the rubber band from her hair before tussling the waves into her face. "Motherfucker's due on rounds any second. Don't let him catch you with the ponytail. Too easy to grab. Too pretty not to."

"Tell me about the dreams. About interpretation. How do we make them stop?"

"That's the thing, Gilly. I don't think we can. They keep beaming them into our heads and we keep dreaming them. We can fight them. But we can't win." He rolled up his sleeve, showing off a long red scratch. "Woke up with this on my arm. Motherfucker bit me last night. Bit me! Why would I ever dream some motherfucker with sharp-ass teeth bit me? Damn chemicals they force us to take. Checked under my tongue." A palm to his ear, three smacks in succession. "Chemical dreams. Dreaming someone else's dreams. Always dreaming other people's . . . "

"But they must be our dreams. Our fears. Some of them at least."

He shook his head. "Maybe."

"Representations," said a deep voice.

Gillian nearly wrenched her neck looking around to find no one there.

"Nathan?" She felt a hand on her shoulder and lifted her own to cover it.

"Keep him talking."

"You're hallucinating, Gilly." Patrick inspected her face. "Put your head down. I'll wake you if you twitch."

"I can't. I need you to talk to me. Tell me how to get them out of our heads."

Patrick tugged at his hair, yanking hard enough to jerk his face to the window. "Fucking prick catches you by the hair before he— you know—"

"I know." Gillian caught Patrick's hand in her own. He paused, eyes clearing for a single moment of sanity.

"Don't let him catch you, Gilly. I can't protect you as much as I like, but I'll always try. You know that, right?"

"I know."

SOMNIUM

Nodding, Patrick tussled her hair again. "You look so pretty in the daylight. Anyone ever told you that?"

"You have."

"Too pretty for such bad dreams." Grinning like a child caught stealing a cookie, he snatched his hand away and flipped through the composition book to a drawing of a sea serpent.

Patrick's skill with pen and pencil brilliantly highlighted the creature, the eyes both sinister and human as they glared from the depths of his darkest fears. At its feet, three boys ran for their lives, the largest protecting the smaller twins, shirts marked with an individual letter of E, P or J.

"He's the serpent," Patrick said and tugged his hair again. "See here? See the eyes? It's him, Gill. I don't have to tell you why I picture him that way. We gotta look for the details. The things that show us who they really are. Who they represent. Look for the ones we don't know. Those are the ones that aren't ours. When we slay the interlopers, we'll be able to sleep again. I know it."

The hospital shifted, the asylum suddenly nothing but ash and quiet, the laundry room surrounding them once more.

"Patrick? Patrick!" Gillian clutched at a hand that no longer existed. At her feet, the burned edges of the manifesto flickered in an unseen breeze to land on the image of the serpent swimming the seas of a lost boy's memory.

"Who was he?" Nathan asked gently.

"My protector. My friend. The only one I ever really had before Jenna." She lifted the book. Letters and words lay scrambled on the page, unreadable. "I lost track of him after he turned 18 and they forced him to leave. But I saw him once, years later. On a city street when I went for a job interview. He followed me inside. Called my name over and over until security escorted him out. But I didn't answer. Didn't acknowledge him. Why didn't I answer, Nate?"

Nathan caught her shoulders and forced her to face him as the laundry flickered into mist. In an instant he sat behind the wheel of a 1970 International Harvester Scout II. It ran backward down a steep hill, rolling out of control. Shifting gears, he slowed the speeding car. "Because you wanted to be normal. There's no crime in that."

"Yes, there is," Gillian said. "He loved me. Protected me in that god-awful place. And I denied even knowing him. What does that say about me?"

A gust of wind shook the Harvester, the scent of sea air seeping into the cabin. Nathan slammed on the brakes and screeched to a halt inches before the ruptured edge of the highway. A wall of water crested over them, the rogue wave hurtling down to engulf the car, both staring in awe as Gillian gasped.

"Fucking hell."

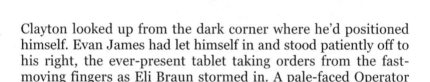

Clayton looked up from the dark corner where he'd positioned himself. Evan James had let himself in and stood patiently off to his right, the ever-present tablet taking orders from the fast-moving fingers as Eli Braun stormed in. A pale-faced Operator stumbled behind him. Clayton remembered the boy's face but not his name as Braun raged.

"What in God's name do you think you're doing?"

Dr. Phil Dietrich muttered an insult under his breath and checked on MCL McDonough. The sleeper lay undisturbed in a small room beyond one-way glass, as if he were under interrogation at a police station, the only difference, a bed in place of a desk. The plethora of noisy equipment didn't disturb him, the MCL apparently able to drop off in any situation without the need for strong sedatives.

At the edge of the bed, a square black console waited for input from the electrodes on McDonough's forehead. White stenciling on the side of the box identified it as Prototype F-DIT.

"Shut up and let me work, Braun," Dietrich said. A large screen filled with shifting static stood near the middle of the room. Seconds later, the hazy image of a human flashed, as if someone had taken a picture with a high-speed aperture. "Get that in focus. *Now!*"

"You don't have the authority to . . . " Braun said.

Dietrich chucked his chin toward Clayton. "Take it up with him."

"I've given my authorization to start the human tests."

"McDonough is under my command." The challenge in Braun's voice was unmistakable. "My authority over the MCLs is . . . "

Clayton held up a hand. "He volunteered."

"Volunteered?"

"You heard the man," Dietrich said. "Now unless you want to witness history, I'd suggest you get your ass out of my lab."

Anger filled Braun's cheeks with warm color. "You have no right . . . "

"I have every right," Clayton said, voice low and dangerous. "Don't test me."

Braun huffed. "Billings is dead because of you."

"Billings is dead. That's all we know for sure. I imagine you would prefer I didn't order another MCL expulsion."

"It's my fault," Eric Wilson muttered. "This is all my . . . "

Laura Taylor jumped in. "Focus enhancement complete, Dr. Dietrich."

Dietrich bustled around the console, checked his watch and nodded. "NREM starting at 4:37 a.m.. He's going down. Operator! Get your ass over here and take over the jump tech for Taylor."

In the corner, Eric lifted his chin, eyes wide and dark, the shock of witnessing a second death still with him. He moved automatically, pulled by the strings of authority.

Braun put a hand on Eric's arm. He hadn't let the boy out of his sight, dragging him from the jump suites to the laboratories the moment one of the second-level MCLs had informed Braun of McDonough's situation. "Eric is in no condition . . . "

Dietrich grabbed a firm hold of Eric's wrist and dragged the boy over to the console. "Is McDonough moving to REM?"

"Any minute," Eric confirmed and sat down.

"Mutiny's such a sting, aye Braun?" Dietrich said. "Maybe if you didn't run your division like the goddamn military, you'd finally get some decent results. Stop losing people and actually start doing some good for this company."

"Stop this." Braun glared at Clayton. "Stop this now."

"Initiating full imaging weave," Laura said from a second station.

"Too late," Dietrich sang as Laura adjusted the feed. "Anything?"

"Image should be coming up now."

Clayton took a step toward the screen as blue lighting shot through the static. The picture came into focus for a single instant, as if someone had managed to find the right spot on an old-time television antenna.

In the bed beyond, McDonough twitched, uncomfortable in his slumber.

A woman's face, a smile as she held a baby. Static reigned once again, a stray image forcing some primal reaction in Clayton's stomach as Braun took a step back and Wilson trembled. Moments later the static disappeared, and a hand reached out, caressing the plump cheek of the child.

"First person." Dietrich smiled. "Excellent work, Ms. Taylor. Your theory seems to have been correct."

Braun gaped at the screen. "How did you do this?"

"Theory?" Eric perked up to glare at Laura. "You said . . . "

She cut across him. "I've been working on the enhancement project for some time. Eric and a few of the other MCL Operators have been very helpful." She settled a hard look on Eric, who slumped at the console. "Should I wake him?"

"No," Dietrich said. "Give him two minutes and we'll confirm."

"You will fry his mind," Braun said through clenched teeth.

"No more than you have," Dietrich bit back. "How many have you lost tonight, Braun? Four? Six? More?"

"Gentlemen," Clayton cut in. "Please."

On screen, the image changed. The MCL chased the woman down a hallway, laughter following, and Clayton felt the intimacy of the dream as hands caught up with her and slid over her hips, lips coming closer until the screen blurred again.

McDonough's legs lurched, kicking at the covers.

"The waves," Eric said, voice so low he barely heard himself. "Dr. Braun. Look at the waves."

Braun's mouth dropped open, eyes following the subtle hitches. On screen, the scene turned dark. The MCL's heart rate rose abruptly. An image clear as any ever put on a silver screen pixelated into reality. The woman stood shadowed in sickness of grief, a knife dripping blood into a silent crib.

"Terminate this test," Braun snapped. "Right now."

Laura bristled. "I'm not going to . . . "

"Do it!"

"Wake him up," Clayton said.

Dietrich nodded to Laura who readied a stimulant syringe and moved to inject the MCL. She checked the time and glared back at Braun.

"He should wake in less than a minute," she said.

Eric gasped as the screen went black. "Did you see that?"

"What was that?" Braun asked.

Dietrich snorted. "Leave it to the MCLs to see things that aren't there."

Braun swung around. "Eric, you saw it?"

"Saw what?" Dietrich asked again, irritated. "There's nothing there to see. The dream was over. Stimulant injected. Done."

Shifting his weight, Eric hugged himself. "A chair, sir. I thought I saw a chair. And the waves were similar . . . at the end . . . to . . . "

"To what?" Clayton spoke more sharply than he had intended, the boy immediately withdrawing from the tone, fear clamping his mouth shut. Braun answered for him.

"To Markway's last jump."

Overhead, the lights flickered.

"MCLs," Dietrich muttered. "Nothing but nightmares on the brain."

In the lab bedroom, McDonough lifted a groggy hand to his head. "Damn that was a vivid dream."

Braun made his way into the room "What were you dreaming of just now?"

"My wife, sir." McDonough darted a look at the two-way mirror. "We were in the new townhouse. Planning to . . . " A blush crept over the MCL's cheeks, and he grinned sheepishly before he frowned and searched the lines of his hands as if they might help him find the right words. "She's been having some postpartum depression." He shivered. "I can remember the details of my daughter's pajamas. The way her skin smelled. Crazy."

"At the end," Braun said. "Before you woke. What did you see?"

"See, sir?"

"Did you see a chair?"

"No, sir. But . . . "

"But what?"

"I felt cold. And I heard . . . "

"What? What did you hear?"

"Laughter. But not girlish laughter. Not my wife's. It was more of a low chuckle. Like some villain in a bad western. And my wife, sir." McDonough curled his hands into fists. "Why would I see that? She would never . . . "

Braun squeezed his shoulder. "Just a dream, son. Let it go." He returned to the lab and addressed Laura. "Did you record it?"

"Of course."

"Show me the playback. The last few seconds."

In moments, the dream was on screen once again. "Come on,"

Braun muttered. Eric leaned close as the black void bounced to static, leaving the two of them staring at nothing.

"Satisfied?" Dietrich asked.

Clayton nodded. "How long before you can test this on an in-process MCL?"

"Another hour to calibrate."

"In process?" Braun asked. "You can't possibly . . . "

"Keller," Laura said, and Eric whipped his face to her. "We should test on MCL Nathan Keller."

In the corner, Evan James checked his tablet. "MCL Parker has just been called. It is far more likely he'll be in process within the hour than MCL Keller."

"You will not touch another MCL," Braun said, deep warning in his voice. "Not until these results have been studied and we can guarantee his safety."

"We need to understand what's happening," Clayton said.

"You cannot disrupt the link. This test barely lasted a minute in REM and those waves were unlike any we've seen."

A small squeak emanated from Eric's open mouth. Ignoring him, Braun continued.

"There's no telling what would happen to the MCL or the Sleep Subject if you were to interrupt the dream reality."

"We have no choice," Clayton said. "Or would you prefer more MCLs die tonight? Ms. Taylor, Dr. Dietrich. Assuming MCL Parker is in process when you're ready, prep for a full test."

Braun snapped his mouth shut and glared at Clayton. "Then you can expect my resignation in the morning. I won't stand for this."

Clayton whirled as Eli stormed from the room. "Goddammit Braun! Braun!"

Braun didn't bother to look back.

"What the hell is this?" Nathan asked, awed by the greenish walls of their watery prison. Beyond the Scout's windows, dark shapes swam in distant slow motion, the silent swish of tails bringing the gray bodies ever closer.

"It's like we've been swallowed by the wave," Gillian said.

SOMNIUM

The Scout remained warm and dry. Even their feet, which should have been swimming in cool water, had only small puddles to contend with.

"Reprieve," Nathan said.

"Not for long. Never for long."

"Long enough."

Gillian ran her hand along the leather seat. "Whose car is this?"

"Mine."

"Always protecting me. Just like Patrick."

"What did he mean, interpretations?"

Gillian watched without speaking as Nathan's hand snuck over and entwined with hers.

"We don't have much time," he said.

"Patrick and his brothers were abused by their father." She lifted her chin to look out into the water. "From the time they could crawl, Mark Dolan molested his sons. Patrick used to say sometimes, like some kind of sick joke, but over and over while he cracked his hand against his head, 'old enough to crawl, they're in the right position.' Chilled me just to hear it."

"Jesus," Nathan muttered.

"He was smart. Smarter than me. When he was clear, he talked about things you didn't even know you wanted to know. One day, I sat and listened while he went through the garden and named every flower. He knew the meaning and the intention behind them. Told me how back in the day certain bouquets carried secret messages to lovers, hidden in plain sight by the choice and structure of the buds."

"Hidden messages?"

Gillian shrugged. "He had a bit of a thing for conspiracy theories. That we never landed on the moon. That sort of thing. Kept his mind occupied so he didn't lose it thinking of his brothers."

"And the dreams?"

"He believed there were outside messages in his dreams, hidden within the symbolism. Interpret the dream properly and we'd be able to pick out the things that shouldn't be there, that didn't belong to us, to our minds. I never once thought he was right."

She squeezed his hand so hard Nathan thought his fingers would break.

"What if I had? What if just one person believed him? Would his life have been different? Better?"

"You took us to him for a reason," Nathan said. "Tell me what he knew."

"He once asked me why, if someone else were controlling our dreams, we didn't always dream happy things. Why, when people like us got caught in persistent nightmare disorder where we were waking up screaming at least once a week, sometimes once a night, why they didn't help us by sending us happy dreams?"

"You can't control the mind."

"Why not?" She slipped her hand out of his. "If your company can do what it says, why couldn't they fix this? Reprogram us?"

"They tried."

"What?"

"I don't know or understand the details, but they tried. Hundreds were helped. But not the Elite. So they enlisted the watchers. Tagged you with trackers to pick up the triggers."

"Triggers."

Gillian gently stroked the pendant at her neck. "You've said that before."

"Most of your dreams are harmless. The nights when you're not triggered, you can dream whatever you like without incident. But the nights when the tech hits you, the trigger, those are the nights I'm called."

"Then why can't I sleep? On those other nights? Why do I still dream my horrible dreams?"

"I don't know, Gill. There's something else going on in your mind, in the minds of all the Elite."

"Patrick used to dream of his twin brothers. Ethan . . . no, Evan. And Jimmy."

"What happened to them?" Nathan asked gently.

"His father . . . " Gillian heaved in a breath. "His father was the serpent. The demon that killed them both before he killed himself. That's what drove Patrick over the edge. He didn't understand why his father left him alive. All he knew was that he couldn't protect his baby brothers. So he tried to protect me."

"Did he have any specific, recurring dreams?"

Gillian shook her head. "Always the same dream. Over and over. He couldn't save them. He never saved them."

SOMNIUM

The dark shapes moved closer, and Nathan judged his next words carefully. "The dream may have driven him there, but . . . "

"But what?"

"I think it was his choice to stay in the nightmare. Just like it's been your choice to stay. Maybe not on a conscious level, but on some level, you've kept yourselves in this state."

"So I really am nuts," Gillian said. "Jesus."

In the water by her head, a flash of silver. Nathan drew her attention away from the slow circling death. "What did he think was hidden in plain sight?"

"Which one of these is not like the others," she said in a sing-song voice. "Patrick thought you could tell by the eyes. By the things you might never have seen anywhere else. Didn't know from your own daily life. Like someone else was feeding you the image."

"Like me?"

"When you first showed up, I thought I'd finally gone completely bonkers." Gillian smiled sadly. "Again."

"But you accepted me."

"Only because I thought you were part of my mind. I'd been dreaming up people and places and situations all my life. You didn't belong in my head, but you were of my head, so I didn't mind."

"But Patrick would've seen me differently?"

"He would've decapitated you the first time he saw you and never given you another thought."

Nathan swallowed hard as the gray shapes came close enough to investigate the tires.

"What did he mean by representative?"

"What does any dream mean? Interpret them. Symbols in the chaos. Dreaming of your house and find a room you never knew existed? Your soul is open to new opportunities. See an old crow? Difficulties lie ahead."

"Rogue waves?"

"Overwhelming emotion," she said. "I used to dream of my grandfather, that he refused to believe he was dead. Had come home from the grave and we all tip-toed around his slow-rotting corpse, wondering what the hell he wanted and why he wouldn't stay dead. Until one day, I realized it was me who had called him back."

"How so?"

"I blamed him for so many things. Took me years to figure out that I was the one keeping him from the grave. When I finally let all my anger at him go, forgave him, I never had that dream again."

"The crypt. You took us there because you still blame him for something?"

"I think I took us there because I knew he would have a way out."

"The key."

Gillian nodded.

"What do the sharks represent?" Nathan asked as a massive shadow drifted across their vision.

"You said it before. Guilt," Gillian said as the creature made a sharp turn. "We are literally swimming in guilt capable of eating us alive."

"Hell of a metaphor."

The resignation in Gillian's eyes chilled Nathan to the core as the shadow of a Great White loomed over the car.

"But this isn't a dream, is it?" she said. "Not anymore."

From the dark, the white snout emerged, deadly jaw gaping to show the rows of razor-sharp teeth churning the water, ever hungry for more.

"What is it then?" Nathan asked, muscles tense as the shark darted toward the car only to break off at the last second. Beside him, Gillian watched with an impassive gaze.

"It's a reckoning."

The suite door opened with a whoosh and Dex looked up as Eli Braun stalked in. He had barely enough time to stuff Laura's work disc under 831's file before Braun stood beside him.

"Keller's under again? Who's he with?" Braun asked.

"831, sir," Dex said without thinking, and then silently cursed his own ineptitude.

Startled, Braun checked his watch to find it nearly five o'clock in the morning. "Still?"

"Dreams must not be too bad."

Scowling at the lie, Braun turned his attention to the screen. The hand that clutched Dex's shoulder reminded him of a junkyard compactor, and he winced under the increasing pressure.

"How long?" Braun asked. "How long has she been like this?"

"A while."

"And Keller?"

"With her the whole time."

"Thank God."

Tension evaporated from Dex, blood flowing into his squashed shoulder as Braun read the waves. His pulse slowed thanks to the relief in the doctor's voice. The lights flickered, the echo Dex had seen before dancing across the screen behind 831's lines, chasing her down once again.

"What in God's name was that?" Braun asked.

"I was hoping you could tell me."

Braun shook his head in dismay. "I've never seen anything like this."

"Not even when you ran the 'Neurodiagnostics and Sleep Science Program' at UNC?" A quick tap to Dex's console brought the screen to life, the classified dossier floating before Braun. "That's where you met her, wasn't it? Where you found 831."

Ripping his eyes from the screen, Braun's mouth dropped open. "How—how did you . . . "

"Gillian Hardie. Designated as subject 10017 in the UNC persistent nightmare disorder study. Now known as Somnium Sleep Subject 831."

Mouth slamming shut, Braun narrowed his gaze before he answered. "Those subjects were blinded to protect their privacy . . . "

Dex continued. "But 831 wasn't the first, was she? Who was SSS 542?"

"How the hell did you find 542?"

"Don't ask what you don't want to know."

"I want to know."

"The Department of Justice never really liked it when I poked my head into their records either. But the records on 542 were deleted, and I mean really deleted."

"Damn well better be." Huffing, Braun shifted his gaze to 831's waves, silence slowly easing from uncomfortable to resigned. "You're right that 831 wasn't my first lucid dreamer. But she has proved herself the best. 542's name was Margot. Margot Braun."

Dex sat down hard. "Braun?"

"My daughter. The only child my wife and I ever had. She would've been about the same age as 831 now."

"Would've been?"

Braun sighed heavily "She wasn't as skilled a dreamer as 831. We lost her in the pharmaceutical intervention."

"Was Margot the reason you joined Somnium?"

Shifting his weight, Braun studied his shoes before he seemed to make up his mind. Chin up, he nodded. "Alistair Wilcox is married to my wife's step-sister. Margot was the reason he made the connection between the dream deaths and Somnium's tech. She was 15 when the nightmares started. I spent my life trying to help her. When Alistair offered me the means to expand my research, I took it. No questions asked."

"You should've asked."

"I won't say you're wrong."

"Why? Why did you subject your own daughter to this?"

"Margot was the reason I was able to start the MCL program. Without Alistair's intervention, Miller never would've bothered."

"What do you mean?"

"Didn't you ever wonder why Miller and Wilcox broke up? Why a man like Alistair Wilcox would choose to forgo the much more lucrative benefits associated with Somnium for a life in politics?"

Blinking rapidly as his thoughts ricocheted off a brick wall, Dex stumbled through an answer. "I assumed it was to pave the way for Somnium's growth. A friend in office."

"Your morals are commendable. More commendable than Miller's at any rate. Alistair Wilcox is the only reason Somnium hasn't done even more damage. When we approached Miller with the connection, Miller said two words. Two simple words that to this day chill me to my core."

"What were they?"

"Prove it."

The skin on Dex's arms contracted. "What?"

Braun shifted his weight, remembering the dispassionate look on Clayton Miller's face when he and Alistair had shown him their findings. Alistair had clamped his mouth shut, grabbed the paperwork and stormed from the office. For the next three weeks, the two shut themselves in an office, seeking a way to prove that subjects who had passed away in their sleep had been murdered by Somnium's tech.

Braun reviewed several autopsies, hoping to find something unusual in the brains of those who had been lost, but the results were inconclusive. Alistair took hypothetical situations to every lawyer he knew, hoping for a different result but each time, he'd received the same answer. Laughter, followed by a quick dismissal and a reminder that the supposed victim had signed up for it all when they'd clicked the I Agree button. Braun relayed all of this to Dex, who sat perfectly still, skin paler than usual in the suite's blue lights.

"Right now you're probably thinking you should've read the damn thing when you signed on to Somnium's virtual reality the first time, aren't you?"

Dex suppressed the urge to vomit with brute force. "I'm thinking about scrubbing my brain with steel wool and then never looking at another computer. Ever."

"Sorry to tell you, it's not that easy. We all agreed to this, Dex. You. Margot. 831. Me. Once we made the connection between the tech and the sleeping deaths, there was no going back. The MCL program was the best chance I had to help Margot and the thousands of others like her. And there were thousands. Given the chance, Miller would've let them all die. Eliminated every last person who could've condemned his tech."

"You should've sued. Done something . . . "

"We did do something." Braun slammed his fist on the desk with the force of his conviction. "Built the MCL program. Wilcox paid for it with everything he had. He's been watching like a hawk from capitol hill ever since."

"How did you find them? The sleep subjects?"

"Once we knew what to look for, it was easy."

And it had been. All he'd had to do was search for a diagnosis of persistent nightmare disorder. Margot, 831, all of the Elite, shared the same symptoms. In all, he'd found more than ten thousand people. Most had already experienced a psychotic break, some suffered hospitalization due to psychosis and drug addiction. In the worst cases, the subjects had been locked away, given electroconvulsive therapy, and when not cured, were forgotten in an over-medicated state until the morning they never woke.

Braun always assumed he'd only found a handful of the actual victims. But back then, the only methods to diagnose were rudimentary. Read the waves. Wake the subject to learn about the dreams. In his trials at UNC, he'd discovered that most subjects forgot what they were dreaming the moment they woke up. Those suffering night terrors never remembered more than a feeling of dread.

"It wasn't enough," Braun said to his captivated audience. "I needed a way into their heads—a way to see their dreams. Margot helped build the sleep subject program, she and Jon Markway."

"Markway was Margot's MCL?" Dex asked.

"He had a nephew in the program at UNC." Braun shook his head and fought off a smile at the memory. "Markway called him 'little man.' He loved the hell out of that boy. When we started the consensual tests, Markway was the first to volunteer." Straightening, he looked back at the waves. "You made the decision to let Keller go before I authorized it, didn't you?"

Dex nodded.

"Then I don't give a damn how you know. But I need to understand why you went looking."

Hands up in submission, Dex said, "I wanted to help her."

Braun studied him for a long time before he nodded. "Tell me what you learned."

"SSS 831—Gillian Hardie—joined your UNC sleep study nearly 15 years ago. Your notes said she was already a lucid dreamer and your study of her gave you the idea for the consensual program."

"We'd been toying with consensual dreaming as a means to determine if interrupting the nightmares from the inside was possible. 831 was the best lucid dreamer we had, but even she couldn't recognize the outside influence. We needed to enhance the connection."

"She's the reason you developed the tech."

Braun nodded.

"Why didn't you tell them? When you built the link? Wouldn't it have been better for the subjects to know someone was trying to help?"

"Just the opposite," Braun said.

It had been his hope that knowledge of their condition would help the Elite overcome it, but during the first years of the MCL program, he'd determined the less the subjects knew, the better. Any time he told a subject an MCL would join them, the dreamers started to look for the MCLs to intervene. It distracted them to a dangerous level, and Braun discovered that on the nights the subjects didn't know they were connected, both subject and MCL performed better.

SOMNIUM

Once a link was established, dreamers usually accepted the MCL as part of the dream reality. The subjects had the same nightmares over and over, why not the same players? For those who didn't, Markway and a few others could alter their appearance. "That's when we started to see some real success," Braun said. "By then, Miller had adjusted the programming per our recommendations. Thousands of the sleep subjects had their issues resolved. But not the Elite."

"Why not?"

Braun shrugged. "Emotional issues, perhaps. Other influences."

"Laura Taylor's been working on a case study around 831." Dex slid Laura's disc out from beneath the paperwork. "I've read most of it. It mentions Senator Wilcox was the original programmer?"

"That's right."

"Then he created the virus?"

Braun nodded. "Once we knew what happened, Wilcox gave up everything he had—his stock options, his shares—in order to form the MCL program. But he made damn sure he maintained ownership of everything we develop here. There's a reason for the tight security between divisions."

"Sway the right people and Miller could reverse engineer the tech, couldn't he?"

"Wilcox and I built a way to enter someone's mind."

Blood pushed against Dex's veins, fingers seeking out Laura's disc. "And Clayton Miller created software that can turn a nightmare into a loaded gun. Put the two together . . . "

"And you can commit the perfect murder. There's no way to trace an assassin who never entered the room. No way to know who it was when the target was eliminated in their sleep. The man who controls both sides of the tech controls the world."

Dex sat down hard. "I think I'm going to be sick."

Braun kicked the trashcan to Dex's feet. "I certainly was. If it weren't for Wilcox . . . " He shook his head. "Wilcox blocked every single one of Miller's attempts to usurp the tech. But I'm afraid we've gotten too big."

Both men looked up as the fluorescents danced, an electric hum accompanying the jig.

"What was that?" Braun asked.

"Watch the screen," Dex said. "At the end."

Braun waited, fingers digging into Dex's desk before he gasped. "That chair. I saw it with the dream imaging test. You've seen it before now?"

"Several times, but that's not the worst of it. It's been changing with each dream cycle. Building over the stages."

"Building how?"

"It started off as a school chair."

Braun looked back at the screen, muscles clenched and short beneath his skin. "But what I just saw . . . That was a fully functioning electric chair. Wasn't it?"

Dex nodded. "That's not all I've seen. Or heard. There's more to these waves, sir. A lot more." He flicked a few switches, music playing softly in the suite. "Tell me, Doc. Have you ever found a way to reach an MCL once they're under? Communicate with them?"

"Never been a need. Although Markway once reported hearing a conversation between his Operator and her boyfriend while he was still in transit."

"If we can reach Keller, tell him what's going on, we might be able to get them out."

"How?"

"I'm working on that part."

"Tell me everything."

Relieved, Dex began to talk as the echo danced across the screen again.

Water poured into the car through multiple cracks, the windshield holding under the force of the first assault, but it wouldn't survive another. On the dash, the radio crackled, static jumping from speaker to speaker.

"Time to pay the price for my sins," Gillian whispered and traced the webs in the safety glass.

Nathan grabbed her hand. "Not if I can help it."

Shaking her head, Gillian's eyes cleared, anger burning. "Why can't you just let me go?"

Hurt, Nathan stared at her. "Don't you know?"

"Goddammit, Nathan . . . "

SOMNIUM

The Great White hit the broken glass for the second time. It crashed inward, the shark hammering the car with the weight of its body as it forced its head inside, nose butting between them. Blood splattered the leather dash as Gillian cried out in pain. Taking a deep breath from the remaining pocket of air, Nathan cranked down his window and slipped into the shark-infested water. Gliding up over the Scout, he pulled himself along by the roof rack rails to the passenger side. The shark thrashed its massive form and he nearly lost his grip. Holding tight, Nathan shifted to the back window and hauled back, cracking it on the third punch before he kicked it in. Gillian sank her fingers into the obsidian eye, and the monster released her arm. Back in the Scout, Nathan caught Gillian under her arms and hauled her out. Light glowed warm overhead, and he swam for the surface. Heaving in air, he climbed onto a tile floor. Ash and soot filled his burning lungs.

Coughing up water, Gillian collapsed, the ever-expanding puddle tinged with blood and then filled with suds and grey clothing.

They were back in Laundry Room 3-B.

"What . . . the . . . hell . . . " Nathan gasped in time with Young Gillian. The astonishment on the girl's face when she entered the room was nearly consistent with his expectations of finding two bedraggled, water-logged humans writhing on the floor.

"No," Gillian said and scuttled backward, pressing herself against the wall as if it might give in to the sheer force of her will to be absorbed. "Wall. W-A-L. W-A- . . . " She punched her thigh and a rain of blood sprayed the tiles. Nathan caught her arm and bound it with a nearby towel. A scream rose within her as she muttered to herself. "Wake the fuck up, Gillian. Wake. The fuck. Up. F-U-C . . . "

On the windowsill, a speaker chained to the bars gave a static belch before it sprang to life with an old song by The Smiths. Nathan couldn't quite place it.

"Hey!" Young Gillian yelled, and a large girl at the line of washers turned around.

The offender stood nearly a head taller than Young Gillian, beefy arms covered in tattoos, the number of piercings in her ears greater than her age. A silver link chain drooped from nose to tragus, the simple scrubs she wore a dull yellow match to the mustard colored walls. Leaning casually against the line of washers, the girl dropped soapy gray underwear to the floor and sneered at Young Gillian.

"What?"

"Those are my clothes!" Young Gillian said.

"So?"

"So? I paid money for that machine. You can't just take it, Frances."

Frances tossed another set of gray sweatpants to the floor. "What are you gonna do about it, Hardie? Tell? Who's gonna believe the little drug addict? You've been stealing Provigil for months. We all know it. And your nutcase boyfriend's money ran out. There's no one left to protect you now."

Rage sparked in Young Gillian's eyes, the attempted intimidation backfiring. "I was here first."

"And I'm here now."

"You have no right . . . "

"I have every right. It's my machine. What the fuck are you going to do about it, pipsqueak?"

In Nathan's arms, Gillian shook her head. "Don't. Oh god, please don't."

On the radio, Morrisey crooned, "There were times when I could've murdered her . . . " before crackling to static once again, a single "Dammit" ringing into the room.

Nathan whipped his head to the window. "Dex?"

Frances edged closer, nose nearly pressed to Young Gillian's forehead. "Gonna hit me? Pipsqueak?"

Frances punctuated her words with a stiff-armed shove to Young Gillian's chest, forcing the smaller girl into the dryer and knocking it askew.

"No," Young Gillian said and with a lightning quick snatch, tore the chain from Frances' face. Blood spurted from the bigger girl's nose as fury rose in Young Gillian's limbs. Taking advantage of her stunned opponent, she threw a hard left, the crack of Frances' jaw resounded in the room. A teeth-rattling upper-cut followed, Young Gillian pummeling Frances' gaping mouth shut.

Screaming in pain, Frances leapt, the two bodies crashing into the dryer hard enough to shift the entire line. Young Gillian's hip left a good-sized dent in the machine and she struggled against the older girl's physical strength.

Cornered, Young Gillian let loose on Frances' gut, fists flying in a rage of indignation until an orderly ducked into the room. Calling for help over his shoulder, the newcomer waded into the fray and caught Young Gillian by the ponytail. He pulled back, kicking Frances to the wall to force the girls apart. Two more orderlies rushed in, catching Frances by the shirt.

The first orderly picked up Young Gillian, who still kicked and spat at her opponent, and slammed her body against the dented dryer.

"Get Stone out of here!" the orderly said, and the two who had caught hold of the bigger girl each grabbed an arm and dragged her away. The first orderly slid a zip tie around Young Gillian's wrist, fending off her fists before he wrapped them together behind her back.

Military trained, Nathan thought as the young man subdued the girl. But something was off, and he couldn't tell what until the orderly slammed Young Gillian's head into the dryer.

"Mike!"

"What?" He leaned heavily on the girl's limp body when another orderly checked in from the door.

"You all right, man?"

"Fine," Mike said and offered the second orderly a grin. "Finally caught me the prettiest fish in the barrel. Get out. I got this."

The orderly at the door hesitated, his gaze on the young woman.

"Don't," Young Gillian said. "Please. Please don't go!"

"Out!" Mike said, and the startled orderly backed away from the angry command, the click of the lock loud.

In the silence that followed, Gillian shivered, ripples of fear overflowing her skin. The orderly released the girl from the pin long enough to slip his hands under her shirt. Stuck against the dryer, Young Gillian struggled away from the unwanted touch.

"Get off me," she growled.

"Now, now, girlie, no need to fight. I ain't gonna turn you in. Not if you treat me right."

"Turn me in," Young Gillian said, only to be met with a low and chilling chuckle Nathan easily recognized.

"Shearer," Nathan muttered. In his arms, Gillian whimpered, whole body shaking.

"Been waiting for you to fuck up, girlie," the orderly said and untied his scrubs. "You're mine now."

Nathan curled himself around Gillian as Michael Shearer slammed Young Gillian's head against the metal for a second time. Dazed, she nearly slipped to the floor when he caught her and propped her up, chest down on the dryer.

"They say the wash cycle does a little something for you girlies," Shearer said. "You let me know if the dryer works too."

Every fiber in Nathan's body revolted as Young Gillian cried out in pain and then went absolutely silent, the only sound in the room the rhythmic pounding of flesh against metal as her body pushed up against it.

Over before it had truly begun, Shearer stepped back with a grin as Young Gillian sank to the floor.

"What is it your little boyfriend used to say? Old enough to crawl." Shearer chuckled again.

The sound would haunt Gillian for the rest of her days. Catching her ponytail, he pulled her face to his. "Anytime I ask, you assume the position, or I'll make you wish you did. Shoot you up with so much shit you won't know who the hell is between your legs. You hear me, girlie?"

"I'll tell . . . "

Shearer laughed. "Who they gonna believe? You? Crazy girl? Little drug addicted whore? You're mine, girlie." Digging into a hip pouch, he checked an Rx bottle and poured its contents onto the floor before her, the oblong white pills sprinkled around her feet like spilled rice. "Well now, what have we here? Looks to me like I've found the little thief whose been pilfering stimulants from the pharmacy. I'd say that might buy you an hour or two in the electroshock room." He leaned in close to Young Gillian's ear. "From what I've seen, that shit don't tickle."

Hauling her to her feet, he pushed her into the hall.

Nathan had nearly let his muscles unclench when the scene started again.

Suds on the floor, screams, flesh against metal.

"Gillian . . . "

Suds on the floor.

"Gillian, stop this."

Screams.

"Gillian, goddammit, stop this. Now!" Nathan caught her head in his hands, the life nearly gone out of her eyes. "Don't you do this."

SOMNIUM

"I can't stop it."

"Yes, you can."

"I couldn't stop it then. I can't stop it now. There's nothing I can do. This is my hell."

"This is a dream."

"This is where I belong. Goodbye, Nathan."

Slapping his hands away, she took off for the door and disappeared into the mist.

On the windowsill, the radio crackled to life once more.

Nurse Angie Babcock slipped, nearly going down on her ample rear as she hurried past a row of unconscious patients. Regaining her balance, she looked back at the floor to find a growing puddle of blood dripping from a peony bloom expanding across one of the white sheets.

"What on earth?" she muttered and flipped the cotton back to find a mangled array of flesh. Despite the brightly lit hall, her skin rippled in cold fear. She'd done intake on every single one of the unconscious souls that lined the hallway, and she knew for damn sure what she was seeing hadn't been there when they'd brought this one in.

But it must've been, because it was bleeding now.

"What idiot didn't treat this?"

Pressing her hand to the wound, she glanced at her patient, whose pale countenance rivaled the pillow for purity.

"I got you," she whispered and set about cleaning the wound. When the blood had cleared, she gasped at the razor-sharp tears. Ten years of working the emergency wards in the Florida Keys taught her to recognize several things, not the least among them the damage caused by sharks.

"Not possible."

She did her best to believe her own lie, but Angie knew. Knew the way she knew how to check blood pressure. Knew the way she could always tell when one of her patient's wouldn't last the night. Knew the mangled flesh before her was a shark bite.

"That's not right. That can't be right."

"Talking to yourself ain't gonna help, Angie."

Angie looked up as an orderly rolled another crash victim into the last available spot on the hall.

"Tell me I'm not going crazy," she said.

"You're not going . . . Jesus, is that a bite?"

Happy the long night hadn't messed with her head, Angie let her breath go in relief. "Can't be, right? She came in with the crash victims."

The orderly paused long enough to run his scanner over the woman's wrist. He smacked it against his palm and stepped away from the body. "Damn thing." Another strike had it working. "Head trauma. EMT said there was a burn on her arm."

"This isn't a burn," Angie said. "It's a goddamn shark bite."

"Must've caught it on the glass. Ain't no sharks in the mountains, Ang."

"Must be a full moon," Angie said, brow creased in uncertainty. She bandaged the wound but didn't have time to consider it further. A fresh load of bodies paraded past. Scanner out to catch the next passing victim, she left Gillian Hardie to her own devices.

CHAPTER FIFTEEN

NATHAN BOLTED INTO the hallway, hoping to catch Gillian but found himself alone. Calling out to her, he looked left and right, seeing only the gray walls of the burnt-out institution and the fast-encroaching mist.

Muttering a curse, he searched his memory for some precedent, some tale from Markway of losing his subject in the dream reality, but nothing came.

Behind him the door to the laundry room slammed shut, the lock clicking in place to cut off any return. Down the hall, a single door creaked open on unoiled hinges. Nathan waited, muscles tense as the soft slush of a body being pulled along a tile floor echoed in the haze. A single hand emerged from the gray, groping along the tiles for some purchase it would never find but still clawing forward. Stepping back from the monstrosity, Nathan dashed for the remaining junction. A second door opened.

Turning the corner, he threw himself to the left, the whirlwind of screaming dust nearly consuming him before he gathered his feet beneath him. Running full speed along the hall, he shouldered a third door closed. A quick glance through the window showed him the English moors where he first landed in Gillian's dream, the chants of zealots ringing in his ears. Smoke filtered under the gap in the steel.

Spinning away, Nathan flew down the corridor while rushing water gave chase. He turned right, then right again, feeling more than seeing the decline of the floor. Doors opened behind him, but he didn't look back. He careened around a soft curve only to backpedal as he came face-to-face with the wraith. Mouth open, she let loose a screech so piercing he felt it reverberate in his eyes.

Water covered his feet, and he searched for an escape only to find he was no longer in the straight corridor of the asylum.

Instead, he stood at the center of a circular structure similar to Frank Lloyd Wright's Guggenheim Museum.

"What the hell," he muttered.

Hannibal Lecter decorated his thousand-room memory palace with frescoes. Sherlock Holmes built a mind palace to store his facts. But Gillian Hardie had trapped the horrors of her dreams behind endless spirals of locked doors in an asylum like no other. Within the awesome array of bolted steel doors, Gillian's nightmares lurked, waiting to pounce. A shifting, slithering noise that reminded Nathan of a monstrous millipede emanated from the closest. Overhead, speakers blasted that same Smiths' song he'd heard in the laundry. Ignoring it, Nathan put his back to the balustrade.

On his right, the wraith blocked his path, mangled arm dripping blood across the floor. On the left, the torso advanced under the impetus of the whirlwind. Water rained from above. Mist rose in an electrified cloud that pulsed in time with his heart.

"Who the hell are you?" Nathan asked but the wraith said nothing. Blue lightning gathered at her hips, leaving him with only one choice. Taking a deep breath, he closed his eyes, pictured where he wanted to land and threw himself over.

A bolt of energy slammed him to the far wall, forcing the air from his lungs before he plummeted into the fog.

Alarms blared in the suite, rattling Dex's frayed nerves.

"That's not possible," Braun said, eyes on the waves. "What just happened to Keller?"

Dex sat down hard, hands tucked in his hair. "You tell me, Doc. I just work here."

"Did we do this?"

"Radio waves never killed anyone. Raise your body temperature, sure, but not like this."

"Is he alive?"

"Barely."

"And 831?"

"Hanging by a thread."

"Are they in the next cycle?"

Dex glanced at the timeline and shook his head. "I don't think so. Not yet. But these waves . . . they're like nothing I've ever seen. Might be external this time. Something about her condition. Jesus, this would be easier if we knew what happened to her, what is happening to her."

"Then we'll get her." Braun moved to the intercom on the wall, barked instructions to whoever answered and faced the screens only to stop short. "The link's been breached. Someone else is in there with them."

Glancing up sharply, Dex saw the echo cross the screens, the third wave now as strong as Keller's. Galvanized, Dex set his fingers to his console, hands flying before he shook his head. "Hasn't been hacked, but damn I've never seen this kind of . . . fuck me."

"What?"

"I don't think it's a . . . " Dex paused, eyes on the waves. " . . . a living consciousness."

Braun stared at him. "Talk to me."

"See this?" Dex said and indicated the repetitions in the wave. "It's too uniform to be human."

"What do you mean?"

"I think it's tech." Dex shook his head as if to clear it, thoughts racing too fast for his mouth to keep up as the third line disappeared.

"Where'd it go?" Braun asked.

"Stronger. It's been getting stronger. Following the cycles but this time it wasn't within the dream state. It's learned the cycle. Punctured N3. It can't still be functioning unless . . . "

"Stronger how? And what do you mean it follows?"

Outside the suite, a parade of people moved through the corridor. Braun darted to the door to discover the party included Laura Taylor and Eric Wilson.

"It's Dietrich. Stay here."

"Wasn't planning on going anywhere else," Dex muttered absently.

Braun met Laura and Eric as they entered the suite.

"What's going on?" he asked.

Without looking at him, Laura rolled the ImaDream prototype next to Keller's head. "Parker's subject hasn't gone down. We're going to test on Keller."

"On whose authority?"

"Clayton Miller's."

"We can't," Dex said soft enough no one seemed to hear him. But a 'what if . . . ' played at the edge of Dex's brain, and he wondered if a second path into the dream reality might offer a much needed option. "Maybe . . . yes, maybe it could."

"Could what?" Dietrich asked.

Unwilling to share his thoughts, Dex shook his head.

Huffing, Dietrich addressed Laura. "How long until you're ready?"

"I'll need to recalibrate for Keller and 831," she said. "Half hour."

With a shot of warning to Dex to keep silent, Braun gave an abrupt shake of his head. "Keller will be awake by then."

"Will he?" Dietrich smirked. "Rumor has it Keller's been under for quite some time."

Dex drilled Laura with a hateful glare, the Weaver staunchly refusing to meet his gaze. "What did you do?"

"Suffice it to say some people prefer science to nightmare voodoo bullshit," Dietrich said. "So sit down and do your job, Operator."

"And if I don't?"

"Your contract will be terminated."

Bristling, Braun came to Dex's defense. "You don't have the . . . "

"Authority?" Dietrich scoffed. "You quit, Braun. Someone had to take over the MCL division. Might as well be me."

"My resignation isn't written yet. You will not touch Keller," Braun said, voice low and even, the tone never heard before by any of his underlings. Dex shivered with awe and more than a little pride.

Laura smirked. "I would advise you, Dr. Braun, for your own good, not to let your feelings for the subject cloud your judgement."

"My feelings for the subject are the only thing keeping my judgement sane." Braun whirled on Dietrich. "If you lay a hand on Keller . . . "

Dietrich batted away the threat with a dismissive swat of his hand. "Take it up with Miller."

"I will. Let's go."

Braun shot his eyes to Dex and with a nod, left the room. Grumbling directions to Laura to prep for his return, Dietrich followed. Laura immediately got to work and then lifted her head to the music with a smirk. "'Girlfriend in a Coma'? Really, Dex? Such an obvious choice. I would've thought you had a better sense of humor than 1980s synth pop."

"What'd he offer you?" Dex asked.

Laura paused, her refusal to look at him telling, and something Dex didn't know he relied on disintegrated in his chest.

"Promotion. Head of the Dream Imaging Division. Money. Power. All the things you've never wanted. All the things those pretty girls hoped you had when they agreed to a first date. If you join my team, I'll make sure you finally get a second."

"You're willing to kill to get them?"

"Don't be so melodramatic," Laura said and plugged ImaDream into the pod while Eric wheeled in a screen.

Never before had Dex felt the urge to hit a woman, but it took everything he had to suppress it now. "There is no telling what will happen to 831 if you turn that thing on and you know it."

"What is it you think it's going to do, Declan?"

"Give the buggers a way out."

"Buggers?" Laura laughed without mirth. "Really, your word choice is so juvenile."

Dex squeezed his fists tighter. "You think I'm such a fucking rube? Fine. Let me explain this to you in terms you can understand. Yours." Lifting her work disc, Dex stabbed a finger at the plastic as if it would speak. "You said it yourself right here. The initial tech was treated like a virus."

Laura's eyes narrowed. "You read my file?"

"If what you've surmised is true, then the viral glitch was never actually fixed. Wilcox just found a way to make it go dormant so it would stop affecting new initiates to the software."

"So?"

"So, even dormant it can still learn. It's been learning. Years longer than anyone thought possible."

In the corner, Eric gasped.

"That same glitch forced the Elite's neurons to backfire," Dex said. "To act the exact opposite of how they should, causing the sleep subject to experience their dreams as if they were actual, or near actual, reality. The AI would interpret the dream reality as the proper state. Would try to simulate and emulate. It would learn from the dreams. Learn the situations the Elite experience."

Laura shrugged. "Again, I say, so?"

Eyes rolling, Dex grabbed a chunk of his hair and pulled. "It's artificial intelligence. Its sole job is to interpret and spit back out the same or similar reality, just enhanced with the product weave. In the game field, it learns your habits and then makes the game harder. You see what I'm saying?"

"Spell it out for me."

"The programming is still there. It's still learning. It's been learning. Every time an Elite was triggered by Somnium tech. But the dreams are getting stronger for a reason, aren't they, Laura?"

"You have no proof of that."

"Yes we do." Eric sank to the floor in the corner.

"Shut up, Eric," Laura warned.

"Bad dreams," Eric said and looked up at Dex. "They were the ones that made the best impressions. We thought the ImaDream programming would enhance the image, but it didn't. So we turned it back on, the original virus. Enhanced it to get the images clear. We made the dreams more real. We did this."

"There was no other way," Laura said. "The dreams needed to be stronger. Glimpses were all I was getting. If we wanted to see images, then the dreamer . . . "

"Their names were Jon Markway, Kevin Davis, Marcus Blake, Kaylee Hess, Jake Billings and Matthew Anderson," Dex said.

" . . . needed to be stimulated."

"Stimulated?" Dex asked, aghast. "You call this stimulated?"

"I call it successful. The dreams are stronger. The electrical impulses within the brain are strong enough to make the images clear. We can see their dreams and the possibilities are . . . "

Eric rose to his feet and cut her off. "Braun said the realities are shifting. When Markway died. He said the dream reality was getting closer to normal reality. If the AI somehow learned to simulate the normal neuron function . . . "

"Normal function," Dex cut in. "But the Elite have never been normal. If the virus builds its model using the faulty neural networks, it would draw the conclusion that it's real and the subject is the dream. The virus is upping the ante. Using the bioelectric energy from brain and body to its advantage, to become a living, breathing part of the dream reality."

Laura shook her head in amusement. "You can't be serious . . . "

"Why not?" Dex called up the timeline of Keller's jump, backtracking to the extended echo.

"What is that?" Eric asked.

"You tell me," Dex said and glared at Laura.

"It's nothing," she snapped.

"Nothing? Or is it the result of your tests? Because it sure looks real to me. Real as a third consciousness. One that just might figure out how to manipulate the environment as well as the dreamer. And if it can do that, it might just decide that it wants what the dreamer wants."

"To wake up," Eric muttered. "A reverse jump."

Dex nodded. "She goes much longer, and it will find a way out, and a thinking mind, one without emotion, without feeling or conscience will reach the real world."

Laura dismissed him. "Don't go all *Ex Machina* on me, Dex. It's a computer program. Nothing more."

"So it doesn't know it's wrong! It's interpreting data generated from the bioelectric energy associated with the dreamers' fears and drawing conclusions. The wrong conclusions."

"I don't think . . . "

"Doesn't matter what you think! You're not the one doing the thinking. It is. When did you trigger the virus?"

"Three months ago," Eric said.

Dex sank into his chair. "Months?"

"The more time spent in the dream state, the stronger the images were." Eric looked at Laura. "The longer the nightmare, the better the image."

"The longer the dream, the more it learns." Dex gasped. "And 831 has spent more time with it than any other sleep subject."

"8924 and Markway," Eric said. "He was second only to 831. And he's dead. Markway's dead. They couldn't wake up. Not in time. But then, how is 831 still alive?"

"Maybe the coma actually saved her?" Dex said. "Think about it. What does a coma do? Lowers the body's electrical impulses. Reduces the body's response rate to focus on healing whatever has gone wrong. What if the lowered electricity within her body somehow stalled the AI? Knocked down her electrical impulses to a lower level. Forced the AI into a slower build when her neurons slowed." Realization rushed through Dex's skin, pushing at his arteries. "Which means if she surfaces from the coma, and she doesn't wake up right away, she's going to be dead before she can flutter her eyes. How did you deliver it?"

Eric stood, face pale in the blue light. "It's riding the jump tech. Buried in the link. The MCL carries it in on the current." He moved toward the console. "You have to disconnect. We can find a way to quarantine it. Delete it . . . "

Dex shook his head. "We disconnect and she dies."

"If we don't disconnect, that virus is going to build to a final nightmare, one with enough juice that it can ride the current back . . . "

"To Somnium," Dex muttered, eyes wide as he caught Eric's thoughts. "It'll take over. Infect the servers. Anyone connected to the dream weaves is going to experience Gillian Hardie's worst, most lethal nightmare."

"The bugger really is trying to get out. Jon Markway was smarter than we thought."

"Stop it," Laura said. "Both of you. This is all just the conjecture of two science-fiction obsessed little boys. You have no way of proving it."

"Yes we do," Dex said, eyeing the prototype.

"We did this to her," Eric said. "There's got to be a way to undo it."

"What if we weave into the imaging tech?" Dex said. "Would that establish an alternative jump path?"

"You will not touch my tech," Laura said only to be ignored by two young men who had once hung on her every thought.

"It's a risk," Eric said. "But it might work. We'd be able to send in help, another MCL." He shook his head. "But it might also put Keller at risk of losing his way back. His consciousness might get lost in the dual paths."

"You got a better idea?" Dex asked.

All three froze as the door opened. Evan James stood in the pod entrance, his ever-present tablet facing out to show a view of the security cameras, deep blue eyes flicking over the trio as he smirked.

"Ms. Taylor, Dr. Miller has requested your presence in his office. He would like you to join the discussion . . . " Evan's lips twitched at the word. " . . . between Drs. Dietrich and Braun. Now, please."

"Of course," Laura said and plugged in her passcode to lock down the prototype. Sidestepping Evan, she cast a glare over her shoulder at Dex, snatched her disc and left the room.

Evan stepped forward as the door closed, fingers busy typing on his pad. Overhead the hum of the security cameras ceased and the image on his tablet went black. "Mr. Cooper, we need to talk."

"Mr. James," Dex said, heart running at hummingbird speed as he waited for the inevitable axe to fall. "I can explain."

"I'm sure you can." Moving silently to Keller, Evan let his impassive gaze linger on the dreamer, fingers dancing beside his thigh as if he were still typing. He reached up, almost as if to push a set of glasses up the brutally straight perfection of his nose. "And while a discussion about your interest in the personnel files would no doubt be—enlightening—that's not why I've come."

"Then why . . ."

Evan faced them, a quick jerk of his hand to his neck stopped with a grimace before he smacked himself. Curling the hand into a fist, he leveled his gaze at Dex. "This plan of yours. To send in a second. Will it work? Will it keep her alive?"

"No guarantees," Dex said. "But I think it will work."

"Then do it," Evan said.

Eric cut in. "We just lost access to ImaDream. I don't know Laura's passcode."

"I do," Dex said. "Gave it to me herself."

Eric shook his head. "We still need a second MCL . . . "

"What you need," Evan said evenly and looked down at Keller. "Is someone who knows exactly what she's been through." He lifted his deep blue gaze from the pod and finally released his hand to do what it wanted, three hits to the side of his ear before he steadied it once more. "Get me in."

Dex locked eyes with him, seeing something familiar in the look, before he nodded. "I'm on it."

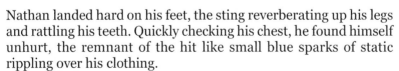

Nathan landed hard on his feet, the sting reverberating up his legs and rattling his teeth. Quickly checking his chest, he found himself unhurt, the remnant of the hit like small blue sparks of static rippling over his clothing.

His clothing.

Black pants. Black t-shirt. Black boots.

In a dark corner, the Wraith stood silent, watching him with gleaming eyes through a cascade of dark hair. Far above, a glittering dome poured rain into the atmosphere, but it didn't reach him. Water had filled the upper levels, sloshing against the balustrades like a tumultuous ocean. At the core, all was quiet, calm and cool.

The Wraith pointed off to the left before she vanished into the creeping mist. A massive oak, its base broad as a train, soared upward. Sunlight shone through a canopy of amber and rust-colored leaves to cast a kaleidoscope of color on his skin.

A wooden staircase spiraled around the thick trunk. He climbed toward a structure hidden in the branches, ascending until he reached a porch of rustic pine. Ducking through a carved archway, Nathan entered a simple room, the treehouse decorated with stacks of books and old records. A small radio played that same Smiths' song, the refrain barely registering as Nathan spun slowly to take it all in.

Windows without glass had been cut into the wood. No doors covered the archways and Nathan suddenly understood the layout of her little cabin as he hadn't before, the small space offering the safety of seeing everything at once. No one would ever surprise her again. In the corner, an extra-large easy chair, worn and comfortable, awaited an eager reader. And while his mind registered these little comforts, it was the walls that caused him to gasp.

On the right, every inch of space had been dedicated to her family. Laughing images of her brother as they played on the swings; her mother at the kitchen counter cooking dinner; her father tossing a ball to her in the yard. On a different wall, images of Patrick's deep blue eyes plucked at his memory strings, but he couldn't place them before they gave way to Jenna and the cabin Gillian now called home.

Locations to which she had traveled in her youth, before the dreams made it impossible for her to leave her house, filled a separate space. He recognized some of the places she had taken him in her nightmares. An arched hallway in Powers Court and the ruins of Bective Abbey in Ireland. The pink sands of Bermuda. Everywhere he looked, he saw a pattern of motion, the constant beauty her mind sought and clung to. He let his fingers drift over the pictures before he faced the large fireplace.

Failing flames generated little more than a breath of heat as he looked on the two stunning images that crowned her collection.

SOMNIUM

On the left, Toby as Nathan had seen him when he'd visited Gillian's childhood home.

On the right . . . He stepped forward, a hand out to trace the lines of his own face, seeing the sharp cut of his cheeks, the intense blue of his gaze as he watched her over his shoulder. It was a face both fierce and handsome, one he had never seen in the mirror, and he felt his spine straighten with pride.

"Is this how you see me?" he asked.

Gillian stepped up beside him. "I'll admit, the first time I saw you, I didn't find you quite so attractive."

"The Picture of Dorian Gray," he muttered.

"Except this soul doesn't reflect a monster."

"You so sure about that?"

"I keep those upstairs."

Nathan finally looked at her, the tired, gaunt image breaking his heart. Unless something changed soon, he knew with a certainty he didn't want to believe she wouldn't last another cycle. "You did make yourself some rather intriguing circles of hell."

"Dante couldn't have done it better," she said with a hint of a smile. "How did you get here?"

"Not important. What is this place?"

"Toby and I built this treehouse. After my father called Davidson. He sat with me the whole morning, holding my hand, and together we built a safe place for me to go when things got too tough. He said it'd be like summer camp and promised he'd visit."

"Did he?"

"He left for Fort Benning that June. I never saw him again." She collapsed into the chair and Nathan sat down beside her. "He wouldn't have had to go if it weren't for me. It was my fault he died."

The flames dimmed in the fireplace.

"What do you mean?" Nathan asked.

"Everything my parents had went to Davidson. All the money for college was gone. He had to enlist. When he died . . . " Gillian reached up, redrawing the faded lines on her cheek. "I knew because the letters stopped. Just stopped. My father came to tell me a few weeks before I got out. He had to get permission from my shrink in case it set me off. But I already knew."

The treehouse dimmed. A cold mist slipped through the windows and settled on the floor.

"I'm sorry he's gone," Nathan said. "But Toby made a choice."

"And Shawn? What choice did he have?"

"Who?"

"Jenna's boyfriend."

"You should've ruptured both his 'nads. Keep that shit from reproducing at all."

Gillian huffed. "And Shearer?"

"Don't get me started on that piece of . . . " Unable to find a word strong enough, Nathan merely shut his mouth and seethed.

Gillian lifted her chin and blinked to find they were back in the laundry, suds on the floor, the dented dryer rattling as if a pocket full of coins had been tossed inside. "I belong here."

Nathan reached out to take her in his arms. "No one belongs here."

Anger flared bright in Gillian's eyes. "Just who the fuck do you think you are? You don't know me."

"Yes I do."

"You think sharing a few dreams and a roll in the sheets means you get to know all my secrets? Means you know who I am? What I've been through? You don't know shit."

"I know what you've shown me. And there's a reason you keep coming back here."

"You have no right to judge me."

"I'm not the one judging you. You are. Why are we here?"

"Because this is hell. And it's where I belong."

"You keep saying that."

"It's true."

"No one belongs here, least of all you."

"I was raped. Right there on that fucking dryer. It was my first time but it wasn't close to the last. For 427 days I endured that motherfucker's every whim . . . "

"It's not the reason you keep coming back here." Nathan caught hold of her. "Why here? If this is a reckoning, why the hell are you here? This was done *to* you, not by you. So why do you keep coming back?"

"You want to know? You really want to know why I come back here? To this fucking room, to this fucking place, to this fucking time? You want me to shatter the image of your dream girl so profoundly you never knock on my door? You got it. I lured him here."

In the corner of the room, an old television sparked to life, a wall eye image of the laundry room in its heyday crystal clear before them.

A finger of dread ran down Nathan's spine. "What?"

"You heard me."

On the television, a sitcom entrance of a young woman, smiling at the camera and curtsying cutely. She pulled back her hair, tying it into a ponytail and advancing into the room with a sly and dangerous smile.

"That machine shocked the living shit out of me not three hours before. I knew the wiring was faulty. When he came for me that night, I fought back. He hit me so hard I couldn't see straight for days. But I knew where to run."

The floor shifted beneath them, the walls soaring like a funhouse mirror as the show took on a first-person perspective. Blood on her hands, she dashed forward, the shambling shuffle of her worst nightmare somewhere down the hall. Bloody palms skidded across the top of the dryer, leaving a mark like an arrow pointed toward the lint trap. Gray sweatshirt pulled down over her fingers, she turned the nobs. A spark behind the machine forced her to jump back before she tried again. A rattling sound, like the metal runners of a shower curtain drawn aside, sprang to life. She rushed to the sink and jammed a set of panties in the bottom before she turned the water on full blast.

"I brought him here," Gillian said. "I made sure the machine was running and the floor was wet."

From the doorway, the low chuckle Nathan had come to abhor.

"And when he came in, I pushed that ass into the metal," Gillian said. On the television, she backed away from the jiggering body, the slat-back chair getting her feet off the wet floor as fire sparked in Shearer's skin.

"He laughed when the electricity arced. But it was me who was laughing when they found the body. I couldn't stop."

The air filled with the acrid smell of burnt flesh. Lights flickered like an old school movie projector. Gillian sat perched like a parrot on the wooden chair.

"What did you do, Gillian?"

"I murdered a man. Intentionally murdered another human being. And when I did, when I committed the sin of all sins, I laughed until my stomach hurt." She faced him. "So what the hell do you think of me now?"

Nathan slammed the television into the wall, caught her face in his hands and bored into her eyes. "I think you're the strongest woman I know."

She slapped his hands away. "Fuck you."

"You handed him a far easier death than I would've. But that's not what you did. What did you do, Gillian?"

"Are you even listening to me? I murdered him." Gillian set her back against the wall before sliding down to the floor. She drew her knees to her chest and wrapped her arms around them. "Damned myself to eternal hell. And fucking-A did I ever find myself in hell."

"You ended the life of a rapist, not an innocent." Nathan knelt before her. "He had no respect for life. Not his, not yours, and not the lives of the countless others he hurt or would've hurt. His death was not a reason to trap your soul in this room, or to live your life stuck in a nightmare. So tell me, what did you really do?"

"Quit asking me that! I was happy he died. What kind of a person would be happy to murder another?"

"Look at me."

Shaking her head, Gillian tucked her cheek to her knees and began to spell out "m-u-r-d-e-r-e-r." He grabbed her chin and forced her to face him.

"I went to war, Gillian. I took my morals with me and learned the hard way that there are things in this world that simply need to be done. You think you're the only person who's ever done something that didn't sit right after? Who's had feelings associated with those things that come back to haunt you late at night? Ask any soldier suffering PTSD about it. They've all got a different version of the exact same story. So tell me, Gillian Hardie. What did you do?"

"I killed him . . . "

"Why?"

"To save myself."

"To survive," Nathan said but it didn't soften her guilt. "By whatever means necessary."

"God doesn't forgive . . . "

"I don't care about your god! Countless young women survived and thrived because you did what you had to do. How do you think they'd feel about it? If someone else had stopped it from happening to you, how would you feel about it?"

She stared at him, eyes begging for something he knew from experience only she could give. "How do you feel?"

He put his forehead to hers. "Proud."

"You mean it?"

"I mean it." Nathan took her hands in his and drew her to her feet. "And if that means I'm condemning us both to hell, so be it."

Wiping her nose, Gillian looked up at him, the scent of the woodfire beside them as they returned to the treehouse. "Will you still come find me? If I wake up?"

"I'll be knocking on your door by the time the coffee is ready."

"Who the hell are you really?"

"Nobody special. Just an idiot who's been through some serious shit and came out smelly on the other side."

"So you recognized my stench?"

"Picked it up the very first time I saw you slice open a zombie without batting an eye."

Spluttering through her tears, Gillian nodded. "Thank you."

"You're welcome," he said. "Now let's figure out a way to get the hell out of here."

Gillian laid a gentle hand on his cheek as the radio abruptly stopped.

A strange voice flickered like candlelight between the static, growing in urgency as it consumed the room.

" . . . in . . . danger . . . Repeat . . . extreme danger . . . "

Astonished, Nathan caught Gillian's hands and squeezed. "Dex?"

"You did what?"

Clayton Miller felt his blood pressure rise as he faced the windows in his office. The discussion had turned ugly, as he had known it would from the moment Eli Braun and Phil Dietrich stormed into his office. The two men were already at each other's throats. It had taken a good ten minutes before he'd been able to ascertain what the issue was, and only when Laura Taylor slipped into the office had either of the men made any attempt at civility.

"I authorized her removal from the local hospital," Braun said again. "She'll be here within half an hour."

"And what the hell are you going to do with her?" Dietrich asked.

"If you're going to experiment on an Elite then it makes more sense to have her onsite."

"You've been experimenting on the Elite for years and you never bothered to meet even one of them. You are just trying to delay my testing . . . "

"Gentlemen! Please!" Clayton said and turned away from the darkness of the pre-dawn forest. "I happen to agree with Dr. Braun. We'll wait for the delivery and then proceed with the test. Dr. Dietrich, Ms. Taylor, go to the jump suite and continue your preparations. I'll join you shortly."

Dietrich nodded but Laura paused, puzzled. "Excuse me, Clayton, but why did you ask me to join you?"

Clayton looked up, brow crunched. "I didn't."

"But Mr. James . . . "

"He must've been mistaken," Clayton said dismissively. "Call me when you're ready."

Laura nodded and followed Dietrich out the door.

"If you'll excuse me," Braun said. "I'll see to 831's intake."

"Braun," Clayton said. "A moment?"

The doctor paused at the door, back to Clayton. "What is it?"

"Are you still planning to submit your resignation?"

"No," Braun said. "In fact, I've decided to stay as long as it takes."

Clayton rounded his desk and stood, hands in his pockets as he eyed the doctor. "Then may I remind you that you are an employee of Somnium, and not the United States Government. The next time Alistair Wilcox receives a phone call about any of the activities that occur under this roof it will be from my personal phone and my phone alone. Do you understand me, Doctor?"

"Yes sir," Braun said with a steady, unnerving smile. "I understand you perfectly. But you won't get what you want, Clayton. Not from me. And not from Alistair."

"Dammit Braun, do you have any idea how much the combined technology is worth?"

"Yes," Braun said simply. "A life. And while insurance companies and governments can put a price on it, I cannot. So after tonight, there will be a new and higher security level in the jump suites, and you will not gain access to my technology no matter who you send to steal it." Braun looked around. "Alistair would like this office, I think."

"I'm not going anywhere."

Braun stepped up, nose nearly touching Clayton's. "10,000 people, Clayton. More than that if Alistair and I were to look deep enough. And I won't have to prove a goddamn thing if 831 wakes up. One word from her in the media and everything you've done will spread like wildfire."

"No one will believe . . . "

"No one has to believe. They just have to wonder. And I bet the families of the people you hurt will do a good bit of that. And when they add their voices to 831's, you will go down. Someone will actually read that monster of a legal disclaimer and despite the fact that you covered your ass, you'll be tried and found guilty in the court of public opinion. Then all this," Braun raised his hands. "Everything you built will fall. Without one goddamn shred of proof."

The muscles in Clayton's jaw twitched as he clamped his teeth together. "What do you want, Braun? Name it and it's yours."

Braun smiled, a cold and mirthless stretch of his lips. "I want my daughter back, you prick."

Spinning on his heel, Braun stalked out of the office. Clayton watched him go, mind mulling over the veracity of Braun's threat before he crossed to the bar, a stiff drink swallowed as the sky began to brighten.

"Ang? Hey Ang!"

Nurse Angie Babcock took the stethoscope from her ears and looked up. Down the hall an orderly flagged her over. With a quick sign off on her current patient, she trudged down the hall, unsteady on her own feet, every muscle in her body stretched to its last limit.

The accident scene had finally been cleared of all those still breathing, the ambulance parade ceasing. The hallways were crowded, every one of her nurses on duty and running on pure adrenaline, just as she was. She reached the orderly, who stood over a comatose victim, the peony bloom of dried blood on the sheet marking the body beneath as the mangled arm she had fixed earlier. She wondered how she had forgotten to change the sheet.

"What is it?" Angie asked.

"Requisition from on high," he said and handed her the paperwork. Angie looked it over, the two men waiting just behind the orderly finally coming into view. After reviewing the summons, she handed it back without signing.

"You can tell your Dr. Braun she's in no condition . . . "

"We've been authorized to take her, Nurse," one of the men said. "She'll be transported to a state-of-the-art facility via a medical helicopter with a full team of medics on standby. We're relieving you of a burden. So if you'll just sign the release . . . "

"Where's she going?"

"That's classified."

"Does this have anything to do with the bite?"

The two strangers exchanged a glance. "What bite?"

Angie flicked the sheet to the side, the bandaging still in place. Only a hint of blood had seeped through her expert wrapping. The newcomer stepped up, fast-moving hands unwinding Angie's careful work. If nothing else, he proved himself a member of the medical community, easing Angie's fear of the strange request. But her anxiety bounced back when he revealed the smooth skin beneath the gauze.

"What the . . . " Angie breathed in sharply and ran her fingers over the red lines. The hair on her arm raised in a wave, as if pulled by the static of a passing balloon. A sting of electricity plowed through her fingers. Overwhelmed by the strange feeling, she stumbled backward, the orderly catching her before her knees gave out.

"I don't understand," Angie said and rubbed her fingers.

"You don't have to understand. All you need to do is sign."

Ignoring him, Angie examined the remains of the bite without touching the skin again. The marks looked almost like a child had drawn them with a crayon, the skin stitched back together by an expert hand without the use of string. "How can this be?"

"Nurse, we're short on time here . . . "

Angie looked up. "I have your word she'll be treated well?"

"We'll take excellent care of her," the second stranger said. He put a reassuring hand on Angie's arm. A bolt of static jumped in a sharp blue zap from Angie's skin to the man's uniform. "You've had enough to deal with tonight."

Angie couldn't help but agree and signed her name at the

bottom of the request. Absently wiping her hand on her scrubs, she watched the two men wheel the body down the hall. Lights brightened as they passed, the fluorescents buzzing like a beehive in summer and igniting in a glow so fierce Angie had to hold up a hand to shield her eyes. By the time she could see again, the strangers had gone.

"Goddamn full moon," she muttered and smoothed down the hairs on her arms, the last of the strange static dissipating. She spun on her heel, her step light and quick as she returned to her patients.

CHAPTER SIXTEEN

DEX WATCHED THE WAVES, fingers drumming as he waited for any kind of response. Adjusting the frequency, he tried again.

"Repeat. Keller, 831 is in extreme danger. If you can hear me, change the song."

Across the desk Evan James leaned over his tablet and kept watch on the cameras in Miller's office. By the jump pod, Eric Wilson worked frantically on the ImaDream prototype, its black casing lying on the floor as he altered the circuit boards within.

"The argument's winding down," Evan said. "How long until you're ready?"

Eric let loose an emphatic 'yes' before he clipped a cylindrical object to the mess of wires and got to his feet. "We're in. I need five to calibrate Keller's jump frequency."

"Hurry," Evan said. "Dietrich and Taylor are on their way."

Dex exchanged a worried glance with Eric before he leaned into his task once more. He'd been testing different frequencies, hoping to find one that would carry his voice into the dream reality, but so far, nothing had induced even a flicker in the waves. "Say again. Keller, if you can hear me, change the song."

Eric set two wireless electrodes on the desk, checked Keller's wavelengths and sat down beside Dex. Fingers flying, he muttered under his breath. "Just need to hit the right . . . " In minutes a solid line joined Keller's screen. "Frequency calibrated. Now all we need is a jump suite."

"Go," Dex said. "Keep eyes on Keller. Laura will want to test as soon as she's back."

"On it," Eric said and headed for the door only to pause.

All three men faced the pod as a slow melody filled the room, the music seeming to rise from Keller's skin.

"Got him!" Dex said. "Keller, my man. Listen up. I don't know how long this connection will hold or if it will. Your dream girl is in trouble. There's a third consciousness in there with you. It's a viral AI and it's highly developed. It's been following you through the cycles. This thing is strong. It's the reason the dreams have gotten worse, and we think it's trying to find a way out. We're working on sending in help. Gillian's been hurt, but it's been keeping you both alive. The closer she comes to waking, the stronger it will get. If you can hear me, change the song."

Several long moments of silence passed.

"Keller?" Dex cursed under his breath. "Keller, do you read me?"

A second melody drifted over the room.

"They're at the airlock," Evan said.

"There's no time to explain but, Nathan," Dex said, with renewed urgency. "They're going to test ImaDream . . . "

The music cut off abruptly and a hissing static filled the room.

"Cut off," Dex said, awed gaze on the screens. "Jesus, I think it just cut me off."

"How the hell did it do that?" Eric asked and Dex shrugged, baffled.

"Then all we can do is hope he heard," Evan said and laid a hand on Dex's shoulder. Dex looked up, the lump in his throat too large to speak. "You did good."

Relieved, Dex looked to Eric, who nodded in approval, before he swallowed hard and squared his shoulders. "We get one chance at this. Are you sure you don't want to bring in another MCL? Someone experienced in the jumps? Reese or maybe . . . "

"4-2-6," Evan said and leveled his gaze at Dex.

"What?" Eric asked, brow crunched.

Dex rose to his feet. "SSS 426 died nearly 10 years ago."

At the door, Evan faced him, lips twitching, his right hand clenched into a fist at his side. "And here I thought you'd done your research."

For the first time in Dex's presence, Evan James' face flickered into a bemused smile, and while it chilled him to the core, it also lifted Dex's spirits. If Evan had been one of the Elite—if he was, in fact, Somnium Sleep Subject 426—then he had survived without MCL intervention. Survived and thrived.

Dex pressed his fist to his heart and then slapped a hand to a non-existent patch on his arm. It was the only salute he could think to give, and he felt a stirring of true pride when Evan inclined his head in appreciation. For the first time since Keller had gone under, Dex believed they might actually be able to bring 831 home alive.

<hr />

"What do you think he meant, viral AI consciousness?" Gillian asked as the radio popped and crackled into silence.

"Must've had something to do with the glitch in the system when you were inducted," Nathan said. "Rumor has it they used a virus as the base for the tech transfer."

"And that's made the dreams stronger? To what end?"

Nathan shook his head, uncertain. "Upping the fear wouldn't do much more than increase your adrenaline, which should've woken you faster. Dex said he thinks it wants a way out. A way back to the mainframe at Somnium where it would be able to expand exponentially. I think the real question is what does it get out of your nightmare? What does adrenaline do for it?"

"Maybe it's not the adrenaline it wants," Gillian muttered. "You said yourself it's some sort of tech, right? So how did it get into me in the first place?"

"Somnium induction programming subliminally readies the brain to accept the waves emitted by the dream technology."

"How does it reach me? Through television?"

"Any smart tech," Nathan said. "Dex could explain it better, but basically, the product weaves ride the tech, mixed with the waves . . . "

Gillian cocked her head. "Waves?"

"Bioelectric energy formed in the human body."

"You mean neural activity? Like an EEG?"

Nathan nodded. "Dex reads it to determine where we are in the sleep cycle. He says he can tell when you're dreaming by the fear response in your waves. They spike, like watching lightning during a storm."

"So the stronger the dream, the bigger the wave?"

Nathan followed her thoughts. "The stronger the fear response, the more neurons fire . . . "

SOMNIUM

" . . . the more bioelectricity generated by mind and body. Waves." She sat down on the arm of the thick chair. "The memories we've been through. They're like matches to my nightmares, aren't they? Ignite the right memory, trigger the right trauma, and it sparks the bad dream."

"Which spawns a new array of electrical impulses."

"Stronger dreams generate stronger currents. Nightmares stimulate the body, the electricity charges my cells. Get enough of a charge together and I should wake up."

"But Dex said you've been injured." He chuckled and shook his head at the silent radio. "Of course, 'Girlfriend in a Coma.' He's been trying to reach us for a while."

"A coma would definitely explain why I haven't been able to wake up. So with each cycle, I'm generating more energy. But if the injury trapped it, then it's accumulating within my body. If this tech wants to find a way out, could it tap into that energy?"

"It would need to find a pathway. Something to ride back to the original mainframe."

"Ride the lightning." Gillian dug her fingernails into the padded arm beneath her. "The chair."

"What chair?"

"The one I've been seeing since the first dream cycle." Gillian described it for him, beginning with the simple structure of uncomfortable wood she had seen on the moor. With each memory, it had added to its complexity until it had become a fully functioning electric chair. "If I build up enough energy . . . "

"The bugger gets out," Nathan finished.

Gillian shuddered. "What do we do?"

"Dex said it follows." Nathan looked up through the leafy canopy at the spirals of her trapped nightmares. "So we go on the offensive."

Gillian stood and shook her head. "Uh-uh. No way. You can't mean . . . "

"He's shown up in nearly every landscape."

"And damn near killed me every time!"

"If we seek him out, find him before he finds us, maybe we can destroy that chair."

Gillian huffed in disbelief. "With what? Harsh language?"

Nathan stroked a hand over his black t-shirt and moved to the window of the treehouse, scanning the darkness below before he answered. "They're your dreams, Gill. Your fears. You know where they come from. Your mind created them. It's like your friend, Patrick, said. Interpret it and you'll stop dreaming that particular dream. You can find him."

"I don't know how!"

"Yes, you do. All you have to do is open the right door . . . "

"And Michael Shearer will devour me in my sleep."

"That's not his goal."

Gillian scoffed and slapped her hands to her thighs in annoyance. "Correct me if I'm wrong but wouldn't, oh, I don't know, the funneling of every last micron of my bioelectrical energy basically result in my death? Sort of puts a stop to that whole neurological thing where my brain sends a signal and my heart beats."

"This isn't your body. This is your mind."

"And the mind controls the body," Gillian said. "Every idiot who ever watched *The Matrix* knows that."

"But what controls the mind?"

Gillian rolled her eyes. "Don't get philosophical on me. If you're asking me if the soul exists, I think we both already know I'm a god-damned believer. And I do mean god-damned."

"Think about it. The manipulation of bioelectric energy has been at the heart of ancient healing techniques for thousands of years."

"Now is not the time for acupuncture, Nathan!"

"If the soul is that energy, the electricity, the current within your body, it controls everything. If you can consciously direct that energy, you can use it against him."

"I'm not conscious," Gillian said with all the petulant stubbornness of a three-year-old child determined not to eat broccoli.

"Yes, you are. But you have to take control. Direct it."

"And just how do I do that, Master Yoda?"

"Face your deepest fear."

Gillian gripped her elbows. "I do that every night."

"Not this one."

Nathan stepped to the side, the image behind him a nightmare in a white sheath. Gillian opened her mouth, but words failed her as a screech tore through the treehouse and a ball of light slammed into her chest.

In the jump suite, the screens on the left ignited in a flash of blue fire. Dex stumbled backward as all three screens blew up and then went dark.

"Jesus Christ, what the hell was that?"

He ran a diagnostic before he ripped the main cord from the Chicken Coop and plugged it into his laptop. In seconds he had a pattern again, but the sight didn't stop his heart from skipping a beat.

"I'm not seeing this," he muttered. It did nothing to convince him. On screen was a pattern he had seen only once before, but he recognized it instantly. He opened a channel on his wristband.

"Dr. Braun?"

"Not now, Dex."

"Now may be all the time we've got. Do you have her?"

"Just picked her up from the medevac helicopter. We're on our way to Medical."

The elevator doors pinged, a mechanical voice announcing its rooftop arrival.

"She took a hit. Same as Keller did before, only bigger. Wiped out my screens."

Static cracked on the line and Dex looked down at his wristband as if it might somehow show him what was happening in the elevator. When Braun finally answered, the cadence of his voice had slowed.

"What do you mean, same?"

Dex looked back at his laptop and then at the unaffected screens on the Coop. Keller's waves were dominant on all six active screens. "I mean it's the exact same jolt we saw Keller take earlier on a much grander scale. The one we couldn't explain."

"That can't be."

"I'd like to believe you, Doc, I really would. But I'm seeing what I'm seeing. Again."

"Read me her vitals."

Dex relayed the slowing numbers, her heartbeat stuttering with each second.

"Dex, I need you to listen to me. I'm going to take her to the MCL medical ward, do you understand?"

"Sure," Dex muttered, uncertain what Braun was telling him—there was no designated MCL medical ward and Braun knew it. But he was also smart enough to know that if Evan had been listening, someone else might be too. With luck, Braun would be back before Dex needed to figure out where he planned to stash 831.

"I need MCLs Reese and Ingram to meet me at the elevators on Sub-Level 5," Braun said. "Quick as they can. And I need you to connect me to a secure outside channel. Can you do that now?"

The second line secured and active, Dex sent a quick message to the two MCLs. Both had been personally recruited by Jon Markway early in the program. Neither were married, and like most single MCLs, resided on Sub-Level 2. They responded immediately, and Dex breathed a sigh of relief as Braun disconnected from the secured channel. "On their way."

"Good," Braun said. "Is Dietrich back?"

Dex checked his feeds. "Passing through final stage security now. I'll hook you in, just in case you need . . . " A glance at the waves brought Dex to his feet. "Doc . . . "

"What's going on?"

Alarms pierced the air in the suite, a single, jarring note drowning out the monotone mechanical voice announcing the elevator had reached Sub-Level 5. "She's crashing!"

"Starting CPR."

Dex fell to his knees while Braun counted off compressions, prayers dripping from his lips while he watched for a tremor in the waves.

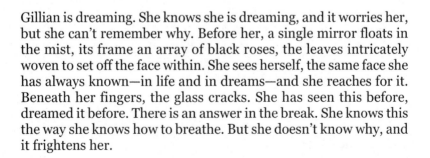

Gillian is dreaming. She knows she is dreaming, and it worries her, but she can't remember why. Before her, a single mirror floats in the mist, its frame an array of black roses, the leaves intricately woven to set off the face within. She sees herself, the same face she has always known—in life and in dreams—and she reaches for it. Beneath her fingers, the glass cracks. She has seen this before, dreamed it before. There is an answer in the break. She knows this the way she knows how to breathe. But she doesn't know why, and it frightens her.

SOMNIUM

A memory surfaces, congeals behind her. Her grandmother lies in a bed, light shining on her the way it does through windows on a late summer day. But it is too golden. Too perfect. She approaches the bed with trepidation. Her mother sits beside the old woman, stroking the remaining gray hair, the last tendrils tied in a pretty green bow.

"Go," her mother whispers.

In her hand she holds a compact under Gillian's grandmother's chin, breath forming and fading on the tiny disc just once more.

For the first time, Gillian knows she is dying.

"Gillian!"

Turning, she sees herself in the treehouse, suspended in mid-air. In the doorway the Wraith waits, disjointed fingers gathering a second fiery orb from the electrified atmosphere.

Betrayed. She has been betrayed. By the only man she ever loved.

He brought the Wraith. Brought death. Broke the spell of her safest place. Water pours over them from above where the nightmares trapped within the asylum rage. She feels an absurd need to stick her thumb in her mouth, and finally sees what Nathan already knows.

The elevator doors opened and two MCLs grabbed the gurney, racing with Braun toward the emergency Medical Lab. Careening around a corner, they entered the makeshift hospital room. Lights dimmed and charged with a life of their own.

"Take over," Braun said and immediately MCL Reese pressed his hands to the woman's chest. Braun dashed out of the room and passed the nurses' station in search of a defibrillator cart. Overhead the lights went out, this time for good, and he cursed vehemently.

"Dex? Are you still there?"

"Here."

"We've lost power in the Med Lab. I need you to be my eyes on her insides."

"On it. Screens are still down, but I've got her on my laptop. Just need to adjust."

Familiar with his surroundings, Braun turned in a slow circle.

In the dark everything seemed to have moved of its own accord, so it took longer than expected to find the battery-powered AED kit on the wall. Pack in hand, he dashed back to the room, the MCLs maintaining a steady cadence of compressions and breaths while he charged the pads. Setting the AED on the gurney, he waited for the tell-tale beep.

"Dex? Anything?"

"No heartbeat. Brain activity declining."

"Start the three-minute countdown."

"But . . ."

"Just do it. If I can't get her back before brain death, we'll at least have enough time to get Keller out. I won't let them both go."

Dex set the clock and spoke the required words in a tight, mechanical voice. "Initiating preparation for MCL expulsion due to Sleep Subject brain death. Three-minute countdown commencing in five . . . four . . . three . . . two . . . "

On the gurney, the little AED pack let off a loud beep. Braun placed the shock pads on his patient's chest, thumb poised over the delivery button.

"Clear!"

Gillian stands in a stark room, alone but for the body laid out on the cold steel table. A simple white sheath covers the pale form. She remembers it now. Gillian wore it herself. More times than she can count. She sees herself on the table, the pain from the electroconvulsive therapy so intense she had to leave, the Wraith the shell left behind. Separated but always together. Cracked.

Electricity courses through her, jolting her further from herself, and she passes through the mirror. The frame now holds Nathan's receding image, her body sheltered in his arms, his lips still forming the first letter of her name. She understands without needing to that time has slowed. That she has been given a moment of grace before hell swallows her whole.

On the table, the Wraith sits up, chest heaving. A low growl of warning emanates from her lips. Gillian wipes the foam of drool from the young woman's chin. Rage bubbles like maggots beneath the ice-cold skin. Parting the girl's hair, she looks on the scarred face beneath and fights the urge to scratch her own cheeks bloody once more.

Eyes burn bright moss green, enhanced by the dying light of hatred, all the anger Gillian denied over the years pent up within this casing. This part of herself she fears to face, neglected to acknowledge for nearly 20 years.

Around her, familiar voices whisper.

"Face your fears," Toby says.

"Only you can mend the crack," Nathan says.

"See what is yours," Patrick says. "And you'll know what you need to destroy."

Trembling, Gillian stares at the girl, who stands so still in the mist and knows that this Wraith is hers, that she is of her mind and her mind alone. A purple rubber band encircles the Wraith's wrist, and Gillian remembers everything. The rape had been the fissure, the ECT treatment the earthquake that broke her in two. And she knows without knowing how that this is the crack she must mend.

"I see you," Gillian whispers.

"You fear me."

Gillian nods. "I am afraid. To feel what you felt. To know what you know. That if I do, I'll lose all that's sane in the mind I have left."

"And so we are here."

"So we are here." Trembling fingers take the Wraith's hands. "I'm ready."

"They're supposed to use anesthesia," the Wraith says and lays down on the table. "Shearer reduced the dose."

"You protected me."

"And you deserted me."

Shame creeps over Gillian, heart breaking for the child she had been. She wants to weep but there are no tears. Instead, she reaches out and places her hands on the Wraith.

"I am not afraid," Gillian says.

Electricity courses through her, a searing torture that burns her skin, clenches her teeth and contracts her muscles so tight she fears her bones might crack.

On the table, the girl eases.

A second jolt races into her muscles, the pain blinding, but Gillian takes it. Whimpering, she drops to her knees and feels a gentle hand stroke her hair. Opening her eyes, she sees the Wraith, who looks at her with the hope of a chastened child, and climbs to her feet. She runs a hand over the Wraith's arm, redrawing the lines of the shark bite that still leaks blood. Blue sparks dance from her fingers, like a static-filled blanket pulled away in the dark, but she feels no pain. The mangled arm heals, spiders of energy sealing the wound.

She puts a hand to her own chest, but within all remains silent.

"We have a few places to go," the Wraith says.

"I know."

The Wraith takes her hand, electricity encircling her wrist in a bracelet of light, and they stand once again in Dean Abbott's office. The Wraith nods at the young woman sitting before the desk. Gillian slips into her old skin and feels again the churn of her stomach. She wonders if this time someone will believe her.

"Give me a reason, Gillian," Dean Abbott says. "Any reason and I'll find a way to let you stay."

Taking a deep breath, Gillian sneaks a peak at the Wraith and then lifts her chin. "I was raped, Dean Abbott. And when he grabbed me, I reacted as if he were the man who had done that to me. I didn't mean to hurt him."

Dean Abbott looks at her with sympathy, comes around the desk and sits beside her. Reaching out she takes Gillian's hand. "You never told anyone, did you?"

Shaking her head, Gillian squeezes the Dean's fingers.

"Why not?"

"Because I didn't think anyone would believe me."

"I believe you, Gillian," Dean Abbott says. "Others will too."

Behind her, the sharp pop of cracking knuckles. The Wraith's disjointed bones heal, the hands now younger versions of Gillian's own. Rising, she takes them once again, and they stand in the golden light of the name McBride. A shifting whirlwind of ash congeals into her grandfather, who holds his head bowed before her.

"Gillian."

"Poppop." She looks at the man who had long been the bane of her dreams. Warm eyes look down at her, and she notices for the first time that they are the same green as her own. "Thank you for giving me a way out."

"You're welcome, child," he says and cups her cheek. "I'm sorry I never knew how to show you I loved you. But I did. Truth to God, I did."

"I know," Gillian says, and takes a deep breath, the truth that she must acknowledge painful as the years of rage and blame she mistakenly laid at his feet. "I loved you too." She falls into the old man's embrace.

A sharp sizzle mends the burn, the Wraith's forearm clean and clear as her own. The door opens to the stairs where she had last seen Toby's corpse. Her brother waits on the landing, whole and handsome and she throws herself into his open arms.

"I'm so sorry," Gillian whispers and her brother laughs.

"For what?"

"Everything."

"You have nothing to apologize for, little sister. I made my own choices. Who was it I always wanted to be when we played *Aliens*?"

Gillian smiles sadly. "Corporal Dwayne Hicks."

"Colonial Marine and absolute bad ass. The Rangers weren't exactly the same, but they were a pretty close substitute. So you see, there's nothing to apologize for my little Ripley." He catches her cheeks in his hands. "I always meant to come see you, you know. I wrote to you every day."

"I know," Gillian says and smiles, heart breaking as he fades from her eyes. The Wraith's face smooths over, healed of the hideous scars she'd inflicted on her cheeks when the letters stopped for good. Down the hallway, a light burns in the darkness. Gillian steps inside her old room to find her younger self alone on the bed, curled into a tight ball.

Gillian approaches her carefully and sits down beside her. The girl tugs herself away, the soft words she speaks, simple letters, forming the words "fish" "dog" "ghost" and "lost" until Gillian strokes her hair.

"I see you," Gillian says, and the girl looks up, seeking her with a longing so fierce it brings tears to Gillian's eyes. "I will always see you."

She takes the child in her arms, and gasps as the girl melts into her, as if she were a Russian babushka doll with smaller versions nesting within. She stands and faces the Wraith, who now sits laughing on the slate-backed chair while Shearer jiggles a deadly dance.

Ignoring the nightmare, she squats before the Wraith.

"I am so proud of you," she whispers and brushes the girl's hair from her face, the last of the welts on her forehead fading. She takes the purple rubber band from her wrist and ties the girl's hair back.

They stand together in the mist, the mirror of black roses before them. Nathan waits on the other side, and Gillian's heart leaps. She takes the Wraith's hand and they both gasp.

"So that's what it feels like?" the Wraith asks.

Gillian smiles through her tears. "It is."

The power within the Wraith glows bright. Gillian touches a hand to the mirror, the crack mended but the barrier is still there. She faces the Wraith. One doll left to nestle in her breast.

"Bring me back to him," she says and takes the Wraith's hands. "Bring *us* back to him."

The Wraith says nothing. Instead, she tugs Gillian away from the mirror. A tunnel of warm light stretched out before them. A silhouette stands at the end, and with a leap of joy, Gillian races down the sunny path.

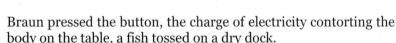

Braun pressed the button, the charge of electricity contorting the body on the table, a fish tossed on a dry dock.

"Dex? Talk to me!"

"Nothing," Dex said. "Brain activity is . . . Wait." Dex shifted in his seat, uncomfortable with the strange pattern of neural activity. "Doc, I don't know what I'm seeing."

"What do you mean?"

"Her neural activity just leapt off the charts." Dex rose to his feet, uncertain what to do.

"Charging," Braun said.

"Doc . . . I don't think . . . "

"Clear!"

The security camera in the Med Lab jolted as if it had been struck by debris. Dex caught the laptop in both hands, gasping as he watched Braun and the two MCLs slam into the walls.

"Doc!"

The electricity in Gillian Hardie's brain jumped with the influx from the AED, but nothing accounted for the return of the disconcerting patterns.

"Doc! Can you hear me?"

In the lab, one of the MCLs lifted a hand to his head. A long low groan emanated from the other. Braun struggled to his feet, pulling himself up on the gurney before he slowly backed away from the body.

"Dex, are you seeing this?"

"I am," Dex said, awed by the scene, the players clear, the light source uncanny. "But I'm not sure I want to."

"Get Keller out."

Dex shook his head. "We've got 60 seconds left."

"I can't get her back," Braun said and looked directly at the camera. "Initiate expulsion. That's an order."

"You can't get her back," Dex said. "But you're not the only one trying."

"What do you mean?"

Dex sank to his seat and cut the feed, the image of Gillian Hardie's body crackling with light in the darkened hospital room one he would take with him to the grave. He looked at Keller's waves, the intermingling of their consciousness still active, and then at the heightened activity in the neural patterns on his laptop. He held out a hand to the screen, nearly touching Gillian's lines. A bolt of plasma leapt out to greet him, the sting forcing his fingers to curl. The echo danced across the darkness.

He folded his hands into a fist before his mouth.

"Hold strong," he whispered to the lines. "Just hold strong for one more minute."

A woman stands within the light-filled tunnel. Behind the familiar form, Gillian sees a pinpoint of darkness that fills her with vague unease.

"Hello, my love."

She falls into her mother's arms, the warmth of the embrace deep and joyful, and Gillian floats within. "Mom. I was coming to see you."

"Take my hand, we'll go together. Toby is waiting. Waiting for us both."

Gillian steps out of her mother's embrace. Mist closes over the tunnel, the rose mirror almost lost and she hesitates.

"What is it, child?" Amy Beth asks.

"I . . ."

Amy Beth follows her gaze. "There's nothing holding you here."

"He . . ."

"Peace awaits you. Awaits us both. Come with me. I need you now."

Her mother's hand clenches Gillian's until she squirms for release. "Nathan is waiting for me."

A troubled frown forms on Amy Beth's lips. Behind her the darkness grows, emulating a familiar shape while a sulfurous stench triggers a warning in Gillian's chest. The first ripple of fear darts around her brain like an erratic thought.

"You would return? To the sleepless nights? The bad dreams? For what? For him?" Amy Beth strokes the hair from Gillian's forehead, tucks it behind her ear and smiles with too many teeth. "Don't be stupid, girl. You've never even met the man."

Tears slide down Gillian's cheeks as she lifts her shoulders to her ears. "I know him. I know his heart."

"But he doesn't know yours, does he?" Amy Beth slaps at Gillian's tears. "How dangerous you are? To know him is to kill him. And you will kill him, won't you, girlie? Just like you killed your brother. Just like you killed me. Just like you killed yourself. Face it dearest, you've damned your soul to hell."

Gillian backs away as her mother's façade slips. "I didn't . . . What did you call me?"

The mask disintegrates and Michael Shearer stands where her mother stood, the lines of his skin knitted back together like trails on a map. Sulfurous yellow fire sparks from the chair behind him. "You and I are the same. Sinners. And there's only one place for sinners. A death for a death, girlie. It's time to pay the price."

"I have sinned," Gillian says. "But not against you." She holds her hands out from her thighs, fingers splayed as if she were clutching a bowling ball.

"I'm ready," she says, and feels the pain, the horror, the unbearable sadness move into her limbs, but this time, she bears it. It is hers, and she welcomes it. Cool blue fire engulfs her, the Wraith no longer with her but within her. She breathes in and feels a hard thump reverberate within her chest. Lines of blue fire arc toward the chair. The force throws her back, shattering the mirror.

Shearer charges but the glass seals before he can follow, the reflection showing only a gaseous mix of sulfurous yellow and crackling blue lightning before it fades into the mist.

Gillian is dreaming. She knows she is dreaming, but it no longer worries her. She places a hand on her chest. Beneath her fingers, a reassuring thump. She breathes in.

"Holy shit . . . " Dex muttered as the echo crossed the screen and entwined itself with 831, choking the pattern like an invasive vine. It consumed the shade of blue that was Gillian Hardie's mind, nearly eclipsing it with a musty yellow. Where her patterns had been subsumed, a single green line remained. "Doc, I wish you could see this."

"Talk to me."

"It's the echo," Dex said. "I don't know how to describe it. It's like it's eating 831's neural patterns. Almost as if it's taking control of her brain." He stopped short and rose to his feet. On his screen, 831's remaining waves seemed to brighten, forcing the echo to release its hold. Blue light flexed and then pulsed, the echo shattered in a rain of yellow sparks.

All three screens on the left side of the Coop fired up, a warm blue light beating on the screen until it settled into the patterns he associated with Gillian Hardie's neural activity.

"She's back, Doc. Holy shit! She's back!"

Braun leapt to his feet, fingers to the cool skin of his patient's neck. A strong beat met his touch. The lights flickered and then held steady. A series of consistent blips from the AED confirmed what his hands already knew. "Abort the expulsion. Now, Dex. Now!"

In the jump suite, Dex slammed his fingers to the keyboard, commands halting the countdown with less than ten seconds to go. "Expulsion aborted."

"Oxygen!" Braun called and MCL Reese placed a mask over the woman's face. "How the hell . . . "

"Doc," Dex cut him off. "Company is headed your way in the form of three very stern looking men with guns."

"How long have we got?"

"About two minutes."

"Can you stall the elevator?"

"Not from here."

Cursing under his breath, Braun ripped the AED pads from his patient's chest, the blood-stained sheet back in place. He looked from the gentle lines of her face to the hard men before him and made a decision from which he might never recover, but for the first time in years, felt like the right choice.

"Gentlemen," he said. "I'd like you to meet Somnium Sleep Subject 831. Her name is Gillian Hardie, and she needs you now more than she ever has before."

The MCLs spun toward her, their backs straight, as if they were in the presence of royalty. In unspoken unison, the two men put a fist to their hearts and then slapped the patch on their shoulders. MCL Reese stepped up and gripped the cool hand in his own. Braun felt a tug of respect, his men's devotion to the Elite reaffirming the pride he felt in his program. He put a hand on Reese's shoulder as he spoke.

"What I'm about to ask of you is nothing short of treason when it comes to Somnium's rules and policies, but this woman must be protected at all costs. Is that understood?"

"Sir, yes sir," both men said.

When the elevator doors opened moments later, MCL Ingram stood before it, blocking the view of the men within as the freight elevator doors slid quietly closed.

CHAPTER SEVENTEEN

A N ICE DAM broke within Nathan's chest, relief running through him like the first thaw of spring as Gillian gasped in his arms. Around them, the treehouse solidified, the fire burning bright and warm.

"Welcome back," he said.

Eyes bulging, Gillian scuttled away from him and put her back to the wall. Looking around the room as if it were the first time she'd seen it, she peered at him with open suspicion.

"Nathan? Is it really you?"

"Are you all right?"

"Answer me, dammit! Is that you?"

Nathan grasped her shaking hands, the touch warm and reassuring. "You know that place between sleep and awake, that place where you still remember dreaming? That's where I'll be waiting."

Gillian relaxed. "And I have been happy to find you there." She pressed her forehead to his, the tremble in her fingers diminished before she lifted her eyes. "Thing is, I'd rather find you in my bed."

Nathan grinned. "Then let's get the hell out of here, shall we?"

A strange static burned through her when she pressed her lips to his, a tingle transferred from skin to skin before she pulled away.

"How did you know?" Gillian asked. "That the Wraith was a part of me?"

"She brought me to you." Nathan helped her up. Beyond the canopy of leaves, the nightmares rumbled to life. "She could've taken me out, back when you were trapped in the coffin, but instead she helped. I didn't understand it then. But when she sent me here, I knew."

"She was there when I needed her most."

Nathan nodded at her feet. "Got your boots back, I see."

Probing her pockets, Gillian held up a serrated knife. "I think we're back in business."

"Unstuck," he muttered. "Think that means you're waking up? Coming out of the coma?"

"If I am, then everything is about to get worse. What was it Dex said?"

"Closer you come to waking up, the stronger it will get. If the virus wants a way out, Shearer's going to burn through you to get it."

"He damn near did it," Gillian said, brow crunched in confusion, uncertain of the words even as she spoke them.

"What do you remember?"

"I don't know," Gillian said, the memory slipping away even as she spoke. "A face, torn in two. Like he was wearing a mask." She shook her head. "It's fading now."

"Dreams usually do."

"You still think the offensive is the way to go?"

"Only thing we haven't tried," Nathan said. "Gives us the element of surprise if there is such a thing in the dream reality. He won't be expecting you to seek him out."

"What if I'm still stuck?"

"Fight or flight. Either way we keep opening doors until you wake."

Circles of doors rose high over Gillian's head. "So many charming options. Question is, where will the Laundry Room be?"

"Seemed on the way down that your most recent nightmares were on the top level."

"Lovely. So we have to go all the way up?"

"Did you think it would be easy?"

Gillian shrugged. "Have to admit, I kinda hoped it would be. Do we need a memory? Something to activate the nightmare?"

"Do you have one?" Nathan asked.

"No," she said and grasped his hand. "There's only one thing left that can scare me."

"Then stay behind me."

Scowling, she hefted a crossbow to her hip. "And miss all the fun?"

Nathan grinned. "That's my girl."

They had nearly reached the bottom of the treehouse staircase when Nathan felt the first twinge. A sharp headache, as if he'd eaten something cold far too fast.

"Gill . . . "

"Are you all right?"

Nathan shook his head to clear it, the twinge gone as quickly as it came. "I don't . . . "

A second bolt of pain burst across his eye. Nathan slapped a hand to his face.

"Nathan?"

"I'm . . . I'm all right." Around him the ground swayed and dipped, Gillian fading in and out of a static-filled grayness. He wondered briefly if he had somehow lost the link when he heard people talking. "Do you hear that?"

Initiating weave.

"Hear what?"

"I think it's . . . " Nathan shook his head again. The pain faded and he centered his mind, thoughts on their next move and her choice of weapon.

"You'll do better with the short blade," he said. "Gun. Anything that's a natural extension of your arm. We're going through. No stopping to fight. Wound it. Kill it if you can. But don't stop. We'll handle whatever follows when we reach higher ground."

"Straight up. Straight through. Got it."

Before he took more than two steps, Nathan roared in pain and dropped to his knees. Pixels of light flashed behind his eyes, threatening to dislodge the orbs from the sockets as blood pulsed hard against his veins. He felt Gillian's hands on his arms.

"Don't," he said and pushed her away. Something adjusted within his head. "Dammit, Dex. What the hell are you . . . " He screamed again, the pain a guillotine slicing through him with a blade so sharp he felt he'd been split in two. Forehead to the dirt, he opened his mouth and vomited black blood across the dying grass.

Dex sat heavy in his chair, the sound of the flatline still ringing in his ears despite the life-affirming blips in 831's vitals. He silently thanked every deity he could think of for the reprieve. When he finished the list, he ran his hands down his face as if to wipe it dry, then set his fingers to task once more.

"Eric?"

Wilson responded instantly. "We're next door. Evan's ready whenever . . ."

The door opened and Dex cut off Eric's mic. He watched silently as Laura crossed the room, and noted the slight easing of her shoulders when she looked at the ImaDream prototype.

"She's still under?" Laura asked and pulled up a chair to her makeshift station. The ImaDream screen showed nothing but static. She plugged the prototype into the jump pod and then attached two wireless electrodes to Keller's forehead.

"Stupid question," Dex said.

"Holding on?"

"Barely."

"I understand Dr. Braun is bringing her onsite. That should make you happy."

"It does."

"Do you plan on saying more than two words to me?"

"Never again."

Laura glared over her shoulder at him, and Dex shifted to a more leisurely recline, feet up on the desk to watch her work. He had stacked his files on the console, allowing him to keep views of Eric and Braun open on a laptop Laura couldn't see. He watched silently as Eric looked directly at the camera, a slight shake of Dex's head acknowledged. Braun and his patient had disappeared, the two MCLs flanking the elevator bank to stop anyone from entering the Medical Lab.

"Calibrations are ready," Laura said and opened a line. "Clayton, it's time."

"On my way."

Laura smiled in triumph. "The show will go on."

"Good," Dex said and gave her a cold smirk, his own interest in seeing the output of the lines he knew so well firing like the last corn kernels in the kettle of his stomach. He set his feet on the floor, folded his fingers into a fist beneath his chin and gazed at the screen, but his body felt off. The anxious buzz made it hard to sit still, the sense he had missed something vital not letting him relax. He went over his conversation with Eric until with a slap of his hands on his desk, he found the missing piece.

"Eric said you made the dreams stronger by activating the virus. That it rode the jump tech. Is that right?"

"Yes," Laura said. "Your little snit didn't last long."

Dex tapped several fingers on his forehead. "Rides the jump tech. It goes in with the MCL."

"That's right."

Troubled, Dex muttered the answer several more times, trying to articulate what was wrong with it. "Rides with the MCL."

"So now you're just going to repeat everything I say five times?"

"Shut up and let me think. The virus is riding the jump tech. It goes in with the MCL. So how does it separate?"

"Separate?"

"When it's in the dream reality? How does the virus separate from the MCL's consciousness?" Dex looked up to find Laura studiously avoiding his gaze. "You did separate it, didn't you?"

"It's harmless."

"Nothing is harmless when it comes to this tech." Dex shot to his feet. "She's coming out of it."

"What?"

The door opened to let Clayton Miller and Phil Dietrich bustle into the room. "Are you ready, Ms. Taylor?"

"Initiating weave," Laura said. The prototype hummed, filling the cool air. Phil Dietrich assumed a position to the left of the screen while Clayton took a spot on the right.

Dex tucked his hands under his pits, hoping his twitching wouldn't give anything away. The new weave intermingled with the waves before shifting apart then gliding back together.

"NREM," he muttered, eyes alight. "Definitely on her way up."

"What's that, Operator?" Clayton looked directly at Dex then let his gaze flick to the lights, which dimmed and brightened as if they were beating in time with Dex's own heart.

Dex cleared his throat. "She's in a standard cycle. Currently in NREM." He checked his link to Braun, hoping the doctor would hear him. "A fully normal cycle."

"Which means?"

"Which means, for Sleep Subject 831, REM will commence in approximately two minutes, and the dream should be strong enough to wake her in less than 20."

On the middle screen, the crashing lines moved closer, intertwining twice more before they wove into a pattern Dex had never seen.

"What's happening?" Clayton asked.

"We're getting similar results to a first connection," Dex said. "But . . . "

"But what?"

On Dex's laptop screen, Eric frantically drew a line across his throat. *Evan*, Dex thought and looked up with a confidence he didn't feel. "Nothing," Dex said. "I'm sure it's nothing."

Nodding, Clayton faced the ImaDream screen. A flicker of motion. A hint beyond the static of something bigger. The sound of water rushing. Then it was gone, back to static.

"What's wrong?" he asked.

Laura's brow creased. "We're getting some interference. It should clear." She made several adjustments and the image surfaced again. "There. Images should come up in a few seconds."

Awed gazes from around the room focused on what appeared to be falling leaves. Rain dropped from a glittering canopy far overhead. The suite's lights stuttered again, the buzz of the fluorescents overpowering the simple sound of water emanating from the prototype's speakers.

"What are we seeing?" Clayton asked.

"We're in," Laura said. "We should be seeing first-person from Keller's point of view."

"That doesn't answer my question. Operator?"

Dex reviewed the waves. "She's not in REM yet. Images should be stronger when she re-enters the dream cycle."

"What do you mean she's not in REM? If she's not dreaming, how are we seeing anything?"

"She's cycling up. She'll be in the next dream in a few minutes. Probably catching the first snippets of neural activity."

"And what happens when she reaches REM? What will we see?"

Laura spoke up. "If it works, we should have an excellent view of 831's dream reality."

"Which means we'll all be pissing ourselves," Dex muttered and then flashed a toothy grin. "Hope you all availed yourselves of the facilities. 831 is one helluva dreamer."

The room fell silent, all eyes on the ImaDream screen except for Dex, who watched the waves. He sat forward and chanced a glance at Eric, who gave him a thumbs up. Evan was in.

"She's reached REM," Dex said as the image on the screen shifted. "Hold onto your butts."

Gasping, Phil Dietrich put his back against the door. Laura

SOMNIUM

Taylor let out an involuntary cry and Clayton Miller took a step back before forcing himself into position to view the image clearly. He swallowed hard.

"What in God's name is that?"

Every instinct told Gillian to flee as the first, and worst, dream from her youth clawed its way out of the earth. The old hag had been ugly enough when she was young, but now the greenish tint of her skin had taken on a new hue, the gaseous emissions of an aging bog accompanying her rise.

It started as nothing more than what appeared to be a tree branch. Nathan on his hands and knees, the vomit he'd spewed spreading like a pool of hot metal and opening a gash in the earth. Gnarled extensions clawed out of the hole. The decaying head followed, chin hanging low as the pus-swollen flesh erupted like lava over the bones. It pulled itself out, shook like a dog and turned black-hole eyes to Gillian.

"Steady," Nathan muttered and climbed to his feet.

Gillian shook her head. "I can't do this."

"Yes, you can."

"I really, really . . . "

Snake-like branches shot across the grass and wrapped around Gillian's ankles to drag her forward. A limb slapped Nathan away, and he hit the base of the treehouse with a dull thud. Gillian landed hard on her ass, smaller shoots searching for purchase and digging into her skin. Before she could react, a broadsword descended to slash the branches in two. A hand wrapped around her waist, yanking her up and away from the spray of black liquid.

"You're far too pretty for such bad dreams, Gilly."

Fear ebbed as Gillian recognized the deep and distinctive voice.

"Do you know me?" he asked.

Gillian nodded but didn't take her eyes off the flailing limbs. "Patrick."

Reassured that he did indeed recognize the scraggly waves of unwashed hair and deep blue eyes under the layer of black dirt, Nathan placed himself between Gillian and the roaring hag. "We need to move . . . "

"You can stop it," Patrick said to Gillian.

"How?"

"What does she represent?"

Gillian shook her head. "No idea."

"How old were you when she first came?"

A vine snuck through the grass, curling itself around Gillian's ankle and winding its way up her torso to constrict her lungs.

Dreams of the old hag were the first to truly terrify Gillian. The suffocating she associated with the creature was like a swimmer unable to surface from the weight of the water. The worst occurred when she thought for sure she had emerged from the dream yet still couldn't move. Paralysis froze her limbs, her lungs stifled.

"I can't . . . breathe . . . "

Patrick struck out at the vine. "Who made you feel suffocated?"

"I don't . . . " A distant memory rose up to mock her. Instantly, Gillian's throat opened, and she heaved in air. "Shelly Finch."

The Hag whipped its massive head toward Gillian, opened a mouth full of rotten teeth and screamed. Nathan leapt onto its back, glinting blade slicing its throat. Black blood gushed from the wound as rage threw him into the tree.

"Who was she?" Patrick asked.

Gillian got to her feet, an axe in her hands. She advanced on the Hag, who seemed to shrink before her. "The biggest bitch on the summer swim team."

"What did she do to you?"

"Made fun of me. Endlessly teased me for a crush I had on one of the older boys."

"Defend the girl you were."

Fury built within Gillian's chest, rage crackling her blood. She launched at the Hag, the sharp blade of her axe slicing through the creature's arm and rending it from its body. The Hag's mouth dove down toward her, teeth snapping close to her cheek. Spinning away, Gillian sent a second swing at the Hag's leg. The axe struck home and stuck. Black ooze coated Gillian's fingers and vines circled her ankles once more. She tucked a hand into her pocket, fear easing when she grasped the lighter. Letting go of the axe, she allowed the vines to take firm hold. The Hag dragged her up by the foot until she was upside down and nearly face to face with its rotten breath. Its eyes glowed red in the darkness, triumph lit within until it heard the flick of flint. Fire sprang to life and the

Hag's hair burst into flames. It hurled Gillian away. She landed hard and rolled to stop in time to see flames consume the creature. Screaming in agony, the Hag dropped to its knees. Rising, Gillian strode across the room and wrenched her axe free.

"You were never anything more than a fucking bully," she muttered and raised the axe. She brought it down on the Hag's neck, the force separating head from the body. Silence filled the room, its screams abruptly cut off. The head rolled heavily to the base of the tree, where it dispersed into the air like a horde of flies.

Nathan dropped from the treehouse branches and grinned at Gillian. "Remind me not to piss you off."

"This is going to be more fun than I thought," she said, boot probing the pile of leftover ash. Above them, the walls shook with silent fury.

"We need to move," Nathan said.

"Where to?" Patrick asked.

"Laundry Room 3-B," Gillian said.

He looked at her sharply. "When?"

"Two days after you left."

Patrick let loose a string of curses before he calmed himself. "You found your core?"

Several doors swung open on the mezzanine of Gillian's asylum, the sound like a snickering of cicadas rising from a prolonged slumber.

"What do you mean, core?" Gillain asked.

"The core of your fear," Patrick said. "It would've taken form in your dreams."

"Shearer?" Nathan asked.

Patrick shook his head. "It would've represented a side of Gillian she didn't want to acknowledge. A part of herself she was afraid to see."

"The Wraith," Gillian said and cracked her knuckles.

"Is she still a threat?"

"Not to me."

Pride glowed in Patrick's eyes. "I knew you'd find your way. Use her now."

"And just how do I do that?"

"Tap into the emotion she represents."

"Will that work?"

Patrick's skin shifted, an array of blue-green scales blooming across the surface of his body as his eyes narrowed to dangerous, yet human, slits. "I know it will."

He shot forward, slithering his way between a horde of zombies and knocking them to the side like bowling pins.

"I'll be damned," Gillian said, awed gaze following Patrick's path. The serpent that had plagued his youthful dreams flipped an inquisitor into its mouth and swallowed the robed heathen whole.

"You know, I think I like him," Nathan said.

Gillian grinned. "He has a way of growing on you. Like a fungus."

"You ready?"

"Straight up," Gillian said and raised her axe.

"Straight through," Nathan said.

"Let's do this."

Braun slipped into the jump suite and circled behind Dex's desk. On screen, the battle continued, the audience enraptured by the multitude of creatures Keller and 831 left in their wake. They were nearing the top of the asylum when Braun put a hand on Dex's shoulder.

"How are her vitals?" he asked.

"Off the fucking chart," Dex muttered and perused the waves. "She's tapped into activity levels I've never even seen, and quite frankly, didn't know existed. But she's surfacing, Doc. And there's something . . . " Dex shook his head. "I can't put my finger on it."

"How's Keller?"

"Holding strong."

"She's still in REM?"

"Ten minutes and climbing," Dex said. "But I don't think we can even call this a cycle anymore. I think she's come out of the coma. Which means . . . "

"She's in serious danger." Braun shifted his stance. "And there's no telling how long it will last."

Before them, Keller turned into a hallway, the wide open doors showing nothing but mist on the moors. He paused before Laundry Room 3-B, waiting for 831, who limped slowly toward him while some sort of serpent swayed behind them.

"We're here," Nathan called and opened the door.

"Is he there?" 831 asked.

"The MCL carries the virus into the dream reality," Dex said. "But it doesn't separate." Dex addressed Laura. "How does the MCL carry the virus to the sleep subject?"

"I told you, it rides the tech."

"What tech? It's not part of the weave, is it?"

"It's programmed into the MCL."

Dex froze. "What do you mean, programmed in?"

"Subliminal. Like the original code."

Braun's hand clenched Dex's shoulder. "What did you say?"

Laura smirked. "I couldn't access your systems, so I accessed your MCLs. Most of them were easy. Flirt a little and they'll do just about anything for you. I was able to incorporate it into the daily dose of tech they already received, but Keller was a little more difficult. I had to access his personal log."

"You hacked his private files?"

"Really, Dr. Braun, if you would just share your . . . "

"He doesn't know," Dex cut in. "Markway would've never gone in if he knew he carried that virus with him. Never would've put 8924 at risk. Neither would Blake or Billings. 8924 and 9998 died because they carried it in without knowing what they did." Dex's wristband buzzed with a message from Eric. He puzzled over it before turning to Braun. "What does he mean? 9998 isn't dead?"

Braun shook his head. "No, thank God. He flatlined at the expulsion. We lost the connection, but his watcher found him up and about, disoriented and frightened, but no other harm done."

Dex thought back to his conversation with Eric at Macho Nacho. *Markway died almost two minutes before 8924. Died before. Before.* "How did Markway die?"

"Two puncture marks appeared on Jon's neck," Braun said. "But cause of death hasn't been determined beyond neural trauma. I'll need to do a full autopsy . . . "

"Billings died after the expulsion. His mind would've still been in a heightened state of activity. Almost as if he were still dreaming. But 9998 lived." Dex gasped, the connection he'd been struggling to find finally clear and goosebumps erupted across his flesh. "It wasn't his dream."

"What?"

"8924 couldn't wake up because in the end, it wasn't his dream.

He wasn't in control. The virus was. Markway carried it in. So did Billings. And so did Keller."

The lights dimmed in the suite. On screen, Keller slammed into a dented dryer, mist obscuring a fight at the heart of the room. All they saw was a dull yellow glow rising like fire in the haze.

"What are you saying?" Braun asked.

"Keller's going to kill her." No longer worried about who saw what, Dex slammed a hand to his laptop, opening the mic to Eric. "Talk to her. Use the radio frequency!"

On screen, a presence emerged from the mist. The whole room caught its breath as one. No one moved, the image riveting as Keller reached for Gillian.

"Initiate emergency separation," Braun said. "Do it, Dex! Now!"

Dex flew into action, the sequence nearly complete when a single note erupted from six different screens at once.

Nathan reached the door first, chest heaving, an unknown substance covering most of his right side. He'd been scratched across his stomach by one of the mutant hawks, but they'd made it through. Behind them, Patrick's serpent blocked the hallway, giving Gillian a chance to limp toward him.

"We're here," he said and swung open the heavy door.

"Is he there?"

The stench of the bog hit him like a hammer, Laundry 3-B just as dank and disturbingly normal as they had left it but for the smell. Water gushed over Nathan's boots as something large slammed into Patrick. His serpentine form thrashed violently from side to side before it dwindled to puny human and a deluge of water pushed him into the hall.

Gillian caught Patrick's arm and rode the wave, one hand wrapped around Patrick and the other stretched out to Nathan, who caught her at the elbow and hauled them in. He put his back to the door, Gillian slamming against it to fight the rising water. Together they were able to close off the room just as a giant fin slid past the murky window.

A paint stroke of blood on the wall marked Patrick's descent as he slumped to the floor. Gray haze coated the air. Mist rose from the water and cascaded down concrete walls, obscuring all but the closest objects from view.

"Jesus," Gillian muttered and caught Patrick before he folded face-first into the puddles beneath her boots.

"I'm fine," Patrick said. Blood gushed through his fingers.

"You're really not." Gillian touched his cheek, and a spider of blue electricity sprang from her fingertips. It scurried down his body and disappeared into the wound. "Close your eyes."

Patrick held her gaze before doing what she asked. She took a deep breath and felt a drawing from within her, tingling heat running along her veins before it crested in her fingertips and released into Patrick's skin. Beneath her hands, Patrick slammed his teeth together, chest rearing off the wall before he settled again, flesh sealing beneath the pale blue glow.

Static rippled around his head, the faint hum of a panic-filled voice catching Gillian's attention. She leaned close to discern the rush of words, but barely caught more than a few disjointed thoughts. The sound ebbed and flowed, like a hint of music playing in someone else's headset. She struggled to decipher the message as Nathan called her attention to the center of the room. The mist parted to reveal its prize.

The electric chair sat on a raised dais, right where Gillian's dented dryer should have been. Nathan recognized the wood structure at its base; it was the same he had used as a weapon the first time they'd found themselves in this room. But what stood before them now was a far more deadly version of the out-of-place school chair in Dean Abbott's office. If Gillian had seen it on the moors and in the driveway of her childhood home, then it had been with them the whole time.

"That's it, isn't it?" he asked. "The chair?"

"It is," Gillian said. "He's here."

Beyond the door, waves crashed incessantly against the wood. Water penetrated the stronghold and covered the floor. From the center of the mist, a hazy, mustard-yellow light burned. Gillian braced herself as a dark shadow slid a hand over the chair.

Michael Shearer stood beside his throne, body whole and handsome.

"Back again, are we? Admit it," Shearer said and reached out to stroke Gillian's cheek. She ripped her head away, skin oozing blood from his corrosive touch. "You liked it."

Gillian tensed, flesh cold and hard. Behind her, Patrick pushed himself to his feet.

"You sick son of a bitch," he said.

"Well now, if it isn't a little Davidson family reunion," Shearer said and leered at them. He snatched a handful of Patrick's hair and pulled him close. "You didn't really expect me to honor that little deal we made, did you? Not when there was such a pretty little fish to fu . . . "

Patrick rose up before him, the scales on his back spreading into the hood of a king cobra and he lunged forward. Shearer sidestepped him with ease, and Patrick hit the wall headfirst before he collapsed into silence.

Nathan caught Shearer by the waist and slammed him into the tile hard enough to break it. With a laugh, Shearer wrapped an arm around Nathan's neck, the limb extending at unnatural angles before he spun his prey out from beneath his grasp with all the ease of a lead partner on the dance floor. Nathan hit the door and dropped.

"Stop this," Gillian said, voice nearly lost in the rising hum of electricity from the warming chair.

"It's not me who needs to stop," Shearer said and positioned himself before her, his massive form towering over her. "Give me what I want, and I'll let them go."

Water gushed over her boots, rising above her ankles and quickly overtaking her shins. A tingle of current flowed through her fingers. "You don't scare me anymore."

"Then why do you keep coming back?"

"This is my head, and you're of my mind," she said. On the far side of the room, Nathan stirred. "We're playing by my rules."

"Rules? There are no rules here, girlie. No rules that affect me. You and the intruder have killed me before. Didn't work out so well, did it?"

"Defend the girl you were," Patrick said.

A bolt of yellow light flew across the room and Patrick slammed into the wall. "Stay where you are, fuck face," Shearer said. "This is between me and the pretty little fish."

"You're damn right it is," Gillian said. "You're mine."

Blue light traveled the length of her legs and churned the water at her feet. Electricity arced across the surface, seeking a home it had known once before and slammed into Shearer with the force of a raging bull.

His skin cracked, body deteriorating under the onslaught. The flesh blackened before the outer layer split and the ruin of raw meat surfaced. At his center, a puddle of gore spread out across the scrubs, his oozing frame growing in size. He began to laugh with a mirthless glee that chilled the air.

Gillian stumbled, the effort to maintain the current forcing her to her knees.

Water parted like the Red Sea before him, and Shearer advanced across the floor. He caught Gillian by the throat and lifted her into the air.

"Did you think it would be that easy?"

He flicked his wrist and Gillian sailed across the room. She landed hard against the dented dryer, wrist skidding across the arrow of dried blood. She pushed back but he was already on her, the pressure of his body against hers freezing her to the core.

"My turn," he said.

All the fear Gillian had known as a girl gathered within her, the idea of what came next so repulsive she nearly vomited. She closed her eyes and stood once again before the mirror of black roses, the Wraith glowing within. She reached out, fingertips echoed on the other side of the glass.

Heal the crack.

And Gillian suddenly understood what she had to do.

"It's me who keeps coming back," she said. "Not her. Not the Wraith. Me." In the mirror, the Wraith absorbed the blue hue and raised her chin as her skin luminesced in the darkness. "You're here because I called you. Because I felt I deserved to torture myself with my sins. But there's only one path to redemption. Only one way to heal a torn soul."

"Don't." Shearer held up a hand as if to ward her off.

In the mirror, Gillian's own reflection smiled back.

"I forgive you," she said and felt a gentle lifting, like ice melting to water then releasing to gas. It blew through her, clearing the dams and she felt power surge from her core. "For all that you've done. And all that you have to do."

Blue light emanated from her in bright waves. She took Shearer's face in her hands, her touch now as corrosive as his.

Within her grasp he writhed like a trapped animal, but she didn't let go. "I forgive you, Michael Shearer. For everything you ever did to my body. But more than that, I forgive myself for ever giving you domain over my dreams."

Shearer screamed, the yellow light within him oozing out of the crevices until it flayed his remaining flesh, exposing tendons and bone. Gillian held on tight, their light mingling to a sickish green hue before the blue emerged victorious, the last hint of yellow fading into a pile of dust.

She dropped to her knees. Sparks of blue light danced at the end of her fingers like a faulty wire, and she felt a draining, as if someone had unstopped a tub within her. As she watched, the light crossed the floor, skittering along the tiles to Nathan.

"Gill," he muttered and stumbled toward her.

"I'm all right," she said and got to her feet, exhaustion pulling at her limbs. "You?"

"I'll live."

"Patrick?"

In the far corner, he muttered something indistinguishable. One of the skittering blue spiders of current crossed the water and entered his fingers, rising to stitch together the wound on his forehead. Nathan and Gillian crossed the room and helped him to his feet.

"You know how to get out?" Nathan asked and held out a small, single-shot handgun, the kind a lady in the roaring '20s might've carried in her purse.

"I got it," Patrick said.

Blue eyes gazed softly at Gillian, and Patrick leaned forward, lips to her forehead. "I'll see you in the real world."

Gillian nestled her cheek into his hand, and he looked at her with longing before he dropped the gun and fired, the report loud in the rising mist. He kept his eyes on Gillian until he flickered and disappeared.

The chair loomed and Gillian stepped up beside it. "Why is it still here?"

"Does it matter?" Nathan asked and caught her face in his hands, lips to hers. "He doesn't scare you anymore. It's time to wake up."

Gillian shook her head, troubled, and moved to put the chair between them. "You're right. He didn't scare me. Not even when he had me over the dryer."

"The end of the nightmare," Nathan said.

"Then why are you still here?" Gillian asked, hands digging in her pockets as he circled the chair. "I start to wake up and you get kicked out. That was the deal, wasn't it?"

"Stop this," he said and reached out to caress her cheek. "It's done. Over."

She stepped into his arms and kissed him fiercely. "Forgive me."

Nathan's eyes went wide as she slipped the serrated knife deep into his gut. He pulled away, a hand to the wound, hot blood flowing over his fingers. "Gillian?"

Tears streamed down Gillian's cheeks, hands trembling with the uncertainty of what she'd done. She fought the urge to go to him. "You're not of my mind."

"Gill . . . "

"Don't. Don't use his voice. Don't you dare. Whatever you are, you're not him."

Nathan dropped to his knees. "What have you done?"

"There was only one thing left that scares me." Gillian sobbed before him, mirroring him as she collapsed. "I'm so sorry."

"Why . . . why . . . would you . . . "

"Shearer was mine. He was of my mind. But you're not. You never were. You're the only thing that doesn't belong to me. The only thing that followed me through every stage."

The puddle of blood around Nathan's hand expanded, life seeping out his body to combine with the mist and dust that skittered like bugs across the floor. He collapsed, limbs silent, only wisps of air left in his lungs.

"I'm sorry," Gillian sobbed and crawled toward him, certain now that she'd misinterpreted the message, the frantic voice from Patrick's skin that had confirmed her fear. Nathan no longer belonged to her. And she'd killed him, just as her mother predicted. She'd done it again. Committed the sin of all sins, only this time, she'd murdered an innocent.

And for that she could never forgive herself.

"This is where I belong," she whispered and picked up the knife. She placed it carefully between her bellybutton and ribs on an upward slant, the sharp tip cutting into her flesh just as Nathan's legs twitched to life.

Worms dashed along the paths of his veins, searching for a way out and finding it in the puncture wound Gillian had inflicted. She lurched upright and scrambled away until her back hit the wall, eyes wide in horror. Elegant snow-white limbs exploded from the ruptured skin, tearing at the flesh of Nathan's torso until it discarded the body like a heap of dirty clothes. A scream tore out of Gillian's throat, the giant albino spider scuttling across the floor and growing larger with every extension of its disjointed limbs.

It reached the chair and reared up on its back legs, the remaining four limbs poised like snakes about to strike. On each side of the bulbous body, two segments intertwined to form a single extension. Fingers sprang from the fleshy protrusions and a low chuckle rumbled over the tiles.

Slapping a hand to her mouth, Gillian dropped the knife and watched in dread as the spider's body contorted again and again until a familiar horror stood before her.

"Well done, girlie."

Gillian crawled to Nathan and put a hand on his chest, finding life remained within. There was still time to save him. Closing her eyes, she hoped for a spark but there was nothing, no power left. Drained, she lifted his head into her lap and tried again. Two pitiful jolts opened his eyes, and he cringed in pain. Within her chest, she felt a backward pull, the mist sucked toward the hum of the monstrous chair.

Hand pressed to Nathan's wound, Gillian felt the hot pulse of his life slipping past her ineffective fingers. The effort to speak drained color from his face, but still he reached for her.

"Never hurt . . . " he said.

Gillilan's heart cracked. "I know."

"Don't let . . . bugger . . . out."

"I won't." She grasped his hand and placed it against her cheek. "You know that place between sleep and awake? That's where I'll always love you."

"I'll be waiting," he whispered, and his fingers slipped from her grasp.

She watched his chest for any sign of breath, but nothing moved in the silence. Beneath his body, light danced along the receding water, the floor visible as the chair sucked everything toward it.

Kissing him gently one last time, she set his head back on the linoleum. Rage flowed like hot steel through her body, and she rose to her feet, hands cupped by her thighs. Hair draped over her eyes as her knuckles cracked into distended claws. Cheeks burning with freshly cut scars, she opened her mouth and screamed.

At her feet, the water reversed, waves crashing against each other as if unsure which direction to run while the mist flowed backward and into her body, a blue aura rising around her.

Across the room, Shearer completed his preparations and stepped onto the dais to settle into his creation. "Time to wake up."

"Not for you."

Gillian plunged her hands into the water, the room erupting in a spray of mist. She rode the rising tide forward, the tsunami pushing Shearer from the stage. He slammed into the line of dryers as blue flame crackled around her, water hissing to steam at her feet. She approached the chair, electricity sizzling from her fingers. The chair began to glow, a nebula of blue light connecting with the walls, as if she were the heart of a plasma lamp. A single touch to the chair's elements would be all she needed to ignite what remained of her world, and she knew without knowing how that once she put her hands to those pads, she wouldn't be able to remove them until the walls crumbled.

Until she crumbled.

On the floor, Nathan's body lifted from the puddle. Blue flame consumed him, Gillian's hands hovering over the pads until his wound stitched itself back together and his chest rose.

"Take him home, Dex."

Smiling in triumph, she placed both palms squarely on the steel pads.

Shearer roared. Skin tore from his frame, crumbling into pixels of gore, a sonic wind flaying his body until nothing remained but a heap of blackened bone. His muddy yellow light faded to ash gray, the walls of her asylum cracking open.

As the wind snatched at her flesh, Gillian closed her eyes, thoughts on the way Nathan smiled and the joy she felt when she'd seen him gazing at her from the pillow next to her own.

She didn't notice when the charred bones shifted, and a single skeletal finger hooked itself into her heel as the dream world disintegrated.

"Take him home, Dex."

"You got it," Dex said as if Gillian might hear. "Initiating return in three . . . two . . . "

Light consumed the screen, the tsunami of activity reaching its peak..

"Did you get him?" Braun asked.

A flatline raced across Dex's screen. "No. No, no, no . . . Dammit big guy, don't you do this!"

"Good god, what is happening?" Clayton Miller asked.

"System's overloading!"

The room flared bright. Fluorescents popped in a spray of sparks. Clayton caught hold of Braun. "Where's the subject? Where did you take 831?"

On the ImaDream Screen, blue flames engulfed 831, illuminating them all for a split second in the spectral glow before the noise reached an ear-piercing crescendo and machinery exploded.

"Get down!" Braun shoved Clayton to the floor and vaulted the console. He threw himself over Dex as the room ignited, every button glowing brighter until they blew in a rain of fire, tech shattered into a million embers of hot metal.

In the silent aftermath, with ears still buzzing, Clayton got slowly to his feet. Light emanated from his phone to reveal the ruined suite. He picked a shard of metal from his cheek, dialed a number and barked a single instruction. "Initiate Protocol 37." By the light of his screen, he slipped through a gap in the door, Laura Taylor quick to follow.

Dex tapped his wristband and a personal security light brightened the darkness. Phil Dietrich lay silent on the floor by the door, a piece of metal embedded in his eye. Braun pulled himself across the linoleum and touched his fingers to the man's throat, shook his head and rose on unsteady legs. In Keller's dressing room, Dex found the emergency kit and flicked on a powerful flashlight.

Braun stumbled to the jump pod and looked down at the dark liquid. "Did you get him?"

"I don't know," Dex said.

"Help me get him out."

"Dex? Dex do you read?"

"Eric!" Relieved to hear his friend's voice, Dex tapped his wristband. "Are you still on the frequency? Is Keller alive?"

"I can't see shit. The suite's fried. Evan's manually overriding the door now. We're on our way."

Dex joined Braun, who hauled Keller's torso out of the muck and then collapsed on the floor. The trickle of blood from Braun's side gushed into a steady stream.

"Dex . . . " Braun gasped for breath. "Get . . . Keller . . . out."

Nodding, Dex pulled Keller's lower half out of the pod and gently placed him on the floor.

"Alive?" Braun asked.

Hand to Keller's chest and ear to his lips, Dex waited for any sign. "He's breathing."

Braun pushed up on his elbows, the ashen color of his face leaving Dex certain of only one thing, and he shifted his attention to the doctor.

"Get to 831," Braun gasped. "She's . . . Markway."

"I got it," Dex said.

"Get her out . . . Alistair . . . coming . . . trust . . . no one."

Dex blinked back tears as the pressure on his hand released. "We'll be okay. Margot is waiting for you."

Braun's lips twitched, a last gush of air rattling from his lungs, eyes set on something Dex would never see. He placed Braun's hand carefully on his chest as Evan and Eric burst into the suite.

"Power's out on the whole Corridor," Eric said and stumbled over to Dex and Braun. "Is he?"

"He's gone," Dex said. "Saved my life."

"Damn," Evan muttered.

"What's protocol 37?" Dex asked.

Evan shot his gaze across the gloom. "Did he initiate it?"

"Tell me what it is, and . . . "

"Dammit Cooper! Did he give the order or not?"

"He did."

Evan nodded, hands silent at his side. "Miller is saving his ass the only way he knows how."

"How's that?" Eric asked.

"He just issued a death warrant for the entire MCL division— including the remaining Elite."

DEIRDRE SWINDEN

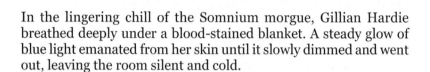

In the lingering chill of the Somnium morgue, Gillian Hardie breathed deeply under a blood-stained blanket. A steady glow of blue light emanated from her skin until it slowly dimmed and went out, leaving the room silent and cold.

CHAPTER EIGHTEEN

RIBBONS OF LIGHT sent Nathan careening back to himself and he bolted upright. Hands clasped him by the shoulders, rolling him onto his side and he vomited, blood splashing across his fingers before it turned to pale yellow bile. He put a hand to his belly, the sense of having been torn apart and stitched back together again still with him when he caught the worried gazes of Dex Cooper, Eric Wilson and Evan James.

"Gill . . ."

Dex caught Nathan's arm and helped him sit up, only to have Nathan grab his shirt and pull his face close enough to see Dex's eyes in the dim light. "Send me back in. Now."

"We can't."

"What do you mean you can't? Why did you pull me?"

"The suite's dead," Eric said. "Lights out. Whatever your girl did, she did it to the extreme. Wasn't us who pulled. She pushed."

For the first time, Nathan noticed the silence. The incessant hum of technology had ceased within the room. On the floor two bodies lay inert, the first man someone he had never seen before, but the second was all too recognizable.

"What happened?" Nathan asked and knelt next to Braun.

"She got you out just in time," Dex said. "Two more seconds and we would've lost you."

The effects of Nathan's return coursed through his body in remnants of electrical impulses, the same way waking from a dream sometimes left lasting impressions in a slowly surfacing mind. "How did he die?"

"He saved me," Dex said and caught himself in a lonely hug. Nathan reached out and put a hand on the boy's shoulder.

"There was a surge," Eric said. "The likes of which we've never seen. Took out the entire grid. Whole fucking place is dark."

"I can't get back to her?" Nathan asked.

Dex shook his head. "Afraid not."

Nathan sat down hard, the ache behind his eyes unfamiliar and harsh. "ImaDream. You used it?"

"You got my message?" Dex asked.

"Loud and clear. What was the last thing you saw?"

"She was with you. She was alive. And that other guy. The virus. It tore right out of you. Headed straight for the chair. She got there first."

"What did she do?"

A voice Nathan recognized answered. "Blew up the world."

The rolling click of recognition accompanied Gillian's voice in Nathan's head. *Ethan . . . no, Evan and Jimmy.* "Patrick?"

"She told you?"

"It came up. Evan and Jimmy. They were your brothers."

Patrick huffed. "Did it help?"

"It did. You gave her a way forward."

"You gave her a way out," Patrick said.

"Didn't work," Nathan muttered. "Did it?"

"Only one way to find out," Dex said.

"I need to find her. Her address . . . it's a cabin . . . "

"We got her," Dex said. "She's here."

"Here?"

"With Markway."

Nathan gaped at Dex. "Jon?"

"Come on."

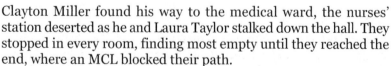

Clayton Miller found his way to the medical ward, the nurses' station deserted as he and Laura Taylor stalked down the hall. They stopped in every room, finding most empty until they reached the end, where an MCL blocked their path.

"No entry," he said. "By order of Dr. Braun."

"Do you know who I am?" Clayton asked.

"Yes sir."

"Then get out of my way."

"No sir."

It had been several years since Clayton lost his temper. The last time it had resulted in the loss of his third wife, but the rage he had been fighting all night broiled under his skin and he pushed his way past the MCL. He stepped into the tiny room only to choke on the smell of cigar smoke. Coughing, he waved a hand before his face as an Irish brogue barreled down on him.

"Clayton Miller. Been ages."

Clayton searched the dark room, the red embers of a cigar tip illuminating the immense figure of Alistair Wilcox.

"Where is she?" Clayton asked.

"We'll get to that."

Alistair nodded to the MCL, who ignited an emergency lamp, snatched Laura Taylor from the room and closed the door. Alistair puffed on his cigar and then held it out before him, admiring the dark brown wrapping.

He was immaculately dressed, loafers sparkling in the emergency lights, the suit he wore pressed and elegant. Its cut was designed to downplay the man's height and girth. Alistair wore it well, although his cheeks had gone slightly soft in the years since he and Clayton first met. A well-maintained beard of soft gray steel covered that slight defect, the intelligent hazel eyes bright.

"Senator Wilcox," Clayton said through clenched teeth, the nails of his left hand digging deeply into his palm. "What can I do for you, old friend?"

"Come now, Clayton. It's been a long time since we were friends." The lights flickered again. "Having a bit of trouble paying the electric bills, are we?"

"We're working on it."

"Course you are. You've been working on it for years now. Made yourself one helluva little fiefdom here, Clay. No doubt about it."

"You've no right to invade . . . "

"You had no right to set foot on my property. The MCL program is mine."

"The idea was mine. The technology was mine. It's only a matter of time before the sleep technology is mine." Clayton's oily smile oozed confidence. "You had your chance, Alistair. You made your bed. Lie in it."

"And dream, shall I? What will it be? Fast food? Soft drinks? Porno? We can't stop you now that you've started. We can't undo what you've done. Instead we just count the dead. Before your little sojourn into beddy-bye time, every decent American had a one-in-eight chance of dying in their sleep. Not bad, but not great, aye? And after the initial wave? What is it now?"

"Where is the woman?"

"She is no longer your concern," Alistair said and rose to his considerable height. "All I need to do is snap my fingers and you'll be under arrest for the murders of Jon Markway, Marcus Blake and Jake Billings."

Clayton bared his teeth. "Prove it."

"I don't have to." Alistair leaned close. Clayton smelled the whiskey on his breath, the hot feel of Alistair's voice against his ear made him twitch as if ice had been dropped down his back. "Did you really think I would just walk away?"

Alistair settled back on his heels. "But I'm not a hard man, and I'm willing to negotiate. So let's talk about our renewed partnership, shall we, my friend? I'll open the negotiations with this: hand over everything you have, and I'll let you go free. The offer expires in ten seconds."

"There is no partnership," Clayton growled.

"No? Let me ask you this. When the woman known as Somnium Sleep Subject 831 wakes up and tells the world what goes on here, what do you think will happen?"

"She'll see reason . . . "

"Reason aye? Maybe so, maybe so. Or maybe—now stick with me here, Clay. Just maybe, someone blows the whistle on you at long last. Tells the world Somnium's advertising to them in their dreams. And that long before last night, those dreams became lethal. Were, in fact, responsible for the deaths of nearly 10,000 people. People just like them. What then, old friend?"

"You wouldn't dare."

"Wouldn't I?"

"They find out about me, they find out about you."

Alistair circled him. "Let me weave you my own little dream. About a man who reveals the truth about Somnium. He'd be famous, wouldn't he? Saving the world from craving one too many cheeseburgers. Might even get himself elected to something more formidable than Senator. Might even get his big ass all the way to the White House. How's that for a dream?"

"And what happens when I tell them you were one of the founding members?"

Alistair made a grand show of spreading his hands to the side in a fantastically large mea culpa. "I walked away, didn't I? Showed my moral fortitude or whatever the fuck those pansies in the heartland like to think we senators are made of." He offered a humble face before a large snarl spread over his thin lips. He held up his phone. "And there's one last little thing."

Clayton's eyes widened, his own voice giving the order. "Initiate Protocol 37."

"Where did you get that?"

"Patrick Dolan's been playing you for years."

"I don't know any . . . "

"Oh but you do," Alistair said, and pressed play on a voicemail he'd received several years ago, when Clayton had first dictated Protocol 37's framework to his assistant. Evan James' deep and distinctive voice echoed along the hallway.

"The moment you gave that order, you were mine," Alistair said and clenched his fist in the air before Clayton's nose. "And now I've got you by the balls."

"831 can change everything," Clayton said. "She's displayed a rare talent this evening, and if she's still alive, she can save thousands. The Elite . . . "

Alistair snickered. "You expect me to believe you actually want to save the Elite?"

Clayton clamped his mouth shut.

"Tell you what, old friend, I'll give you one last chance," Alistair said. "One chance and one chance alone to renew our partnership. Ninety-ten. Your shares will hold their value. But from here on out, I own this company. And I own you. You've got two seconds to nod."

Muscles popped as Clayton ground his teeth, a curt nod all he had left in him. Grinning, Alistair moved to step around him, but Clayton caught hold of his arm. "If she's dead, all bets are off."

"Deal." Alistair said. "There now, that wasn't so hard, was it?"

Clayton glared at him. "Tell me where she is."

At the door, Alistair barked instructions to the MCLs before he paused and blew a cloud of smoke back toward Clayton.

"I'll be in touch."

DEIRDRE SWINDEN

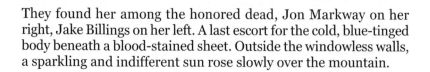

They found her among the honored dead, Jon Markway on her right, Jake Billings on her left. A last escort for the cold, blue-tinged body beneath a blood-stained sheet. Outside the windowless walls, a sparkling and indifferent sun rose slowly over the mountain.

CHAPTER NINETEEN

SUNLIGHT STREAMED INTO the room. Leafy shadows danced on the sheets, the men who surrounded the body on the bed saying nothing. There was nothing left to be said. All the stories had been told. All truths shared.

Nathan stood when a car pulled up the long drive to the cabin, a quick nod to Patrick before he stepped out onto the broad porch. He went no further, merely waited while a black-suited man emerged from the driver's seat and opened the back door. A buxom young woman with bright blonde hair climbed out, followed by the immense frame of Alistair Wilcox. Inside, the little black and white dog let out a volley of angry barks.

"Senator," Nathan said, arms crossed firmly over his chest. He kept them there even when Alistair Wilcox offered his hand.

"Commander Keller. You know my daughter?"

Nathan nodded to the blonde. "Jenna."

The two men stood on the porch, words unsaid between them. When it became apparent that neither would break the silence, Jenna did it for them.

"May I come in?" she said.

After only a slight hesitation, Nathan consented to let the visitors pass.

From his corner, Dex gave a curt nod of greeting, his whistle bringing Jax to heel while Jenna and the Senator loomed over the sleeper.

"Any change?" Jenna asked and Patrick shook his head. "Her mother has been asking for her. She's past the crisis, thank god. Gilly will want to know if she . . . if . . . "

Alistair patted his daughter's shoulder. "These things take time." He spun around, the little cabin bright and cheery despite the abundance of men. Flames danced merrily in the stone fireplace. "Little early for a fire, aye?"

"We thought it might help," Patrick said.

Nathan glared at him, and he snapped his lips shut.

"What can we do for you Senator?" Nathan asked.

"Gentlemen, I have a proposition for you."

"You've got nothing to say we want to hear."

"Don't I?" Alistair looked down at the bed once more. "Whether you're willing to admit it or not, each of you displayed a rather remarkable and rare talent for the dream space. A true prowess in the face of insurmountable odds . . . "

"Cut the bullshit, Senator," Nathan muttered. Dex and Patrick exchanged bemused smirks. "State your business, if you actually have any, and get out. Braun may have trusted you, but I don't. Never did. Even before you made a deal with the devil."

"That deal saved lives. Yours included."

"What is it you want?" Patrick asked and stood to join Nathan. Dex set his feet on the floor, prepared to add his meager weight to the group.

"Only this. If this woman wakes, she may have the answer— no, not the answer—the ability to save the lives of every remaining Elite, and the thousands of others who have been affected by Somnium's tech. It's a very valuable skill, one that many would pay good money to obtain. It's also one that others would pay to eradicate, if you understand my meaning."

Nathan eyed him.

"It's true there's not a trace of tech left in her system?" Alistair asked, eyes on Dex.

"She's clean."

"Given the opportunity, I think she'll want to help those who've suffered like she has." He faced Patrick. "Like you."

"And just how do you think she can help?" Patrick asked.

"She harnessed the healing power of bioelectric energy and used it not only to cure herself but both of you. She could turn the tide on the nightmares for the Elite, with a little help from the three of you, of course."

"You know how to turn the tide?" Nathan said and took a step forward to put himself nose to nose with Alistair. "Turn the fucking tech off. All of it."

"Hell yeah," Dex said from the corner.

Alistair tucked his hands in his pockets. "Jenna, my dear. Will you give us a moment?"

Jenna stood, a last sorrow-filled glance cast at Gillian before she left the men alone in the cabin. Alistair waited until she was tucked into the limo before he spoke again. "We all know there's too much at stake to end it. Too much power. Too many suitors to stop the dance." He took a step toward Nathan. "Somnium may fall . . . "

"Will fall," Dex cut in and nodded to Gillian. "If she has anything to say about it."

"That won't matter," Nathan said, eyes locked in battle with the Senator. "He's got everything he needs to rebuild, don't you? Another name. Another company. And it all starts right back up."

"Highly intelligent," Alistair said as if quoting some unseen dossier. "I've always wondered why highly intelligent men like you choose a life of government servitude. But that's a discussion for another time, aye Keller? I'll get the jump interface working again. Braun had his secrets and he kept them well, but you know I'll make it work. And when I do you're either with me, or you're against me. Which is it to be, Commander?"

Patrick opened the door. "I think it's time you left, Senator."

"If she can save herself, she can save the others," Alistair said.

"And you?" Nathan asked. "What will you do when you have the ability to weave a certain kind of dream?"

"I'm not Clayton Miller. And prior to his death, Eli Braun assured me that you would make an excellent addition to my team. Now, I'm asking you nicely, Commander."

Dex stood up. "Can I ask you something, Senator?"

"Of course."

"How the hell do you sleep at night?"

Alistair pulled a card from his pocket and placed it onto the windowsill. "Think about it. That's all I'm asking."

Nathan followed him out onto the porch, Patrick and Dex stepping out behind him, the three of them forming an arc that blocked Alistair from returning.

"Senator," Nathan called just as the big man stuck a foot in his car. "Get some rest, won't you? Looks like you haven't slept in days."

Alistair tipped his head. "I'll be waiting for your call."

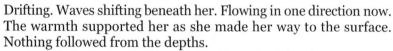

Drifting. Waves shifting beneath her. Flowing in one direction now. The warmth supported her as she made her way to the surface. Nothing followed from the depths.

Satisfied, she broke the crest and breathed deeply.

Outside, a soft breeze blew colored leaves from their perch, the sound like distant applause and she remembered another place, safe from harm. Safe. And she knew without looking that this was that place.

Gillian Hardie opened her eyes.

The first to notice perked his ears. He waited, tense, ready to spring if she moved. When she did he leapt from the couch and trotted across the floor, desperate to hear the only voice in the world that mattered to him.

"Jax?" She reached out a hand to the little dog, only to have it caught between two others.

"She's back!"

Gillian shifted at the scuffle of noise, the bed comfortable beneath her but her body felt as if she had been immobile for days. Muscles refused to answer her command without loud cracks of protest, the effort to rouse her arms to action nearly draining her limited energy. Around her the walls came into focus, the pictures familiar, the view of the trees from the window one she coveted. Turning her head, she gazed upon an array of flowers before settling on a pair of blue eyes she knew well.

"Bloody hell," she muttered, voice thick with a dry rasp. Patrick handed her a glass of water and helped her sit up to drink. Thirst quenched, she gazed around the room in stunned disbelief. "I'm still dreaming, aren't I?"

"Would I have this nose if you were dreaming?" Patrick asked.

"No," Gillian whispered and smiled. "I never would've pictured you with that nose. You look very handsome. Too handsome for me."

"And you're too pretty for me," Patrick said. "Welcome back, Gilly."

Struggling to sit up, Gillian said, "My mother . . . "

"She's going to be all right," Patrick said. "Jenna said she's past the crisis."

Relief flooded Gillian's body and she lay back with silent gratitude. Eyes open once more, she reached out a shaking hand to caress Patrick's cheek. "I'm so sorry."

Catching her hand, Patrick smiled. "For what?"

"Not acknowledging you that day in the city. I didn't . . . "

"Shhhh. I know why you did it. When I saw you, everything came back. I remembered a promise I made."

"A promise?"

"To protect you."

"You didn't have to . . . "

"Yes, I did. I got my shit together, Gilly, thanks to you."

"I believe you," she said with a soft smile. "About the dreams."

"I know you do." He slipped a purple rubber band from his wrist onto hers. "You told me so yourself."

"But that was a dream. Wasn't it?"

A second voice floated across the pine floors. "All that we see or seem is but a dream within a dream."

Startled, Gillian looked to the end of the bed. An unfamiliar face gazed at her, setting off a twinge of fear in her gut. "Do I know you?"

The man seemed to deflate just a little before he shook his head. "Only in a dream." He nodded to Patrick. "I'll leave you two alone."

Something shifted within Gillian, fear diluted by the sound of his voice. "Wait. Please."

He glanced back at her over his shoulder, the light falling on a scar that ran across his scruffy, well-freckled face. A breeze caught a strand of auburn, and it drifted across his forehead.

"You're in that place," she said. "Between sleeping and awake, that place where you can still remember dreaming. That's where I always think of you. No . . . that's not right, is it?"

The man turned back, and she found his face more pleasant than before, the deep scar seeming to recede as he approached the bed. "That's where I'll always find you."

"Who said that?" she asked. "J.M. Barrie?"

"More or less."

Ice-blue eyes caught Gillian's, a light of hope rushing within. "It is you? Isn't it?" she asked. "Nathan?"

"I told you this face didn't get any better in the light," Nathan said and dropped to his knees beside her.

The scruff on his cheek felt rough on her fingers, and she gently traced the soft line of his scar. "Still the only face I want to see on the pillow next to mine."

"You're sure about that?"

"Buy me dinner and we'll see about me making us breakfast."

He leaned forward and softly pressed his forehead to hers. "Tell me I'm not dreaming."

"It's nice to finally meet you, Nathan Keller."

"Same, Gillian Hardie."

Gillian smiled, leaned forward and very softly, pressed her lips to his.

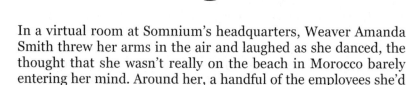

In a virtual room at Somnium's headquarters, Weaver Amanda Smith threw her arms in the air and laughed as she danced, the thought that she wasn't really on the beach in Morocco barely entering her mind. Around her, a handful of the employees she'd met during her first week on the job were happily enjoying the music, the company of virtual simulations indistinguishable from the real people.

She'd just grabbed a drink from a passing waiter when a pair of arms slipped around her waist. Surprised, she turned to find herself in the arms of a handsome young man wearing a pair of muddy yellow scrubs.

"Hello, girlie," he said. "You're a pretty little fish, aren't you?"

Giggling, Amanda offered him a coy smile. He drew her from the dance floor and led her down a dim hallway. She didn't notice the sign by the door when he pulled her inside, only that the bright lights turned to ash as he pushed her up against an old, dented dryer.

THE END?

Not if you want to dive into more of Crystal Lake Publishing's Tales from the Darkest Depths!

Check out our amazing website and online store
or download our latest catalog here.
https://geni.us/CLPCatalog

We always have great new projects and content on the website to dive into, as well as a newsletter, behind the scenes options, social media platforms, our own dark fiction shared-world series and our very own webstore. Our webstore even has categories specifically for KU books, non-fiction, anthologies, and of course more novels and novellas.

ABOUT THE AUTHOR

A successful writer/editor in the corporate world for more than two decades, Deirdre Swinden is currently living and writing in North Carolina. She received an MFA in Creative Writing from Arcadia University and has published short stories in *Griffel Literary Magazine* and *Grim & Gilded*. Early in her writing career, she won the Popular Short Story Contest at the 2000 Philadelphia Writers' Conference with her short work, "Shooting Televisions."

Readers . . .

Thank you for reading *Somnium*. We hope you enjoyed this novel.

If you have a moment, please review *Somnium* at the store where you bought it.

HHelp other readers by telling them why you enjoyed this book. No need to write an in-depth discussion. Even a single sentence will be greatly appreciated. Reviews go a long way to helping a book sell, and is great for an author's career. It'll also help us to continue publishing quality books.

Thank you again for taking the time to journey with Crystal Lake Publishing.

Visit our Linktree page for a list of our social media platforms. https://linktr.ee/CrystalLakePublishing

Follow us on Amazon:

Our Mission Statement:

Since its founding in August 2012, Crystal Lake Publishing has quickly become one of the world's leading publishers of Dark Fiction and Horror books. In 2023, Crystal Lake Publishing formed a part of Crystal Lake Entertainment, joining several other divisions, including Torrid Waters, Crystal Lake Comics, Crystal Lake Kids, and many more.

While we strive to present only the highest quality fiction and entertainment, we also endeavour to support authors along their writing journey. We offer our time and experience in non-fiction projects, as well as author mentoring and services, at competitive prices.

With several Bram Stoker Award wins and many other wins and nominations (including the HWA's Specialty Press Award), Crystal Lake Publishing puts integrity, honor, and respect at the forefront of our publishing operations.

We strive for each book and outreach program we spearhead to not only entertain and touch or comment on issues that affect our readers, but also to strengthen and support the Dark Fiction field and its authors.

Not only do we find and publish authors we believe are destined for greatness, but we strive to work with men and women who endeavour to be decent human beings who care more for others than themselves, while still being hard working, driven, and passionate artists and storytellers.

Crystal Lake Publishing is and will always be a beacon of what passion and dedication, combined with overwhelming teamwork and respect, can accomplish. We endeavour to know each and every one of our readers, while building personal relationships with our authors, reviewers, bloggers, podcasters, bookstores, and libraries.

We will be as trustworthy, forthright, and transparent as any business can be, while also keeping most of the headaches away from our authors, since it's our job to solve the problems so they can stay in a creative mind. Which of course also means paying our authors.

We do not just publish books, we present to you worlds within your world, doors within your mind, from talented authors who sacrifice so much for a moment of your time.

There are some amazing small presses out there, and through collaboration and open forums we will continue to support other presses in the goal of helping authors and showing the world what quality small presses are capable of accomplishing. No one wins when a small press goes down, so we will always be there to support hardworking, legitimate presses and their authors. We don't see Crystal Lake as the best press out there, but we will always strive to be the best, strive to be the most interactive and grateful, and even blessed press around. No matter what happens over time, we will also take our mission very seriously while appreciating where we are and enjoying the journey.

What do we offer our authors that they can't do for themselves through self-publishing?

We are big supporters of self-publishing (especially hybrid publishing), if done with care, patience, and planning. However, not every author has the time or inclination to do market research, advertise, and set up book launch strategies. Although a lot of authors are successful in doing it all, strong small presses will always be there for the authors who just want to do what they do best: write.

What we offer is experience, industry knowledge, contacts and trust built up over years. And due to our strong brand and trusting fanbase, every Crystal Lake Publishing book comes with weight of respect. In time our fans begin to trust our judgment and will try a new author purely based on our support of said author.

With each launch we strive to fine-tune our approach, learn from our mistakes, and increase our reach. We continue to assure our authors that we're here for them and that we'll carry the weight of the launch and dealing with third parties while they focus on their strengths—be it writing, interviews, blogs, signings, etc.

We also offer several mentoring packages to authors that include knowledge and skills they can use in both traditional and self-publishing endeavours.

We look forward to launching many new careers.

This is what we believe in. What we stand for. This will be our legacy.

Welcome to Crystal Lake Publishing— Tales from the Darkest Depths.

Printed in Great Britain
by Amazon

42668465R00136